# SAXON: *The Pope's Assassin*

Tim Severin, explorer, filmmaker and lecturer, has retraced the storied journeys of Saint Brendan the Navigator, Sindbad the Sailor, Jason and the Argonauts, Ulysses, Genghis Khan and Robinson Crusoe. His books about these expeditions are classics of exploration and travel.

He made his historical-fiction debut with the hugely successful Viking series, followed by the Pirate and Saxon series. This novel returns to the Saxon series, and the world of Sigwulf.

Visit Tim's website to find out more about his books and expeditions:
www.timseverin.net

Follow Tim on Facebook:
facebook.com/TimSeverinAuthor

# TIM SEVERIN

# SÆXON

VOLUME THREE

## The Pope's Assassin

PAN BOOKS

First published 2015 by Macmillan

This edition published 2016 by Pan Books
an imprint of Pan Macmillan
20 New Wharf Road, London N1 9RR
Associated companies throughout the world
www.panmacmillan.com

ISBN 978-1-4472-6224-4

1 3 5 7 9 8 6 4 2

A CIP catalogue record for this book is available from the British Library.

Map artwork by Stephen Raw
Printed and bound by CPI Group (UK) Ltd, Croydon, CRO 4YY

Visit www.panmacmillan.com to read more about all our books
and to buy them. You will also find features, author interviews and
news of any author events, and you can sign up for e-newsletters
so that you're always first to hear about our new releases.

# The Pope's Assassin

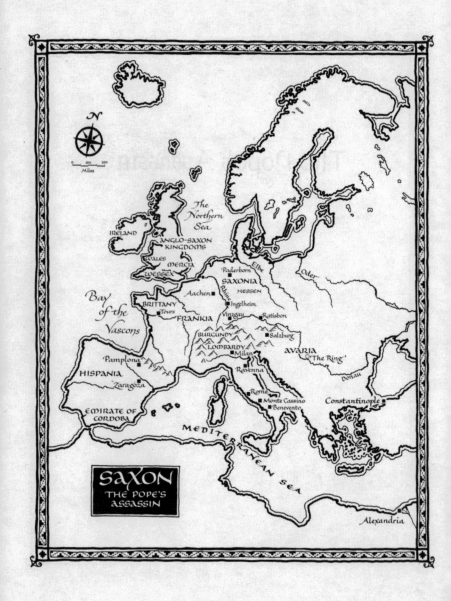

**SAXON**
THE POPE'S
ASSASSIN

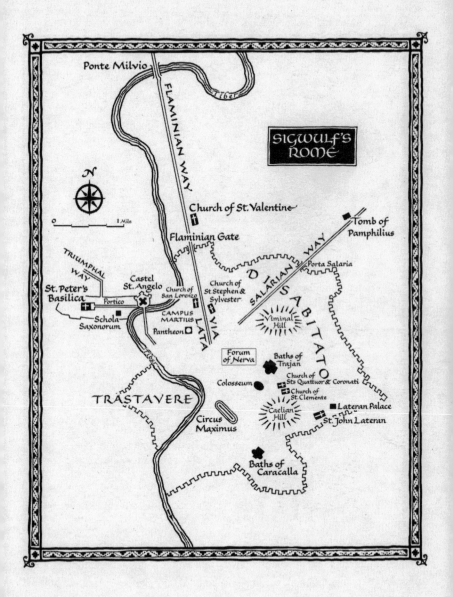

Ponte Milvio

FLAMINIAN WAY

Tiber

N

0          1 Mile

SIGWULF'S ROME

Church of St. Valentine

Flaminian Gate

Tomb of Pamphilius

TRIUMPHAL WAY

St. Peter's Basilica

Castel St. Angelo

Portico

Schola Saxonorum

Church of San Lorenzo

Church of St Stephen & Sylvester

SALARIAN WAY

Porta Salaria

DI SABITATO

CAMPUS MARTIUS

Pantheon

VIA LATA

Viminal Hill

Forum of Nerva

Baths of Trajan

Colosseum

Church of Sts Quattuor & Coronati

Church of St. Clemente

Caelian Hill

Lateran Palace

St. John Lateran

TRASTAVERE

Circus Maximus

Baths of Caracalla

# Chapter One

The cut-throats lurking in the alley were typical of Rome's gutter class. Lank, greasy hair, sallow complexions and a sour smell of sweat-soaked clothes marked them as inhabitants of the grimy slums near the bend in the Tiber. Cheap to hire, they were notoriously unreliable. Their employer, standing with them, was taller by a head. His bulky fur hat was more suitable for a cold winter's day than a bright spring morning in the Eternal City and he had knotted the laces of the ear flaps painfully tight under his chin. The intention was to make his face less easy to recognize. It gave him a pinched and resentful look.

'Reminds me of a hedgepig with gut ache,' whispered one of his hirelings to a companion.

The tall man was listening to the sound of a choir on the steps of the church of San Lorenzo a couple of streets away to his left. It was a last-minute rehearsal of their psalms for that morning's solemn procession. Now, very faintly, he heard the sound of horses' hooves approaching from the opposite direction.

'Get ready. Here he comes,' he warned. The men edged further back into the dark shadow cast by the high side wall of the monastery church dedicated to Saints Stephen and Sylvester.

Gradually, the sound of hooves grew louder. A sparse crowd of spectators lined the Via Lata, the ruler-straight main thoroughfare in front of the church, and now they craned their necks to get a first glimpse of the approaching riders. The choir fell silent, and a large and heavy wooden cross, painted white and yellow, was hoisted in the air above them. It swayed unsteadily, held up by one of the poor from the local hospital, who had been selected for his role. Smaller, more ornate crosses sprouted, their gilded poles spiralled with coloured ribbons. They were the stationary crosses to be displayed as the procession walked out of the city by the Flaminian Gate. On the way they would stop to celebrate the stations at the Church of St Valentine, then cross the Ponte Milvio to arrive at their final destination – St Peter's Basilica and the ceremony of the Great Litany.

The tall man in the winter hat took a half a step out from the shadows so that he could see over the heads of the spectators. He noted that the onlookers were mostly women, with a sprinkling of older men and idle bystanders, and a few of the foreign visitors who came to Rome on pilgrimage. The latter were the only ones gaping with real curiosity, anxious to identify which dignitaries were coming. He could see no soldiers, no guards, no watchmen, and that was very satisfactory.

The horsemen came into view. They were a small group of just seven riders. All but two were beautifully dressed in elaborate church vestments. Their planeta, the long flowing gowns of dark silk, were edged with bands of gold embroidery that glittered in the sunshine. Their leader, a middle-aged man with a podgy, pale face, had a high white headdress and wore a voluminous tent-like garment of patterned brocade. The others had purple skullcaps, ribbed with silver cord. The two more plainly dressed riders were bare headed and in simple tunics of undyed linen.

The tall man watched as the riders came to a halt, only a few yards away, and began to dismount. He waited until all of them were on their feet, and their grooms had led away their mounts.

'Now!' he shouted, and his gang of ruffians burst out from cover. No one had been looking in their direction. The surprise was complete. There were screams as the ruffians pulled knives and clubs from under their clothing and flourished the weapons at anyone who got in their way. The crowd scattered in panic. In a few strides the attackers reached their target, the man in the white headdress. His feet were kicked from under him so he fell heavily to the flagstones. He lay there, winded. The cut-throats turned on his companions, yelling abuse, slashing at the air with their blades. Their victims fled, holding up the skirts of their gowns to prevent themselves from tripping. Only one of them hesitated. A blow in the face from a club sent him staggering back, his nose streaming blood. A hand snatched the jewelled cross dangling on his chest, snapping the gold chain. Then he, too, beat a retreat. In moments the Via Lata was empty of spectators, leaving only the attackers and their hapless victim who was sprawled on the ground.

The tall man in the fur hat stepped up and kicked him hard in the stomach. Tangled in his vestments, his victim could only curl up in a ball and bring up his arms to protect his head. He had lost his black slippers and his costly cloak, and the silk gown had rucked up to his knees, revealing long white linen socks. 'For the love of God,' he gasped.

'Deal with him,' ordered the tall man.

Two of the ruffians grabbed their victim by the shoulders and hoisted him up onto his knees. A third attacker, knife in hand, placed himself in front of the terrified man. The white headdress had fallen off, revealing a scalp spotted with large dark freckles, a rim of thin, greying hair around his tonsure.

The man with the knife hesitated.

'Get on with it!' snapped Fur Hat. When there was no response, he moved around behind the kneeling man, seized him by both ears and held his head steady. 'Do as you were told,' he ordered.

The knife man drew a shallow breath, took a half-step forward and jabbed the point of the knife at his victim's left eye. The kneeling man jerked his head to one side in terror. The point of the knife missed. The edge of the sharp blade cut a long gash in the flesh above the cheekbone.

'Try again!' snarled the man in the fur hat.

The knife-wielder made a second stab, and again he missed the eye. Another gash appeared. Now the face of the kneeling man was streaming with blood.

'Clumsy fool!' cursed the tall man. He let go of his victim's ears, and reached up to suck a cut in his hand. The knife blade had gone past the cheek and sliced him across the knuckles. The men holding up the victim released their grip. The bleeding man in the clerical garb fell forward on his face on the ground, whimpering.

'Time to get out of here,' muttered one of the hirelings. His colleagues were already leaving. One of them was bending down to scoop up the valuable cloak that had come loose during the fracas. The thief who had snatched the pectoral cross had long since disappeared. A little distance away small knots of people were beginning to gather on the Via Lata, gazing nervously to see what was going on. Gang warfare in Rome was commonplace, but the brawls seldom happened so publicly.

'Get the bastard out of sight!' commanded the man in the fur hat. He looked around him. His squad of a dozen had dwindled to just three, the knife man and two more. Fur Hat leaned down, seized his victim by the collar of his gown, and began to drag him bodily towards the door of the church.

His hired men hurried to assist him. They pushed open the

door and dragged their bleeding victim onto the marble floor of the atrium within.

'You were also meant to cut out the tongue,' Fur Hat snarled at the knife man once they were inside.

'Not as easy as it looks,' came the surly response.

'We have no time to waste.' Fur Hat caught his breath and flexed the fingers on his hand that had been nicked. The injured man lay at his feet, groaning pitifully.

Fur Hat nodded towards the door that led from the atrium into the adjacent monastery. 'Put him in there for now.'

Watched by their employer, the three cut-throats man-handled their battered victim through the door and into the monastery, then down a corridor. A door to a cell stood open and they heaved their captive inside; they dumped him on the floor, then shut him in. Returning to the church, the leader of the three men held out his hand, waiting until the man in the fur hat gave him a leather pouch. Then all four slipped out through a side door and back into the street outside. Their employer hurried towards the hill called the Caelian. His accomplices headed in the opposite direction, back towards the slums.

'We should have asked for a lot more money, Gavino,' said their leader, hefting the pouch to feel its weight. His two companions watched him closely, suspicious, in case he was about to run off with it.

'Underpaid, were we?' said the man called Gavino. He had wielded the knife. The dark stubble of his beard failed to hide the rash of pockmarks that marred his lower face. 'We could find out who that fur head is, threaten to report him to the authorities unless we get more money.'

'Too risky. Those Churchmen run this city and the justices dance to their tune.'

'Bloodsuckers, all of them. From top to bottom,' said his colleague. He hawked up a gob of phlegm and spat into the gutter.

'Well, you missed your chance to put your boot into the boss man.'

'You mean that old fart we just gave a going-over?'

The leader looked at his companion pityingly. 'Of course, you oaf.'

'Who was he?'

'He calls himself Christ's Vicar on Earth – His Holiness the Pope.'

# Chapter Two

I was squinting through the iron bars of the palace's leopard enclosure when the bishop's messenger tracked me down.

'You are Sigwulf?' the courier asked politely. The armpits of his brown woollen tunic were soaked with sweat and his face was flushed crimson from the early summer heat. From his accent I judged him to be from somewhere in West Frankia and a stranger to Paderborn. Someone must have told him that I took an interest in the royal menagerie.

I nodded and accepted the folded paper he held out to me.

The flap was held down with a blob of pale yellow wax into which the sender had pressed a simple mark: a plain cross of four arms of equal length enclosed in a circle. I cracked the seal with my thumb and opened the single sheet. There was just one line of neat, church-like script:

> *Sigwulf, I have recommended you to Archbishop Arno of Salzburg.*
> *Alcuin.*

That explained the cross. Alcuin was now the Bishop of Tours though I had known him when he was political advisor and private tutor to the family of our supreme overlord, Carolus, King of the Franks. Eight years earlier it was Alcuin who had chosen me to take a selection of wild animals – including two ice bears

– to Baghdad as a gift to the Caliph from Carolus; hence my continuing interest in the king's collection of beasts.

It was common knowledge that Alcuin still dabbled from a distance in affairs of state and corresponded regularly with members of the king's council. But I felt a tremor of disquiet that he should have written to me directly. I was an insignificant member of Carolus's vast household, a *miles* or courtier-soldier. I held no rank, even if, from time to time, I had been called upon for special duties and had carried them out with moderate success.

The bearer of the letter wiped his sleeve across his brow and stood waiting for my response.

'Did Alcuin provide any verbal message?' I asked.

'No, sir. He only said that I was to bring you to meet with Archbishop Arno.'

'You know where to find the archbishop?'

'Yes, sir. I just delivered another of my master's letters to the archbishop. He's in his office.'

I glanced one last time into the leopard enclosure. I had been hoping that the May sunshine might encourage the mother leopard to show her twin cubs born two weeks earlier. There was still no sign of them. 'Then please take me there,' I said.

The messenger – his name, he told me, was Bernard – led me through the muddle of buildings that formed the royal precinct. Paderborn was only one of Carolus's capitals – he had others at Aachen and Ingelheim – and the king had established it on Saxon territory as a symbol of his victory over their federation. That feat of arms had extended his enormous realm until it now covered half of Europe. The king regarded the Saxons as chronically untrustworthy so a high rampart of wood and earth enclosed Paderborn, and its buildings were crammed inside, higgledy piggledy. It was not always clear which were barracks, storehouses, accommodation or administrative offices. Even Carolus's palace, where

Bernard brought me, was part residence, part audience hall and part basilica.

The ten-minute walk gave me time to compose myself before a meeting with Archbishop Arno. His reputation as a hard task-master was formidable. Not so long ago, Carolus had picked him for the thorny task of turning the fiercely pagan, horse-riding Avars into Christians. The Avars were another of the king's recent conquests. They had plagued Eastern Europe for generations, raiding and demanding tribute. Even the Emperor in Constantin-ople paid them off. Carolus's army had finally crushed them and now he expected their mass conversion. Doubtless the king judged Arno to be sufficiently ruthless to see the job done, and, if necessary, done at sword point.

The archbishop's physical appearance when I was shown into his presence matched his notoriety. Arno was as rough-hewn as the broad, scarred campaign table at which he was seated. Every-thing about the man was blunt and square, from his powerful hands with their stubby, thick fingers and hairy backs to his hefty muscular shoulders and a face whose heavy features were framed by a close-clipped iron grey beard. Dressed in a plain woollen shirt and leggings, he looked like a bricklayer.

I put his age at about forty-five – some ten years older than me – and the keen grey eyes that scrutinized me from under bushy eyebrows held no trace of friendliness.

'What do you know about politics in Rome?' he demanded brusquely. His doorkeeper had withdrawn after introducing me. The only other person in the room was a secretary seated at a writing desk in one corner, taking notes on a wax tablet. The archbishop's voice suited his appearance – it was a pugnacious growl.

'A snake pit, my lord. I spent the winter there some years ago, with a delegation from King Carolus to the Caliph of Baghdad.'

'This time the snakes have stuck in their fangs.'

I waited for him to go on.

'Pope Leo has been attacked in the street by a gang of toughs and beaten up. His eyes were gouged out and his tongue removed.' Arno presented the details without emotion.

My face must have shown my shock. During my time in Rome I had observed Pope Leo's predecessor, Pope Adrian. Crude violence would have been unthinkable against Adrian. People feared him and he had been well guarded. I struggled to imagine how anyone would seek to mutilate the man who had followed him on St Peter's throne.

'Who attacked him?' I asked.

'That is what I want you to find out.'

I goggled at him.

The archbishop was speaking again. 'Alcuin writes to me that you have a useful contact in Rome, inside the Church.'

I knew at once who he meant.

'Paul the Nomenculator,' I said. 'His office dealt with requests to the Pope for meetings and grants. He helped me greatly. But he must have retired by now.'

'Anyone else?'

I shook my head.

Arno took a paper from his desk. The writing was the same as on the message I had received, and the content covered the entire page. 'Find out what really happened, and do it discreetly and fast,' he said.

'I'm not sure if my earlier visit to Rome equips me—' I began.

He cut me off abruptly. 'The king's council wants to know who is behind the attack. The safety and well-being of the Holy Father is a matter of state importance. You may take it that this mission is by command of Carolus.'

I pulled myself together. I had no business to question the wishes of Carolus.

'Is there any background information that might help with my inquiries?' I asked meekly.

Arno's eyes flicked to the letter in his hand. 'Alcuin mentions certain rumours about Pope Leo. Complaints about his private life.'

'What sort of rumours?' I prompted, this time making sure to sound respectful.

'That he has been selling lucrative Church appointments.'

There was nothing new in that, I thought to myself. Paul the Nomenculator had regarded simony as a perfectly normal activity within the Church and had profited from it himself.

Arno had not finished. 'There's also a rumour of adultery,' he said.

I made the mistake of smirking. 'Attacked by a jealous husband, perhaps?'

The archbishop scowled at my levity. 'Don't treat this lightly, Sigwulf.' He laid a spade-like hand on a nearby pile of documents. 'These are all letters received from Rome, written anonymously or by certain senior members of the Church, full of complaints about Leo and his shortcomings.'

'Am I to investigate those letter writers as suspects for the assault?' I asked.

Arno dismissed the suggestion. 'Their turn will come if and when the king's council decides to launch a formal investigation into Pope Leo's behaviour. Right now, your job is to discover who was responsible for the attack and report back to me – and only me – without further delay.'

It seemed that my interview was over.

'My lord, I'll start for Rome at dawn tomorrow,' I said, standing a little straighter. It was obvious that the archbishop preferred his underlings to obey him instantly and without question.

'On the way you can interview an eyewitness to the attack.'

'On the way, my lord?'

'Your shortest route passes through Ratisbon. You'll meet a large party of travellers coming in the opposite direction. They are heading here from Rome. The snowmelt is early this year so they should be through the Alpine passes by now. One of the travellers is a man by the name of Albinus.'

'How will I know him?'

The archbishop gave a grim smile. 'He's got a freshly broken nose. He's chamberlain to Pope Leo, and took a clout in the face from a cudgel, trying to defend his master.'

'Then I take it that Pope Leo himself is amongst the travellers.'

The archbishop nodded. 'After what happened, Leo is frightened for his life. My informants tell me that he is coming here to meet Carolus and seek his protection. The Duke of Spoleto, one of Carolus's most loyal vassals, is accompanying him with an escort of soldiers.'

'Should I interview the Pope as well?'

Arno made a gesture as if brushing off a fly. 'Leo's version of events is not to be trusted. He'll try to implicate his enemies, not tell the truth.'

'What about this man Albinus? He could be a liar too.'

Shrewd eyes held my gaze. 'Alcuin says in his letter that you're no fool. I expect you to know a lie when you meet it.'

The archbishop was already reaching for another document on his table. 'Send me a preliminary report of whatever you manage to learn from his man Albinus,' he grunted. 'My secretary will provide you with money for travel expenses and essential costs. Keep any bribes to a minimum.'

I made my way out of the office, silently cursing Alcuin for landing me in this predicament. Rome was more than two thousand miles away and the troubles of Pope Leo did not concern me. I was perfectly happy to go on spending my days in the undemanding routine of a *miles*. It meant little more than showing up for the occasional muster of the household troops, some arms drill on horseback while being shouted at by a sergeant-instructor, and generally pottering about on the fringes of the king's retinue. It allowed me plenty of spare time to help out the keepers of the royal menagerie at feeding times. I had no wish to be the archbishop's spy.

*

Arno's staff provided me with credentials as a *missi*, an envoy travelling on royal business, so I would be able to commandeer horses as I rode to Ratisbon and beyond. On the fifth day, I came across Pope Leo's entourage resting up in a monastery in the Alpine foothills after they had trudged through the mountain passes. The monastery was a modest enough establishment situated on a spur of high ground that overlooked the road. Its chapel was the only stone-built structure. All the other buildings were made of local timber and roofed with wooden tiles that had weathered to a sombre grey that blended with the drab, rocky countryside. I arrived shortly before noon and the guesthouse was already full to bursting, but royal edict obliged the hosteller to provide food and shelter to a *missi*. Muttering under his breath, the harassed monk found me a corner where I could sleep on a straw palliasse. Then he brought me into the refectory building, explaining that, with so many members in the papal party, he had been forced to arrange two sittings for every meal. Entering the long narrow room with its low ceiling, I quickly recognized Albinus with his broken nose and a face that was covered in large greenish-yellow bruises. He and his companions had already taken their places at table. Apologizing for my late arrival, I made for a gap on the bench beside him, and sat down.

'Some for you?' I asked, reaching for the loaf of rye bread on the table and tearing off a chunk.

'Thank you, no. I have some recently broken teeth and the crust is somewhat hard,' he answered, before sucking gingerly at his spoonful of turnip soup.

'How did that happen?' I enquired cheerfully, as if to make conversation. Albinus was of ordinary height, stoop shouldered and diffident. In company he was the sort of person who would be easily overlooked.

'You'll have heard about the attack on the Holy Father, I suppose,' he mumbled between sips.

'Only rumours. I've been away in the Northlands,' I lied. 'Tell me what happened.'

'It was monstrous. A crowd of villains burst out from the spectators on the Via Lata, right in front of the Church of Saints Stephen and Sylvester. In full view they knocked down His Holiness just as he was about to take his place in the procession of the Great Litany. Quite appalling.'

In telling his story, Albinus had become much more animated. He sat up straight and looked me in the eye. I guessed that he had told the story many times before.

'Is that when you got injured?' I asked him.

'It was.' He paused. 'But not so dreadfully as His Holiness. The attackers gouged out his eyes and cut out his tongue. He was lucky to escape with his life.' Albinus's battered face registered horror with almost theatrical exaggeration. By contrast his voice, though it had become stronger, remained strangely flat and unemotional, as if he was describing something at second-hand.

'You saw all this? It must have been a nightmare,' I said, coaxing him to continue.

'No. I was half-unconscious and driven away by those brutes.'

'What happened to the Holy Father?'

'He disappeared. When I came back with the papal guards, there was no sign of him. Just smears of blood on the pavement where he had been so savagely mutilated.'

'What did you do?'

'I was frantic. I made inquiries, and the next day there came word that the Pope was not dead but being held prisoner in a monastery up on the Caelian Hill.'

This was something I had not heard about from Arno, and the information would have a direct bearing on my investigation. 'How did he get there?'

Albinus turned down the corners of his mouth and simultaneously raised his shoulders in a gesture that I recalled was how the Romans expressed bafflement. 'His attackers must have taken him there. Naturally, as soon as we knew where he was, we organized a rescue. I went there with a party of papal guards and several of my colleagues.'

He looked around us as if to encourage those sitting nearby to listen to his tale.

'We got word into the monastery, to someone there who was as appalled as we were by what had happened. Late that evening, Pope Leo was lowered from a window on a rope. We were waiting in the street below, and brought him back to safety.'

'A miracle,' I said fervently. 'The angels must have been watching over the Holy Father. To lower a blind man, with no tongue, out of a window must have been near impossible.'

Albinus had laid down his spoon. Now he leaned across and gripped me by the wrist. 'But that was not the only miracle. When the Holy Father was incarcerated within the blackness of his prison, the angels came to him. They replaced his eyes and his tongue grew again.'

I sat absolutely still, waiting for him to go on.

'When we received the Pope, he was bruised and sorely

wounded, but he could see and speak!' the chamberlain added dramatically.

'Is he here now in this monastery?' I asked, hoping that I sounded suitably astonished.

Albinus let go my wrist. 'He dines with the Duke of Spoleto in the abbot's private quarters. His Holiness prefers seclusion. He prays that his enemies may be forgiven.'

'A truly amazing tale,' I said fervently. A monastery servant had placed a bowl of soup on the table in front of me while Albinus was talking. I put my face down towards my meal to hide from the chamberlain the doubt in my eyes.

*

Later that evening I wrote a full account of Albinus's story and left it with the Duke of Spoleto's staff. I gave instructions for it to be handed to Archbishop Arno when the papal party reached Paderborn. Doubtless, the duke's people would open and read my report, but that would do no harm. I repeated the tale exactly as I had heard it from Albinus and I relied on the worldly and sceptical archbishop to wonder at the truth in the recital.

# Chapter Three

I entered Rome exactly five weeks after leaving Paderborn and having had a trouble-free journey. Posing as a well-to-do pilgrim, I rented a comfortable room in a recently built hostel a short walk from St Peter's. My fellow guests were eager to gossip about the attack on Pope Leo, but no one could offer an opinion about who might have been responsible. All they wanted to talk about was the miracle that his eyes and tongue had been restored. The only useful information I gleaned came from a chance remark the landlord let drop. He mentioned that the noble families of Rome resented having Leo as the head of the Church. When I pressed him to explain, he would only say that Leo came from a humble family background and that many of the Roman aristocracy thought his elevation to the papacy demeaned the office. I thought it was a poor excuse to have a man half beaten to death but, rather than appear nosey, I decided to wait until I met Paul the Nomenculator to ask what lay behind the landlord's comment.

It was the perfect season to visit the Eternal City. The weather was delightful – cool enough at night to make sleeping comfortable, yet warm enough for me to leave my woollen Frankish clothing in my room the next morning and wear light cotton garments as I strolled down the gentle slope from St Peter's and into the city. I was on my way to inspect the spot where Leo had been attacked. I passed the bulk of Castel St Angelo, crossed the stone bridge over the dingy waters of the Tiber, and cut through the warren of narrow alleys and backstreets where most ordinary Romans lived in mean apartment blocks so closely packed that their balconies almost touched, and the sunshine rarely penetrated into the muddy lanes smelling of ordure. The city was much as I remembered – filthy, run-down and semi-derelict, the monuments of its past glory in ruins or being plundered for building materials. Many churches and monasteries had been remodelled from far older pagan buildings, and the newer commercial construction mostly catered to the burgeoning pilgrim trade. I passed souvenir shops, cheap eating-houses, taverns and money changers. The Via Lata, despite its name, was not broad, but a little more than ten yards wide. Arrow straight, it was paved with the original road surface, the slabs now worn and grooved. When I reached the basilica of Saints Stephen and Sylvester in front of which the attack had occurred, I discovered it was part of a much larger complex. A cluster of dilapidated classical buildings had been turned into the sprawling residence that the locals called a palazzo.

The chamberlain, Albinus, had said that the assault on the Pope had been very public and in full view. Then Leo had disappeared. The basilica was the nearest place where the attackers could have removed their victim, so I crossed the road, pushed open the door and went inside.

The complex was even larger than it appeared from the street. I was standing in the original marble-floored atrium, its centre open to the sky. Columns of dark red granite held up the surrounding red-tiled roof. Beyond them to left and right were several closed doors, while directly in front of me was the entrance to the church itself. Painted on the nearest doorpost was an inscription in red and gold lettering. I went forward and read down a list of names: it was a roll-call of saints and martyrs, more than twenty of them. At the top were Stephen and Sylvester. Many of the names below them were unknown to me and the name at the very bottom – Maximus – had been freshly added.

I was puzzling over the list when a man in a threadbare priest's gown emerged from the interior of the church. His face had once been round and plump, but now the cheeks had fallen in and he looked weary, almost haggard. He suggested that, for a small donation, he could show me the vial of holy water by which Saint Sylvester had cured the emperor Constantine of leprosy.

The priest's Latin was slow and careful. He had recognized me as a foreign visitor and must have thought that all foreigners struggled with the language.

'I'm afraid I have very little money with me, just a few coins,' I answered smoothly. I had learned Latin as a youngster and had used it often when at Carolus's court. 'I was warned to beware of cutpurses and pickpockets in the city.'

'But that is not all there is to see,' the priest coaxed. A bony finger pointed at the names on the doorpost beside us. 'Those are the holy martyrs whose relics have been recovered from their tombs and brought within our oratory. They, too, are on display. Only last month we received the bones of blessed Maximus who refused to worship the emperor's effigy and was stoned to death for his faith.'

It was worth investigating inside the church, so I dropped a couple of the local copper coins into the priest's outstretched palm. His slight grimace managed to convey that he was disappointed by the size of my contribution. Nevertheless, he led me inside. After the brightness of the atrium, it took my eyes several moments to adjust to the gloomy interior. My guide – I presumed he was the verger – was economizing on the cost of candles. Very few were lit. I followed him to the furthest end of the nave, up some steps and into an oratory. There, at eye level, a line of niches had been sunk in the wall. Each was about four feet wide and two feet high and protected by an iron grille. He stopped in front of the fourth niche. The thick bars were spaced far enough apart for me to see inside. Two small oil lamps of clay flickered on either side of a small crystal phial containing a clear liquid.

Laid out in front of the vial were some thin strips of leather.

'The bridle of the saint's horse,' said the priest in a complacent tone.

I stared at him blankly, and he felt obliged to explain. 'In gratitude for his cure, the emperor Constantine offered to serve as the saint's groom, and he went on foot, leading Sylvester's palfrey by those very same reins.' There was a significant pause. 'For a small additional sum you can handle them for yourself.'

'Will that also allow me to see around the rest of the building?' I asked.

The verger was coming to the conclusion that I was too much of a skinflint to be worth further attention. 'The building is private property,' he snapped.

'I've come far to see the sights . . .' I half turned.

The verger cut me off rudely. 'The basilica is cared for by the adjacent monastery – to which I belong – and my brothers do not receive casual visitors. If you wish to see the rest of the building, you need an invitation from the family.'

'The family?'

'This palazzo,' he explained curtly, 'has been owned for generations by the same noble family that has given us two popes: Stephen, the third of that name, and also his brother, Pope Paul. It was the latter, in his wisdom, who generously dedicated this wing to Saints Stephen and Sylvester.'

It was obvious that he was not going to let me nose around the building. 'Then, perhaps you could help me on another

matter,' I said. 'Can you tell me where I might find the Nomenculator Paul who served Pope Adrian?'

My question brought a sharp glance from the old priest. 'As
far as I know, he still lives where he has always done.' Suspicious
eyes scanned my face. 'But if you are going to him, seeking
favours, I have to tell you that Paul retired as Nomenculator on
the accession of our current Pope Leo.'

'Thank you. Then I know where to find him,' I said as I turned
and walked back down the street. Behind me I could feel the old
verger's eyes boring into my back. He was wondering how I, an
obvious stranger, should be acquainted with such a senior former
member of the papal staff.

*

Back in the bright sunshine of the Via Lata, I directed my steps
towards the familiar outline of the Colosseum. I had spent a winter
there, lodged with the ice bears and other animals on my way to
Baghdad. After a couple of hundred yards I turned up a side street
that led me into the area that the locals knew as the 'disabitato'
– 'the uninhabited'. Here large tracts of the ancient city had been
abandoned as its population drained away, moving to live closer
to the city centre. Amongst the derelict houses I noted one or two
quarries and a brickworks, but, for the most part, the people had
gone back to scratching a living from the land. I passed small plots
of land for growing vegetables, chicken runs, gardens converted
into vineyards with bunches of unripe berries tight on the vines,
and orchards where goats balanced on the branches of neglected
fig trees to crop the leaves. In the midst of this decline an occasional building was in excellent repair. One of them was home to
my friend, the former Nomenculator, and I recognized it immediately. It was a substantial square building of rust-red bricks and
would once have been the villa of an important Roman family. A

colonnaded porch ran the full width of the facade, from which a couple of Paul's house servants watched me approach along a broad, carefully tended gravel path lined with salvaged fragments of ancient statuary. Marble torsos without arms or legs, detached heads with blank eyes and battered noses, a plinth that supported only a pair of huge sandalled feet, and a cracked panel from a sarcophagus carved with a hunting scene were all reminders of my friend's passion for the history of his city.

One of the house servants brought me into the villa and to the side room where the former Nomenculator kept his personal archives.

'Sigwulf! A very pleasant surprise to see you back in Rome!' Paul cried, laying down the scroll he had been reading. The scroll curled itself up on the table as he heaved himself to his feet and came forward to greet me.

Paul had changed little. Short and heavy-set, his hair had turned white and had thinned now that he must have reached his mid-fifties. His complexion was as blotchy and veined as I remembered it. The great bags under his eyes and a bulbous nose still made it look as if he drank too heavily. But his eyes were alert with curiosity and held a gleam of good humour. Also, he still displayed the involuntary convulsion that I recalled so vividly: a sudden twitch of the side of his face every few minutes. It looked as if he was delivering a huge, conspiratorial wink.

'How are you?' he exclaimed, shaking me by the hand vigorously. I noted that, though he was retired, he still dressed as a priest.

He stood back and looked me up and down. 'My friend, you're beginning to go grey, just a little, but you look fit and well.'

'You've not changed much either,' I told him, 'and how is it that you still occupy this splendid villa?' I looked around the room in admiration. Its walls were painted with the original frescoes, idealized scenes of the countryside with fields, cattle and harvest. 'When I was last in Rome, you told me you only had the temporary use of this grand house because the previous owner had donated it to the Church and it was due to be turned into a monastery.'

Paul treated me to a foxy grin. 'Time crawls. Temporary so easily becomes permanent. Those inky-fingered *scriniarii* in the papal secretariat are unable to trace the document that allowed me to occupy the building. Until they do so – or locate a true copy – they are unable to evict me.'

I presumed the vital document was pigeonholed somewhere in the room where we were standing.

Paul tilted his head slightly, sizing me up. 'But what brings you here, Sigwulf? Is it something to do with our mutual acquaintance? I hear he has been made Bishop of Tours.'

'Alcuin is indirectly responsible for my visit,' I said, casting a glance towards the open door that led into the hallway.

Paul took the hint. He strode across the room, pulled the heavy door shut, and waved to a second chair beside the table. 'Take a seat, Sigwulf.'

'I'm told you no longer hold the position of Nomenculator?' I said.

'I was retired from the post by Pope Leo soon after his election. Naturally, he wanted one of his own men in the job. I didn't resent it of course. That's the way the papal bureaucracy works.'

'What's Pope Leo like?' I said.

The ex-Nomenculator pulled a face. 'Bit of a nonentity, but cunning. Tends to be underestimated.'

'I hear that he's unpopular with the noble families of Rome.'

'Is this something to do with your arrival here?' he asked. There was a sudden sharpness in my friend's voice as he resumed his own seat. 'The dukes, counts and other nobles dislike Leo intensely because he's not one of them. Leo joined the papal administration as a young man and worked his way up from humble acolyte until he planted his plebeian backside firmly on the throne of St Peter.'

'How did he manage that? Weren't the noble families of Rome sufficiently powerful to have blocked him?'

Paul shifted his position in his chair and leaned back. 'He moved too fast for them. Quite an operator, our Leo. Got himself elected Pope within twenty-four hours of the death of his predecessor.' He chuckled. 'Prepared the ground well. The vote was near-unanimous. That must have cost him a great deal.'

'He bought the votes?'

Paul snorted with amusement. 'How else? For years he had been making sure that either his friends got the key appointments amongst the *palatini* of the Lateran or, if they weren't friends, they paid him handsomely for their promotion. When it came to an election, they didn't want to waste their investment and be turned out of office by a pope they hadn't already bribed.'

'That brings me to the reason why I am here,' I told him. 'A member of King Carolus's council, Archbishop Arno of Salzburg, has a fat sheaf of letters, sent to him by churchmen here in Rome. They accuse Leo of all manner of inappropriate behaviour, ranging from simony to adultery.'

The eyebrows on the blotchy face shot up. 'A reputation to boast about!'

I kept my tone serious. 'Archbishop Arno needs to know if their accusations are linked to the attack on Pope Leo last April. On Alcuin's recommendation I've been sent to find out. Your name was mentioned as a useful contact.'

There was a moment's silence. 'And if the men behind the attack are identified, what then?' he asked cautiously.

'That's not decided. I'm only here to gather background information as discreetly as possible. Will you help me?'

There was another long pause as Paul thought about my request, then he smiled sardonically. 'Sigwulf, of course I'll help you. I'm bored with inactivity. As the Book of Proverbs so aptly puts it, "The Lord has made everything for his own ends, even the wicked for the evil day."'

He stood up. 'But first, let's eat. I always take my main meal at this time of day. Nothing elaborate. I find my digestion can no longer cope with rich food.'

*

Over pickled fish flavoured with sweet fennel, fruit and bread I explained to Paul what Albinus had told me, and about my brief visit to the Church of Saints Stephen and Sylvester.

'I had hoped to look around inside the church. My guess is that the attackers rushed Pope Leo there to get him off the street before his guards showed up.'

'That building was formerly a temple to Sol Invictus,' observed Paul, deftly extracting the backbone from a sardine, 'now it's a house of God, a monastery run by Greeks who moved here from Constantinople.'

'Would the Greeks in Rome have any reason to harm Leo? There seems be a Greek method in what happened,' I said.

'You mean the way the attackers tried to gouge out Leo's eyes and remove his tongue?'

'Isn't that what the Greeks of Byzantium do when they wish to dispose of an unwanted emperor?' I said. It was something that I had been thinking about during my long ride from Paderborn.

The former Nomenculator carefully placed the filleted fish on a slice of bread. 'Certainly that's the treatment Empress Irene meted out to her son Constantine so that she could take sole power. Had him blinded and shut away in a monastery.'

He took a bite of his food and chewed for a while before continuing. 'There are significant differences, though: Constantine's tongue was not removed, and the Greeks use hot coals to blind a man, not the point of a knife.' He let out a soft, satisfied belch. 'Furthermore, the Greeks do the job properly. Constantine did not survive. He died within days.'

I saw the direction his thoughts were taking. 'So you are not convinced that an angel came to Pope Leo when he was held captive, and restored his speech and eyesight.'

'That was a neat touch on the part of Leo or his advisors. It makes a wonderful story. It adds an aura of sanctity to an otherwise sordid event.' Paul dabbed at his mouth with a linen napkin. 'In my opinion, the clues that point to Greek involvement in the attack are altogether too obvious. From what Chamberlain Albinus told you, the men who assaulted the Pope were hired ruffians from the slums, and I may be able to trace them.'

'You have contacts amongst such people?' My voice expressed my surprise.

'Not directly,' he replied. 'You may recall that one of my responsibilities, when I was Nomenculator, was the recovery of the relics of early Christian martyrs. It brought me into contact with a number of middlemen who deal in stolen grave goods. They might have heard something.'

He rose and opened the door and beckoned to a servant to clear the dishes. 'Sigwulf, come back here in three days' time and I'll let you know what I've discovered.'

On my way out to the hallway I told him how grateful I was for his help.

The former Nomenculator waved aside my thanks. 'My friend, three groups run this city – the nobility, the merchants and the clergy. Of these, by far the most devious work up in the Lateran. If it turns out that some of the scheming rogues trying to get me evicted from this comfortable residence are amongst those complicit in the attack on Leo, I will be well rewarded.'

'Even if Arno and the other members of Carolus's council take no action against them?'

Paul's face lit up with mischief. 'Proverbs again: "A good man's house will still be standing after an evil man's house has been destroyed."'

# Chapter Four

THE THREE DAYS dragged by. When I returned to Paul's villa he was waiting for me with a dark-skinned man of medium height, whose tightly curled hair had been shaved to leave a central strip about four fingers wide, a crest. It gave him a menacing appearance that had to be deliberate. He also had one of the thickest necks I had ever seen. It went straight down from his ears until it merged into very wide sloping shoulders. A loose shirt did little to conceal an impressive barrel chest.

'Sigwulf, I would like you to meet Theodore,' Paul began. 'He has been very useful to me in the past when dealing with difficult fellow citizens.'

I nodded politely towards Theodore. He stared back at me, expressionless. His eyes were such a dark brown that they were almost black.

'Theodore lives in the Campus Martius district. He reports that at the end of last April, one of the local street gangs was flush with money. He suspects that they had been paid for carrying out an important job.'

'That certainly coincides with the timing of the attack on Pope Leo,' I agreed.

'Theodore knows where he can find one of the leading gang members. A nasty piece of work named Gavino.'

I glanced again at Theodore. He had not moved a muscle and

was still regarding me with an unblinking gaze that I found unsettling.

'Is Gavino of particular interest to us?' I asked Paul.

'He is.' Paul slid a hand inside his priest's gown and produced a small, flat metal object about three inches long and two inches wide. 'Gavino brought this to one of the dealers who handle stolen grave goods.'

He held the item out to me. It was an ornate gold belt buckle. The centre was moulded into the figure of a beast that was half lion and half eagle, a griffin.

'Where does this come from?'

'From the Avar Hoard. The style is distinctive.'

I had no need to ask about the Avar Hoard. When Carolus's troops, led by the Duke of Friuli, stormed the final Avar stronghold, they made an astonishing discovery: chest after chest filled with gold solidi, the coins minted by the Byzantines. For as long as anyone could remember, the emperors in Constantinople had been paying the Avars to leave them in peace. In some years, the bribe had been as much as 100,000 gold solidi. The Avars had amassed so much precious metal that they scarcely knew what to do with it. Only a fraction had been melted down to make the small items that the Avar goldsmiths could cope with: strap mounts, belt ornaments, decorations for their stirrups and harnesses, and so forth. The remainder had been left in coin. The Avar Hoard which had been brought back to Carolus had filled fifteen army carts; almost all of it was sacks of solidi. The haul more than repaid the entire costs of the Avar war.

'How did this get into the hands of a Roman gangster?' I enquired, turning the buckle over in my fingers. The workmanship was competent rather than delicate. I remembered hearing that Carolus had sent a good portion of the Avar booty to Rome as a thank-offering to the Church.

'That's a question I've asked Theodore to put to Gavino,' my friend said. 'And without delay. The moment that Gavino hears that Theodore is showing an interest in where he acquired that buckle, he'll make himself very scarce.'

His statement made me wonder about Theodore's reputation amongst Rome's underclass.

'If this was part of Gavino's pay for the attack on Leo, I should be present during the questioning,' I said, handing back the buckle.

Paul treated me to a sly look as he slipped the buckle into a pocket. 'I thought you would say that. Unfortunately, Theodore is not happy about taking you along to the interview. Gavino lives in a very rough district, very rough indeed.'

I took mild offence. 'I trained as a cavalryman in Carolus's army. Just give me the loan of a good sword and I can look after myself.'

'No sword, Sigwulf. Anyone walking into the Campus Martius with a sword on his hip would be looking for trouble. In the slums they use daggers.'

There was a twinkle in Paul's eyes as he added, 'I've persuaded Theodore to take you into the Campus Martius if you wear this.' He clapped his hands, and a house servant appeared carrying a soldier's mail shirt.

'Where on earth did you get it?' I asked as the garment was held out for my inspection. The shirt was an antique, its links rusty, the leather backing spotted with green mould. The shape and design were centuries old.

Paul chortled. 'It's a fake but good enough to turn a knife point.'

Mystified, I stared at him.

'A confidence trickster tried to pass it off on me. He said he had found it in a Christian grave, and that it was the very same mail shirt worn by St Hippolytus, the Roman soldier torn apart by horses for his faith.'

I took the shirt and inspected it more closely. Under the rust and mould it seemed reasonably sound.

'The attempt to age it was not very successful,' said Paul. 'The rust is superficial and rubs off easily. Also, I can assure you that the pattern of the rings is not correct for the period.'

I glanced across at Theodore. 'Will it satisfy you if I wear this?' I asked.

He gave me a reluctant nod. 'Put it on under your shirt,' he said and glanced up at a cloudless sky. 'The best time to find Gavino at home is in the middle of the day. He, like everyone else, tries to get out of the heat. We need to get going.'

*

As the two of us walked into the heart of the city, I was reminded how heavily a mail shirt weighs down on one's shoulders. It is not so noticeable when mounted on horseback, but on foot it is a real burden. Theodore advised me to take as much as possible of the weight on my hips by cinching my belt more tightly. Nevertheless, by the time the two of us reached the Campus Martius, I could feel raw rubbed patches on my shoulders. As my companion bluntly informed me, it was important not to draw attention to ourselves. A broad straw hat covered Theodore's distinctive hair style, and neither of us were carrying weapons. The plan was to stroll casually to the area where Gavino lived in a room on the first floor by himself, question him about the gold buckle, and then discreetly get clear before any of his fellow gang members knew we were there. Quite how Theodore proposed to conduct the interrogation was left unsaid, and I wondered if Theodore's obviously daunting reputation would be enough to get Gavino to provide the information I needed. I doubted it.

We entered the slums – a web of small, crooked streets, often no wider than the space for two men to walk abreast. The buildings were shabby and mean, three or four storeys high, their flaking walls defaced with graffiti. The footings of the walls were stained with patches of green and black mildew and Theodore pointed out the watermark left by the floods when the Tiber burst its banks each winter. There was rubbish everywhere. Thin cats picked their way across open drains, and packs of mangy dogs nosed bloated and unspeakable things in the gutters. The air stank of rot, decay and much worse. Crudely lettered signs indicated the shops and taverns, though most of them were shuttered against the midday heat that had driven the people indoors. We saw the usual shoals of urchins and a few slatternly looking women, some hauling buckets of water. I recalled Paul telling me that many of the aqueducts that once brought water into the city had fallen into disrepair. People had to draw water from local wells and carry it home.

We kept our pace slow and relaxed. Under his hat brim, my companion's glance was flicking from side to side, checking the side alleys. Once or twice he drew me into a doorway and we paused, waiting to see if we were being followed. Soon I had lost all sense of direction and we were deep within the tangle of streets when, abruptly, Theodore darted into passageway so narrow that I was obliged to walk behind him. On either side rose the scabby walls of centuries-old warehouses converted into dwellings. The all-pervading stink of urine caught in the back of my throat. From an open window high above us a quarrel was in progress between a man and a woman, their angry yells bouncing off the walls.

A dozen paces down the passage, Theodore put his meaty shoulder to a door and quietly forced the lock. He went up the sagging treads of a worn stairway to the first floor, then turned into short corridor lined with half a dozen doors.

Treading lightly, Theodore stopped in front of the third door and knocked. I waited half a step behind him, hearing the bawling of a baby somewhere further off. There was a smell of boiled cabbage. There was no reply to Theodore's knock and, for a moment, I thought we had wasted our time. I eased the mail shirt on my shoulders.

Theodore knocked again, more insistently, and this time there came a response. The words must have been in the local Roman dialect, but it was clear that the occupant of the room was telling us to go away. In reply, Theodore mumbled something indistinct, using an apologetic tone, and rapped on the door a third time. There was a burst of obvious profanity, then the tread of approaching feet.

The door opened a few inches and I caught a glimpse of a sleepy, unshaven face with black stubble and a rash of pockmarks on the cheeks and jaw. The man's gaze focused on Theodore. The eyes widened in alarm, and the man jerked back, pushing the door shut. Theodore was much too quick for him. He had a foot in the gap and, a moment later, his weight hit the door and he burst in.

Gavino, for it had to be the man we were seeking, was as quick as a stoat. Dressed only in a long shirt, his skinny bare legs propelled him across the room as he bolted towards the open window. He flung one leg over the sill and was about to drop clear when Theodore grabbed him by the shirt tail and dragged him back. I was still standing in the open doorway.

'Shut the door behind you,' Theodore ordered me in a quiet voice.

I did as I was told and turned back to see that Theodore had twisted Gavino's arm behind his back and clamped a hand over his mouth. Gavino was of my own height, scrawny and rawboned, with sunken, watchful eyes.

His room was a mess. A rumpled sheet on a narrow bed

against the wall showed where he had been asleep. Some clothes hung from nails driven into the plaster. Other garments stayed where they had been thrown on the scratched and stained floorboards. The stale remains of a part-eaten meal lay on the single table; next to it were a couple of stools. In one corner a half-full bucket served as a lavatory. There was also a pail of what passed for fresh water, though it had a murky scum.

The gangster's eyes rolled upward in fright as his attacker dragged him backwards towards the bed and thrust him face down into the soiled mattress.

Kneeling on Gavino's back, Theodore lashed his victim's arms behind him with a thin leather thong he produced from his pocket. He stood up, expertly turned Gavino over, and propped him up so that he was sitting with his back against the wall.

'This gentleman wants to know whether you were part of the group that attacked Pope Leo,' Theodore asked.

Gavino's eyes slid in my direction. 'If he wants to know, he should pay me,' he said.

Theodore punched him expertly in the mouth. A short, precise blow that split the lip. Gavino's head slammed back against the wall.

When Gavino came straight again, he said something ugly to Theodore in what I supposed was local slang. Again Theodore struck him, a sharp jab that travelled no distance and struck at precisely the same spot.

'Speak only Latin so this gentleman can understand,' he growled. 'Were you with the men who attacked the Pope?'

Gavino glared back at him, and remained silent.

Theodore turned to me. 'Top up that bucket of piss, will you,' he requested.

It took me a moment to realize that he wanted me to tip the water into slop bucket. I did as he asked. Now the bucket was nearly two thirds full with a vile mix of watered-down urine. In it floated a lone turd.

Theodore's hands moved fast. He seized Gavino by the ankles and lifted him into the air, hanging head down. The gangster could not have weighed much – he was all skin and bones. Theodore took him across the room like a farmer carrying a chicken to market. 'Keep the bucket steady,' he told me.

I held the bucket as Theodore lowered his victim's head towards it. Gavino wriggled like a hooked fish, avoiding the plunge. Calmly, Theodore raised him enough to be able to knee him viciously in the face. While Gavino was still stunned, Theodore plunged his victim's head into the bucket and held him there. After several seconds he lifted him up and Gavino's head reappeared; his long black hair was dripping.

'Answer my question,' said Theodore.

Gavino was still upside down, spluttering and gasping for breath. 'Put me down. I'll tell you what you want to know,' he said, gagging.

Theodore set him back on the bed. Gavino wheezed and coughed. Unable to wipe his face, he screwed up his eyes and shook his head from side to side.

'Don't keep me waiting,' warned Theodore.

'I was one of them,' Gavino admitted.

'Who hired you?'

'I have no idea. The word was passed: where to muster and to bring a knife or a cudgel.'

'Never told about your target?'

'Only that it was an easy hit. One man amongst half a dozen high-ups, all unarmed.'

'What else?'

The gangster made the mistake of running his tongue over his lips and had to spit to clear the taste. 'We were to wait till they got off their horses, then go for the leader, only him. He was our mark.'

I intervened. 'How were you to know who their leader was?'

Gavino squinted at me. His eyes were red-rimmed and oozing. 'He would be the one wearing the really flash costume with all the gold trimmings. As it turned out, he also had on a different-coloured hat from the others – a tall white one.'

'And that was enough to pick him out?' I said.

The gangster sneered. 'No problem. The others had stupid-looking purple caps. A couple of them weren't even wearing their fancy dress.'

Theodore took over the questioning. 'Anything else in your instructions?'

'A promise of a bonus to the man who took out the eyes of the mark, and cut out his tongue.' Gavino began to cough, a sustained strangled sound as if he was choking. Theodore slapped him across the face. 'Enough of that. Don't waste my time. Tell me what happened.'

'We did as we were told, knocked him down, cut him up a bit, then dumped him in that church nearby.'

'Then what?'

'Collected our cash and left. Never saw Fur Hat again.'

'Fur Hat?'

'Fellow who showed up and gave us our last-minute orders. Tall, looked like a halfwit with his head in a winter hat.'

'How much were you paid?' I asked.

'Not enough,' came the quick answer. Gavino was regaining a little of his bombast.

Some instinct made me ask, 'That gold buckle must have fetched a good price?'

Gavino unwisely chose to be obtuse. 'What gold buckle?'

It was a mistake. Theodore grabbed him again by the ankles

and began to lift. 'Stop!' the gangster begged him. 'That buckle was different.'

Theodore let him drop back on the bed. 'Explain.'

'The lads and I decided that we hadn't been paid enough. Thought we would top up our wages, take what we deserved.'

I was puzzled. 'Take from whom?'

'From those others that we'd chased off.'

'But you said you didn't know who they were,' said Theodore. There was a dangerous warning note in his voice.

'Not until we'd done the job,' said Gavino. 'It was Beppe who told us that the fellow we'd knocked about was the Pope.' He shifted nervously.

'Surely you knew the Pope by sight?' I scoffed.

'I don't go to church myself. Once they're dressed up in their ridiculous hats and robes and jewels, I've no idea who is who.'

'Back to that gold buckle,' Theodore prompted. 'Where did you find that?'

'Beppe told us that he knew where one of the other fellows lived.'

'What other fellow?'

'Another of the high-ups. We reckoned he had gone running for help and his place would be wide open. Beppe knew where to go, and there could be rich pickings. He'd been wearing a jewelled cross on a gold chain. Had it snatched off him.'

'So what did you do?'

'All of us went off to this house. The house servants were too scared to stop us. We strolled in and grabbed what was on offer. That's where I got the gold buckle. The others got quite a bit too. Nearly doubled our wages for the original job.'

Theodore turned to look at me. 'Heard enough?' he asked.

I nodded.

Theodore ripped two rags off the bed sheet, balled up one of them and stuffed it into Gavino's mouth. The other he used as a gag to hold it in place.

'Time to go,' he said to me as he ushered me out of the room. We had stayed too long.

As we stepped out of the side alley and into the empty street, a piercing whistle rang out. It was shockingly close.

Theodore planted a powerful hand in my back and gave me a shove. 'Run!' he ordered.

There was another whistle, this time from somewhere high above us, a watcher on the roof top or an upper window. By then I was sprinting down the narrow street, avoiding the treacherous slime in the central gutter. I had never been a fast runner, and the weight of the mail shirt slowed me even more. I had no idea where I was going until, from some distance behind me, Theodore's voice shouted: 'Second corner left!'

I turned the corner, my heart pounding. I had gone no distance at all, yet already I could feel myself getting short of breath. Ahead of me was a crooked laneway, scarcely eight feet wide. A man stepped out of a doorway where he had been waiting, and moved to block my path. He was small and wiry, with a feral look. He was just thirty paces ahead of me, and in his right hand he held a knife. I had no choice but to keep running. If I came to a stop, the pursuit would catch up with me. I pounded forward as he moved into a crouch, left arm held out to impede my passage, the knife held low. I charged straight at him, hoping to knock him off balance. But he was nimble and experienced. As I closed in, he stepped neatly aside and, with his left hand, he reached up and caught me by the shirt. Then he pulled me in tight and drove the knife into my side, a practised upward strike that should have slid between the ribs.

The blade struck the iron links of my mail. I felt a sharp pain as the point penetrated a short distance. Then, as luck would have it, the tip of the dagger caught in the metal rings. A look of surprise flashed across the face of my intended killer and then I was using my weight to pivot around his grip on my shirt. With my free hand I chopped down on the back of his neck. He grunted and the two of us tipped over in a heap on the road surface. By a second stroke of good fortune my mail-clad body crashed heavily across my opponent's face as we fell. For a moment he was stupefied, one hand groping blindly for the dagger he had dropped. I rolled clear and scrambled up on all fours. I scuttled forward, twined my fingers in his long black hair, and with all my strength slammed his head against the cobbles. There was a thud and he went slack. Twice more I battered his head on the stone as hard as I could, gasping with the effort. Then I rose to my feet, leaving him senseless.

Theodore was nowhere to be seen. There was distant shouting and another whistle, fainter than before. I could only imagine that he had led them in a different direction. Briefly I thought of going back to assist him, but put it out of my mind. Somehow I felt that he was fully capable of dealing with the situation. I took several deep breaths to fill my lungs and steady my nerves, and then I began to run again, this time with less panic. I had to hope that Gavino's gang had posted only a single guard in my direction, and that I could successfully confuse any pursuit by varying my route. So I doubled back and forth, took unexpected side turns, and as soon as I felt it was safer to do so, I slowed to a walk rather than attract attention to myself. It was now mid-afternoon and more and more people were appearing on the streets. I mingled with them, matching my pace to theirs until I found myself in a middle-class district where the passers-by were well-to-do and respectable. Looking about me, I caught a glimpse of the great bulk of the Colosseum, towering over the roof tops. With it as a landmark, I headed for the disabitato.

*

Paul made light of my adventure when I got back to his villa and told him about my flight and the struggle in the street.

'Saved by the sacred shirt of St Hippolytus!' he teased. 'The relic must be genuine.'

I didn't find it quite so funny. 'What about Theodore? He could be dead by now.'

My friend was untroubled. 'Don't worry about him. He knows the back alleys and short cuts. Gavino's gang will chase him out of their territory and leave it at that.'

'But a gang member tried to gut me,' I reminded him.

'That's different. You're an outsider and fair game. If they harmed Theodore, they'd start a feud with Theodore's gang and they wouldn't want that.'

He brought me again to the room where he kept his archives. He waved me to a seat and, taking a wax tablet and a beautifully carved antique ivory stylus, sat down at the table ready to take notes.

'So what did you learn from your interview with Gavino?' he asked.

I told him how Gavino had been recruited with the other members of his gang and how they had carried out their instructions on the day.

'It would be ideal if we could identify Fur Hat,' I concluded. 'But his hat was an effective disguise. We only know that he's a tall man and, apart from him, Gavino never met the people behind the assault.'

Paul tapped the end of the stylus against his teeth. 'You're sure that Gavino wasn't told the precise identity of the man they were to attack? Only that he would be the most richly dressed member of the group of riders, the one with the flash costume, as he put it?'

'That's what he said.'

Paul looked pleased with himself. 'There's our lead. We may be able to trace some of the plotters.'

Perplexed, I frowned at him. 'I'm afraid I don't follow you.'

'Ask yourself why the plotters didn't provide Gavino's gang with a physical description of Leo. That would have been simpler.'

'Maybe Leo is difficult to describe, very ordinary-looking?' I suggested.

'He's unimpressive, that I'll grant you. But consider also Gavino's statement that two of the priests riding with the Pope were not wearing their ceremonial robes. Why was that?'

'Maybe the two priests were late and did not have time to dress correctly,' I said.

Paul shot me a glance of patient reproof. 'The ceremony of the Great Litany is a very major event in the Church calendar, same time every year. No one in the Church needs reminding when it takes place.'

I saw the direction his thoughts had taken. 'You think that two of the riders were incorrectly dressed so that Gavino and his friends would not attack them.'

'Well done, Sigwulf! For a senior celebrant to show up for the celebration of the Great Litany not wearing his formal robes is unheard of.'

Paul twiddled the stylus between his fingers. 'Employing unreliable ruffians like Gavino can lead to all sorts of mistakes. In a wild scuffle the wrong people are hurt.'

'But what about the other priests who were dressed in their robes? They were at risk of injury.'

Paul shrugged. 'That was of little concern to the plotters. What mattered was to get at Leo without endangering those two riders.'

'If you are correct, it means those two priests knew that the Pope would be attacked.'

'Precisely.'

'And can we find out who they were?'

Paul chuckled. 'Easily. Only the very senior office holders accompany the Pope in the procession of the Great Litany. It is a jealously guarded privilege.'

The implication of his remark sank in. 'So the plot against the Pope was hatched right at the top of the papal household.'

The former Nomenculator took the suggestion in his stride. 'The priests who work at St John Lateran on the Caelian Hill are no strangers to intrigue. The higher they rise, the more ambitious they become.'

Now I understood why my friend was so pleased with himself. 'And you have a way to find out which of them did not wear their proper robes that day.'

My friend treated me to a confident grin. 'I retain excellent contacts amongst the *scriniarii*.'

'Please be very careful how you use them,' I told him. 'Archbishop Arno wants these investigations to remain secret.'

'Don't worry, Sigwulf. My inquiries will be very discreet.' There was a brief pause as the side of his face twitched in an involuntary convulsion. 'Vestments worn on great ceremonies are extremely valuable. They are Church treasure – issued on the correct day and returned after the ceremony to the vestararius, who is the keeper of the sacristy and altar furnishings. His clerks write down a strict account of the loans, to whom, when returned and so forth. I know someone in the *scriniarium* who can check the logbooks for me.'

The mention of valuables reminded me of the gold buckle from the Avar Hoard.

'That Avar buckle was not part of Gavino's pay for the attack,' I said.

For once Paul appeared at a loss. 'Then how did Gavino get his hands on it?'

'Gavino stole the buckle from the house of one of the priests in the procession,' I told him and explained about the gang's decision to loot the home of one of Leo's colleagues.

'Did he say which one?'

I shook my head.

'A pity. Gavino will go to ground after what happened today. We won't be able to interrogate him again so easily.'

'Perhaps there is a clue. Gavino claims that a member of his gang had snatched a valuable cross from the same man. He was wearing it on a gold chain round his neck. Maybe that cross will turn up. You might ask the dealers you know.'

Paul's face cleared. I noticed that the whites of his eyes were patterned with thin red veins that matched his sagging underlids, rather like those one saw with certain breeds of hunting dogs. 'The pectoral crosses worn by senior clergy are also closely monitored, just like the ceremonial vestments, though by a different department,' he said. 'They are released on loan by the arcarius, the general treasurer. I can ask my source if a pectoral cross is missing from the treasury, and to whom it was issued.'

He got up and came round the table to lay a hand on my shoulder. 'I apologize for making fun of your escapade in the slums this morning. In case Gavino and his friends are planning to finish you off – or the conspirators behind the plot know why you have come to Rome and are keen on getting rid of you – it might be safer if you avoided your lodgings and stayed here in the villa.'

# Chapter Five

WHOEVER HE WAS, Paul's source amongst the *scriniarii* of the Lateran was very prompt in ferreting out the names he required.

'Paschal and Campulus,' my friend announced to me the following afternoon. 'Neither priest drew his ceremonial vestments from the vestararius on the day Leo was attacked. Yet they were both in the procession.'

'Are they important members of the papal household?' I asked. It was a glorious July day with a few fleecy clouds almost motionless in a sky of purest blue, and we were standing in Paul's garden where he had taken me to show off his collection of salvaged statuary.

He took a moment to flick a dried bird dropping from the marble shoulder of a life-sized female figure. From the neck up, the statue's head was missing, leaving one to wonder if her face had been as perfectly proportioned as her body, demurely clothed in a flowing gown that left one arm bare.

'The very pinnacle. Campulus is Leo's sacellarius. He makes the disbursements from the papal coffers. In effect, he's the papal treasurer. Paschal is, if anything, even more senior. He's primicerius, the head man, of the chancery. He is the director over all the notaries.'

'Why would either of them wish to harm Leo?'

'In Paschal's case, that's easy to answer. He was Pope Adrian's nephew and there was every expectation that he would succeed his uncle on St Peter's throne. Leo outmanoeuvred and out-bribed him. If someone gets rid of Leo, the job might well come back into the family.'

'So Paschal's a favourite of the nobility, I would imagine.'

'Undoubtedly.'

'And Campulus?'

'Another papal insider, through and through. Like Leo, he spent his working life amongst the *palatini*. He's a faction man, and had probably thrown in his lot with Paschal. He would have been very disappointed when Leo got the top job.'

I grinned at my friend. 'They must miss you at St John Lateran. You twitch the spider's web and within hours you know who's got himself in a tangle.'

Paul ignored my frivolity. 'You're forgetting the pectoral cross snatched from the man whose home was ransacked and where Gavino stole the Avar gold buckle. The cross was returned to the treasury a full day after the attack on Leo. The official in charge, the arcarius, had been very distraught about its disappearance but kept quiet, fearing a scandal.'

'Who brought it back?'

'The same priest to whom it had been loaned for the procession: the Pope's chamberlain.'

At once an image sprang to my mind: the bruised and swollen face of the meek-looking churchman seated beside me at table in the monastery on my way to Rome.

'You mean Albinus?' I was shocked. 'He never mentioned to me that his house had been ransacked. And what was an Avar gold buckle doing in his house?'

Paul smiled frostily. 'It doesn't make sense to me either. I've been wondering if Gavino made up his story, just to mislead you.'

He looked past me, over my shoulder. 'You can be sure that Gavino has fled Rome by now or gone into hiding so we aren't able to interrogate him again to check his story. Instead, I propose we take a rather unorthodox approach.'

I turned. Coming towards us was the familiar stocky figure of Theodore. I was relieved to see that he was completely unharmed.

'How did you get away?' I asked him as soon as he reached us.

'Fought, then ran,' he answered flatly.

'Theodore, I need a few more hours of your time,' Paul told him. 'I've decided to make an unannounced visit to the house of Pope Leo's chamberlain. It was Chamberlain Albinus who had his pectoral cross snatched during the attack on Pope Leo, and the chamberlain's residence is where Gavino then got his hands on the Avar gold buckle. But of course Gavino may be lying.' He caught my eye. 'Don't be alarmed, Sigwulf. Albinus is still away in Frankia. There'll be only a few house servants in residence. The two of you come with me.'

Without giving me time to ask exactly what he had in mind, my friend sauntered off down the path to the front entrance of the grounds of his villa. Turning left, he led us into the run-down surroundings of the disabitato.

'Chamberlain Albinus occupies another of the properties gifted to the Lateran,' Paul explained to me as we ambled along. 'A fine, big house – the original owner must have been very wealthy – and it is well sited, with a splendid view over the city.'

'You seem to know a lot about it,' I commented.

'I looked at it myself before I chose my present accommodation,' he said without a trace of embarrassment.

Our route was taking us uphill, the land rising gently. On each side of the track the stones and bricks had collapsed from boundary walls, or been stolen. Some gaps were filled with wooden fencing or woven hurdles so the abandoned gardens could be used as rough grazing for donkeys and cows. In other places nothing had been done, and the plots of land were overgrown with briars and scrub, home to small songbirds flitting amongst the thickets. Weeds sprouted between the original paving slabs of the road surface and silt choked the drains. Where houses had lost their entire roofs, they were abandoned shells. If enough tiles had survived or the exposed rafters could support reed thatch, squatters had moved in. There were scorch marks on the walls where they lit their cooking fires, chickens and pigs rooted about, and their children interrupted their games to run out and watch us pass. At a crossroads a small roadside temple had been converted to a cow byre. The farmer was mucking out with a pitchfork.

After about half a mile, Paul turned down a side lane so little used that a hare lolloped away ahead of us before making a leisurely sideways leap and disappearing into the long grass of the verge. To our right an ancient boundary wall was in comparatively good repair until, after a couple of hundred paces, we stopped where the topmost three feet had broken away. Here we found ourselves looking into the rear of what had once been a grand two-storey mansion. It had servants' quarters, cookhouses, pantries and storage sheds. Immediately in front of us were the remains of a formal garden with a large stone basin and fountain at its centre. The fountain was dry and the garden was a jungle of weeds except for the far corner where a thriving vegetable patch was planted with neat rows of what looked like radicchio and chicory.

'The home of Chamberlain Albinus,' Paul announced, speaking softly, though we had not seen anyone since turning down the lane and the place looked deserted.

'I need to get into the rooms at the front of the house,' he said to Theodore. 'Just long enough to look around.'

'Wait here,' Theodore told us. He scrambled over the broken wall and we saw him carefully work his way across the overgrown garden until he was lost from view amongst the columns at the back of the main building.

'I hope you know what you're getting yourself into,' I whispered to Paul. 'If this venture ends in another chase, people are certain to remember seeing a priest in full flight.'

'I won't be running away on my own,' my friend replied with a mischievous sideways glance. 'I'm sure Archbishop Arno will expect your eyewitness description of anything that turns up.'

He found himself a sharp twig and began to scratch faint lines on the flat surface of a stone. 'Doubtless Albinus has installed himself in the main reception room to the front,' he explained, drawing a large rectangle. 'Here we are on the edge of the garden. These smaller buildings at the side and back will be servants' quarters. Our problem is to get to the front rooms without raising the alarm.'

'What are we looking for?' I ventured to ask.

'Something that convinces us that Gavino was telling the truth and that he did find that Avar buckle in that house.'

In less than five minutes Theodore was back. For such a burly man he was remarkably nimble and moved very quietly. 'Three, maybe four, servants in the house,' he reported, dropping quietly to the ground beside us and dusting off his hands. 'I could hear them talking. It sounds as though they've finished work for the day and are sitting out in the sunshine somewhere in the main courtyard.'

'What's the best way in?' Paul asked him.

'There's a back door that will get you into the outbuildings, but you'll then have to cross open space in full view of the servants to reach the main house.' He reached up and eased his shirt collar that was too tight around his bull neck. 'I can deal with the servants if that's what you want.'

'No violence,' I insisted. 'We can distract them.'

They both looked at me questioningly.

'We passed some goats further back along the lane. They're in an orchard, and no sign of their owner. We could borrow them to create a diversion. Goats love vegetables.'

Paul treated me to a gleeful smile. 'Sigwulf, you ought to join Gavino's gang. You are a natural housebreaker.'

The three of us retraced our steps to where we could round up half a dozen goats. We drove them to where we could hoist them one by one over the broken wall and let them free. Almost immediately the lead goat, an elderly brown-and-white nanny, noticed the vegetable garden. She bounded off, tail high and her long ears flopping, followed by her eager companions. They fell upon the feast.

For another five minutes we waited and watched as the goats gorged themselves. They trampled the neat rows of chicory and radicchio, tore up the vegetables, and stood in a gluttonous trance, leaves and roots hanging from their jaws.

Eventually, there was a cry of anger from somewhere within the servants' area of the house, followed by hallooing and shouting.

'Hurry!' Theodore hissed and led us down the lane a little distance. There he stopped and turned. Clasping his hands together, he made a stirrup so that he could hoist first Paul and then myself over the wall. We landed in waste ground and scuttled to the door in the rear wall of the service quarters. A swarm of black buzzing flies and a strong smell of human excrement indicated that this was where the servants emptied out the night soil. I tugged the door open and Paul and I passed quickly through a pantry where clay storage jars were shelved, then on through an empty kitchen. A quick look into the courtyard confirmed that it was deserted, and we crossed the open space to the main building, hearing shouts, whistles and hand claps as Albinus's staff tried to save their vegetables.

Centuries ago someone had spent a great deal of money on beautifying the main building. Every floor was covered with fine mosaics. There were geometric designs and pictures of animals and plants. Hundreds of the little marble cubes were missing, but it was still possible to recognize scenes from the hunt, the gymnasium and the circus arena. More mosaics were set as panels in the walls. We hurried on through an atrium, Paul leading the way briskly, his long gown swinging, until we came to a pair of double doors. They were unlocked and I followed him into a large reception room. Intricate painted mouldings decorated the high wooden ceiling. Evening light flooded in through tall glazed windows. Some of the panes were of coloured glass and the marble floor was splashed with patches of yellow, blue and salmon-pink. Faded frescoes covered the walls with yet more themes from the classics.

Amid this elegance the domestic furniture was serviceable and plain: a couple of sturdy tables, several chairs and stools, two sets of tall iron candle stands, and some worn cushions. There were no rugs or wall hangings. The room had a faintly musty smell, and it was clear that it was unused during Albinus's absence.

'Not much evidence of wealth here,' I muttered to Paul.

He was moving around the room looking at the quality of the furnishings. 'Albinus won't have left anything valuable on display while he was away,' he answered.

He stopped beside a large chest placed against the wall. 'Did Gavino mention anything about a chest for valuables?'

'No.'

He lifted the lid. The chest was empty. 'I wonder what was kept in here?'

He crouched down and peered at the lock. 'If Gavino really did steal that gold buckle from this house, my guess is that he took it from wherever Albinus kept his clothes. Probably upstairs.'

'Should we look up there?' I asked. I was beginning to wonder if Gavino had lied to me. The room we were searching belonged to a man of simple tastes.

'I doubt we'd find anything. Gavino's gang would have carried off everything they could grab,' Paul replied.

He was still examining the lock. 'This lock is stout enough to withstand Gavino and friends if they were in a hurry.'

He straightened up. 'Let's check the adjacent rooms.'

He went to the door, eased it open and made sure that the coast was clear. Then the two of us made our way quietly down a short corridor to our left.

The first door opened into what had been the original bath-house. It had a tiled floor with a channel to carry away waste water, stone benches along the walls, and narrow windows set high up to let in light and air. An interconnecting door led into the next room. 'Very impressive,' Paul muttered, 'whoever built this house liked his luxuries, with hot and cold rooms.'

Both rooms were abandoned and empty.

We continued to a third and final room. It was a latrine, spacious and still in use though not with the original plumbing. A large chamber pot stood next to a stone bench with its row of four large holes.

Paul closed the door behind us and sniffed. 'Good ventilation,' he commented. He walked over and took a quick look into the chamber pot. 'And Albinus has his servants well trained. They've dumped the contents.'

I recalled the smell of excrement outside the back door and the dry fountain in the garden. There was no longer any running water in the house. Paul must have had the same thought. He was squinting down into the disused watercourse beneath the latrine seats. It would make an ideal hiding place. He found nothing.

'Maybe we should look upstairs, after all,' he suggested, turning away.

At that instant my heart flew into my throat. The door behind us was opening. I expected a servant to enter but it was Theodore who stepped quietly into the room.

'You gave me a fright,' I told him.

'Only the old nanny goat still to be caught.' He grinned. 'She's leading them a merry chase. I thought I had better be with you, if you're discovered.'

Something was naggingly familiar in the room. Then a faint memory stirred. It was of my visit to the church and the verger showing off the holy relics.

'Might be worth checking up there,' I said, pointing up to the rusty iron grille that covered the air vent to the latrine. The vent was a yard wide and half as high, placed directly over the row of lavatory seats. It had reminded me of the niche where St Sylvester's holy vial and reins had been on display.

Theodore stepped up on the bench and tugged at the grille. It came away easily. He felt inside the niche and pulled down a leather mule pannier. There was a faint rattling noise as he handed it to Paul, at the same time treating me to a slight nod of approval.

Paul dipped his hand into the pannier and gave a grunt of pleased surprise as he took out a gold goblet, about eight inches high. For a moment I thought it was an altar vessel, a chalice, and I wondered if Albinus had some honest reason to keep it safely hidden in his home.

Paul twirled the item by its stem. 'Not bad!' he said and there was admiration in his voice. 'Here, Sigwulf, take a look.'

He passed the goblet to me. It weighed at least a pound, and the goldsmith had been a master craftsman. He had fluted the lower half of the bowl with delicate grooves and embellished the remaining space up to the rim with an intricate floral pattern carved into the soft metal.

Paul next pulled from the pannier an eye-catching flagon in the plump shape of a tear drop. From its circular base to the elegant neck it stood a foot high and must have had a capacity of at least two bottles of wine. It reminded me of the graceful vases I had seen in the court of the Caliph in Baghdad. Those vases had been made of fine porcelain while this vessel, by contrast, was cast from massive gold. As Paul held the flagon out to me to admire, I saw the image carved into the surface: a mounted warrior. The detailing was exquisite. He wore the same style of chain mail that had saved me from the dagger thrust in a Roman slum, though his armour was an ingenious three-quarter-length body suit. It reached to his elbows and down to his knees and a coif protected his neck and head. Heavy gauntlets and shin guards completed his full protection and on his head was a conical helmet with a double plume. Over his right shoulder he carried a lance with a swallow-tail pennant and he sat astride a magnificent, high-stepping horse with a plaited mane and tail, and decorated harness. But what drew my eye was what he held in his left hand: the topknot of an unfortunate wretch who was being forced to run alongside his mount. It was his captive, also clad in chain mail, bearded and with a long drooping moustache. The helpless prisoner was being pulled along by his hair, on display for all to see. The goldsmith had sculpted the piece so that the face of the mounted warrior turned outward, towards the viewer. It was a flattish, severe countenance; there was a heavy, well-trimmed moustache above a wide, straight mouth, a hint of a beard, and large slightly slanted eyes staring straight out. The expression was of triumph, self-confidence and haughtiness – the face of a conqueror, a prince.

Dangling from the crupper of his saddle, next to the stumbling captive, was another trophy: a severed human head.

'A little gruesome for my taste,' observed Paul, setting the flagon aside on the stone latrine bench. He then proceeded to empty the pannier of all its contents, placing the items one by one in a line: more bowls, cups and several plates. Some had been wrapped in cloth. All were solid gold or a combination of gold and silver.

Paul gave a wry smile. 'More suited to a pagan banqueting table than the altar. Looks like these too came from the Avar Hoard that Carolus donated to the Church.'

'What do we do now?' I asked.

Paul thought for a moment. 'We return these items to where we found them, keeping just a couple of samples for you to show to Archbishop Arno. Otherwise the good archbishop might not believe your report.'

He wrapped the goblet and the flagon in cloth and put the other items back in the leather pannier. Theodore returned the pannier to where he had found it, and replaced the metal grille.

Paul had cocked his head on one side and was listening. Presumably the goats had gone because there was silence from the vegetable garden. I heard only the thumping of my own heart. Belatedly, I wondered how we would be able to leave the building unobserved now that the servants had, most likely, come back into the house.

Paul seemed unworried. 'Time to be on our way,' he murmured and Theodore and I followed him back past the main reception room and into a deserted entrance hall. The tall front doors of the mansion were warped and very old, possibly as old as the house itself.

'As I had expected – barred, not locked,' said Paul in a satisfied tone. 'Albinus probably kept to the original method as being more secure. And so it is . . . unless you're on the inside.'

Gently he slid back the wooden bar that held the doors closed, and I held my breath, fearing the groan of ancient hinges would betray us. But Albinus's conscientious staff had kept them greased. One leaf opened quietly, far enough for the three of us to slip outside.

'Give me a moment,' said Theodore.

From his pocket he produced a length of cord. Now, to my alarm, he slipped back into the house, reappearing a moment later with the ends of the cord, one in each hand. The cord itself was taut around the door's edge.

'Pull the door almost closed and hold it so that the cord's not pinched,' he said to us. We did as he asked, then Theodore pulled smoothly on the cord. He must have looped it around the lock bar for I heard it slide back into position on the far side.

'A useful lesson in housebreaking for you, Sigwulf,' Paul whispered to me.

Theodore permitted himself a slight smile. 'Only works when the doors don't fit well,' he admitted, releasing one end of the cord and pulling it free.

We sauntered away across the disabitato, careful to go at our previous casual pace. After some distance Theodore turned aside, to go directly back to his home. Paul promised him a bonus. 'That was good work with the bar,' he said. 'When Albinus comes home and finds his loss, but no sign of a break-in, he'll think the servants discovered his hiding place and helped themselves. He may go as far as questioning them, but they will plead their innocence. It will add to the mystery.'

I waited until we had got back to Paul's house and were again in his study, with the door closed, before I voiced the idea that had been forming in my mind. 'Albinus must have gone to the dealers in stolen goods and bought back his pectoral cross so that he could return it to the arcarius and avoid awkward questions about the Pope's ambush. He was already stealing from the Church and did not want to attract attention to himself.'

Paul nodded. 'He's certainly a thief, but I have a suspicion that this goes rather deeper than that.'

'Something to do with the attack on Pope Leo?'

'All three men who've come to our attention had easy access to the papal treasury – Paschal and Campulus under Pope Adrian; then Albinus under Leo.'

'You believe there was some sort of collusion between them?'

He gave cynical smile. 'It would not surprise me.'

'But that makes no sense,' I said. 'Campulus and Paschal belong to the faction that wants Leo replaced. Albinus is aligned with their opponents. He's Leo's appointment and if Leo goes, so does he.'

'That's a conundrum you might mention to Archbishop Arno, and let him work out the answer,' Paul replied. He unrolled the cloth in which he had carried the gold chalice and the flagon with its image of the triumphant horseman and placed them on his desk. 'I suggest it is time for you to report back to him in person, taking our bloodthirsty warrior prince with you. Say where we found him, and advise the good archbishop that there is something very rotten in Rome.'

'What about the chalice? What will you do?'

'I'll keep hold of the chalice and show it to some of my contacts amongst the dealers in stolen goods. If they've been offered it or know of anything similar, it might lead us to that mysterious Fur Hat who hired Gavino's gang or some of his well-placed accomplices.'

He picked up the flagon.

'I had no idea that there were goldsmiths amongst the Avars who were capable of such fine work,' he said. 'Doubtless it was commissioned to celebrate some sort of important victory by that ferocious horseman.'

'I wonder who he was,' I said.

Paul shrugged. 'Who knows? He could have died generations ago. But the piece itself looks quite recent.'

He breathed on the gold surface, rubbed it with his sleeve and then held the flagon up to the light and peered at the engraving.

'What are you looking for?' I asked.

'Something to identify the maker, his mark,' he said, turning the flagon over. 'This is the work of a master craftsman. Even a barbaric Avar would be human enough to leave some sort of personal sign, probably something that's tiny and hidden.' He gave a little grunt of satisfaction. 'As I thought: here's his mark. It resembles the letters that you northerners use. Maybe you can make something of it.'

He passed the flagon to me. 'You'll find the letters just inside the rim of the base, where they would be invisible when the flagon is placed on a table.'

It took me a moment to spot what he had detected, and I understood why he had mentioned the writing of the north. They looked like rune letters.

'Do they mean anything to you, Sigwulf?' he asked.

I turned the flagon this way and that, trying to see the marks more clearly. There were five of them and they were so small as to be almost unreadable. 'It's difficult to know,' I said. 'If I copied them down larger, it would help.'

Paul brought me a stylus and a wax tablet from his desk, and I used them to draw copies of the marks. When I finished, I gazed down at the symbols I had scratched in the wax, and was baffled. 'My father was an Old Believer and he made me learn the runes signs. But I never used them for any practical purpose,' I admitted. 'But I don't recognize any of these marks, though one of them is very like *Lagiz*, the letter L, and another is close enough to our letter Z.'

'Another mystery about our warrior prince,' Paul said. 'Transcribe those letters onto parchment and when you get back to Paderborn, perhaps you'll find someone at Carolus's court who can translate them. I understand that the king surrounds himself with scholars.'

'I was thinking of staying on in Rome and helping with your inquiries,' I said doubtfully.

My friend treated me to a sideways look full of warning. 'Sigwulf, we are dealing with ruthless people. If you were recognized during your little adventure in the slums, they may get wind of who you are and why you came to Rome. They may never allow you to make your report to your master.'

# Chapter Six

I came back to Paderborn at the season when nearly every countryman has a sickle in his hand, and his family is bent double in
the fields, binding sheaves. Long hours of sunshine and a drying
breeze promised a bumper harvest, and Carolus's court was in an
equally sunny mood because this was *pinguedo*, the grease time,
when the red deer stags are at their fattest. Carolus was spending
so much of each day with his hounds and huntsmen that normal
business had slowed to a trickle. Pope Leo and his entourage
should have already started back for Rome but they were still
kicking their heels in Paderborn and waiting for the king's permission to go home.

'What have you got for me?' Archbishop Arno asked bluntly.
He was in his hunting clothes – royal councillors were expected
to participate in the chase – and had come straight to his office to
deal with the paperwork accumulating on his work table. From
where I stood I caught a whiff of leather and horse sweat.

'Hired criminals attacked Pope Leo. Their paymasters were
most likely to have been Roman nobles who resent Leo holding
office. Several senior members of the papal staff knew about the
attack in advance and were part of the plot.'

'Names?' The archbishop glowered at me from under heavy
eyebrows.

'My contact in Rome is trying to learn the identity of the noblemen. So far I have two names from the clergy: one is the sacellarius Paschal, and the other is the head of chancery, a man called Campulus.'

The archbishop's eyes lit up with interest. He turned to his clerk seated in one corner, taking notes. 'Check the files from Rome,' he commanded.

The clerk jumped to his feet and began searching through documents in a flat-lidded storage box beside his desk. He pulled out three or four pages and placed them in front of the archbishop before retiring back to his corner and sitting down again.

Arno quickly read through the documents. 'I thought so. These are letters received from Rome over the last couple of years, complaining about Leo and his behaviour. Campulus and Paschal appear frequently amongst the signatories.' He glanced up, raking me with his eyes. 'Can you prove their involvement in the attack?'

'I interviewed one of the criminals, a petty thief by the name of Gavino. His evidence strongly implicates the two clergymen.'

The archbishop grunted. 'Anything else?'

I reached into the satchel I was carrying and produced the gold flagon with the warrior prince decoration. I placed it on the table in front of the archbishop.

'What has this got to do with your inquiries?' he demanded harshly.

'Perhaps nothing, my lord. It comes from the house of a very senior papal official who was also present during the attack on Leo.'

'Campulus or Paschal?'

'No, the papal chamberlain.'

A puzzled look came over his face. 'That mousey fellow who

accompanies Leo everywhere? The one whose face got a hefty thump?'

'That is correct, my lord. His name is Albinus.'

He reached forward, picked up the flagon and examined the portrait of the mailed rider dragging along his helpless captive by his hair. 'And how did you obtain this?'

'It was necessary to burgle his house. My contact in Rome was looking for a link with the plot against Pope Leo. We discovered a large number of items of value in a secret hiding place.'

'We?'

'I believed you would want an eyewitness account if anything was found.'

The archbishop gave a low grunt. It was impossible to tell if he was satisfied with what I had done. He toyed with the flagon, turning it in his thick fingers so that he could see it from every angle. 'And the link with the attack on Leo?'

'The flagon comes from the same source as other items that somehow got into the hands of the criminals – the Avar Hoard. It is a unique piece.'

Arno turned it upside down. He had sharp eyes, for he noticed the maker's mark at once. Like the former Nomenculator, he took them to be runes, and I was impressed that he tried to read them for himself. I saw his lips move as he tried to spell out the signs, but he was no more successful than I had been.

'I could not make sense of them either, my lord, though I've copied them down for reference,' I said. 'My friend in Rome tells me that the flagon is undoubtedly Avar work, and quite recently made. But nothing more.'

'No matter,' Arno said. He licked his thumb and rubbed it against the image of the warrior, removing a smudge. 'Leave this with me. Tomorrow we give a farewell banquet for the Pope and his people. Be there early – I'll have someone watch out for you – and we'll put Albinus to a little test.'

\*

Banquets during the *pinguedo* were timed to start after the king got back from his day's hunting. So it was an hour to sunset before I entered the great dining hall of the palace. It was a cavernous, gloomy space. The small unglazed windows placed high up in the thick walls allowed in little light so the cressets on the walls had already been lit. A shadowy maze of rafters, struts and trusses supported the roof above enormous smoke-blackened oak beams. Three long tables ran the length of the hall and at the far end on a low platform was the king's table, set cross-wise. My normal place would have been midway down the hall, off to one side, amongst my fellow *milites*. On this occasion, however, an under-steward was waiting for me and he led me to the end of the central table, closest to the royal platform. A slight curl of his lip indicated what he thought of placing me amongst my betters and I attracted curious glances from my fellow guests as they started to arrive at their customary places around me. They were men of consequence: magnates and landowners with great estates. They wore expensive clothes and displayed jewellery to match: rings set with precious stones, bracelets and heavy torcs of gold. They knew one another but not the plainly dressed stranger placed amongst them. No one spoke to me as we remained standing, waiting for the royal party to enter. I noticed there was a gap on the bench across the table and a little down from me, and I wondered if the latecomers would be denied entry. Custom dictated that the king was the final person to take his place at table. At the last minute the same under-steward appeared, ushering in two guests. They were tonsured and soberly dressed in plain, dark gowns. I recognized Albinus, the Pope's chamberlain, but did not know his companion. They reached the seats allocated to them just as the entire company turned and faced towards the dais to acknowledge the entry of the royal party.

Judging by his manner, Carolus was impatient to get the banquet over and done with. His long strides outpaced his companions as he strode to his high-backed chair and sat down while his guests were still milling about and finding their seats. There were no women present. I recognized the great officers of the royal household: the count of the palace, the seneschal and the constable of the stable. A stooped grey-haired figure in a tunic of dark blue silk, I presumed, was the Duke of Spoleto, whose troops had escorted Pope Leo to safety. The duke looked bored, and I had no doubt that he would have preferred to be back on Italian soil. Pope Leo sat next to Carolus in the place of honour, the king towering over him. This was my first glimpse of Leo and I searched for signs of the wounds to his face. In the poor light of the banqueting hall the slash scars high up on his cheeks were barely noticeable. The rest of his face, under a close-fitting white and crimson felt cap, was unremarkable – wide-set eyes, a slightly snub nose, and a small mouth that held a suggestion of a pout. He looked nervous and uncomfortable, as if aware that his host who would have preferred to be staying overnight at a hunting camp. The only man at the royal table who appeared to take an interest in what was going on around him was Archbishop Arno.

I caught the archbishop's eye, and he gave the slightest nod of acknowledgment, then gazed out over the hall, deliberately ignoring me.

My attention now turned to Albinus. He was little more than an arm's length away. The result of a blow in the face from a club during the attack in Rome was more obvious than the injury suffered by his master. The bridge of Albinus's broken nose had set crooked. It would be a permanent deformity. The bruising had gone, but a reddish mark remained. It added to his rather dejected and spiritless appearance. He sat quietly, looking down at the table in front of him, and it was easy to imagine that he was naturally shy and more than a little embarrassed by his appearance.

Servants were passing behind the seated guests, offering ale or wine. Those who chose ale were provided with drinking horns. The beefy red-faced nobleman on my left had brought his own. It was over-sized and silver-mounted. The moment it was filled, he turned his broad back on me and begun to talk in a loud, confident voice to his immediate neighbour. The booming conversation was a rerun of the day's hunt, with a list of the quality and performance of particular hounds.

Meanwhile, Albinus and his colleague had chosen wine and it was served to them in funnel-shaped cups of pale green glass. When Albinus started on his meal – inevitably, venison was served – he used his little eating knife to cut his food into diminutive morsels, then chewed on them listlessly, so that I wondered if his teeth still pained him. He did not say a word. Nor did he raise his eyes from his platter, and I was confident that the chamberlain had not recognized me from our meeting in the monastery.

Sometime later, I became aware that an under-steward was progressing along the line of seated guests facing me. He was the same man who had brought me to my place at table. Now accompanied by two servants he was checking if every guest had enough to drink. Where he saw an empty glass or drinking horn he beckoned and a servant leaned in and poured ale or wine. As they came nearer, I saw that wine was being poured from what I now thought of as the gold warrior flagon.

I watched the servant reach in between Albinus and his colleague. The latter paid no attention. But as the flagon passed into the chamberlain's line of sight, Albinus dropped his knife. He stopped chewing and took a deep breath, then slowly he sat bolt upright and I got a full view of his face. He had gone very pale and his eyes had opened wide. The servant finished refilling the glass, withdrew the flagon, and moved on. Albinus sat for a moment as if stunned. Then with a visible effort he got control of himself. He reached out and picked up the filled glass – I saw how the liquid trembled – and raised it to his lips. As he drank, he half turned and looked up towards the royal table, towards Leo. I tried to read his expression. It could have been shame or guilt or fear, but it seemed to be something else: Albinus was trying to communicate a silent message. Leo was looking towards Carolus and did not notice. The chamberlain turned again to face his front, and I glanced away, too late. Our eyes met, and in that moment I saw the glimmer of recognition, followed immediately by hard and hostile calculation.

I feigned indifference and swivelled in my seat, as if to summon a servant, but in reality to look up towards the royal table above me. Archbishop Arno was staring down at Albinus, his expression grim.

\*

Not long afterwards, Carolus signalled an end to his banquet by rising abruptly to his feet. In the body of the hall there was a general shuffling as everyone got up from their benches in deference to the king. We remained standing until he left, his guests scurrying after him, then we sat down again to the final course of summer fruits, and drinking. I took advantage of the moment to slip away, and found Arno's secretary waiting for me outside. The archbishop wanted to see me in his office, at once.

Arno was standing in front of his work table, feet apart, hands behind his back. Yellow light from a single torch in a wall sconce made his face look even more craggy than usual. He was alone.

'You did well to bring that fancy flagon to my attention.' He made it sound as if he rarely gave his approval. 'Alcuin said you were the right man for the job.'

I waited for him to go on.

'Your part in this business is finished.'

'My lord, I haven't yet established a firm link between Albinus's wealth and the attack on the Pope,' I protested.

'No longer your concern,' the archbishop snapped. 'In the next few days, Pope Leo and his staff leave for Rome and I will travel with them. There I will open a formal investigation into the events of the attack.'

I was feeling rebuffed and irritated, and decided to risk the archbishop's anger. 'Then you should hear what I believe was the real reason for the attack on Pope Leo.'

Arno glowered. 'Tomorrow morning, an hour before dawn, the king rides out hunting. I must accompany him and I want to get a few hours' sleep before then.'

He made as if to brush past me.

'There was no attempt to murder the Pope,' I said flatly.

That stopped him.

'What makes you say so?' he growled.

'No one hires a band of petty criminals to cut out a man's eyes while standing in the street. That's a task for professional torturers, in a prison cell,' I said.

Arno snorted dismissively. 'You saw the cuts on Leo's face. They're not imaginary.'

'The intention was to terrify him, not kill him.'

'Why would anyone want to terrify the Pope?' the archbishop demanded, his tone even more impatient.

'As a warning. My friend in Rome drew my attention to the coincidence that all three priests suspected of knowing about the attack are or were closely associated with the papal treasury.'

The archbishop shook his head angrily. 'Sigwulf, I take back what I said about your intelligence. You are a fool. You dream up conspiracies where there are none.'

'My lord, I believe that Pope Leo's misconduct exposed him to extortion and threats.'

Arno shot me an angry glance from under his eyebrows. 'Don't try my patience, Sigwulf. Your services are no longer required.'

Dismissed, I made a polite bow and turned for the door. I was glad that my role as a government spy was over. Yet as I headed out into the night I had a nagging sense that something was not quite right. The archbishop had dispensed with me far too abruptly and without explanation. It left me wondering whether I had been getting close to something that I was not supposed to know.

# Chapter Seven

IT WAS CLOSE to midnight. The air was sultry and there was no wind. A thin veil of high cloud diffused the moonlight and gave the huddled buildings of Paderborn an insubstantial, almost ghostly look. From my right came drunken singing and the notes of some sort of wind instrument accompanied by an enthusiastic drummer. The last of the banquet guests were still at their revels. I set off along the web of lanes that would lead me to the barracks where I shared my lodgings with my fellow *milites*, and as the sounds of carousing grew fainter behind me, I became aware of the normal night-time noises of Paderborn: the fretful crying of a baby, the occasional cough or a sleeper's snore from windows open to the warm air, and – closer to hand – faint scufflings and scratchings from the eaves of the houses that loomed on either side. The only flicker of movement was a sudden black shape that darted out of a side alley, then shot across the lane; a nervous cat. I was looking forward to getting to my bed. The long, fast ride from Rome had been exhausting and I had gone directly to report to Archbishop Arno. There had been only enough time to unpack my saddlebags and change into fresh clothes before attending the banquet. I turned the final corner and ahead of me, thirty paces away, was the long, low bulk of the *milites* barracks, a stable-like building, every window dark.

I never heard my attackers. As I passed the mouth of the narrow alleyway that ran alongside the barracks, someone stepped out behind me, threw a thick cloak over my head and, before I could react, clamped an arm hard around my throat. There was a painful backwards wrench on my neck. My nostrils were filled with the stale smell of goat-hair fabric and I choked. A moment later, my arms were pinioned to my sides and I was lifted off my feet. I was far too surprised and shocked to put up a fight.

My attackers carried me only a few yards, and I guessed that I was being taken down the little alleyway. Here they stopped and, before I could gather my wits, the arm around my neck was removed, someone put his hand against the cloth that covered my face, and the back of my head was slammed hard against what felt like the wall of a timber house. The impact made my knees buckle. I sagged, only to be held up straight and this time punched hard in the belly. With a gasp I collapsed forward, winded.

Whoever was hitting me was business-like and I was reminded of the beating that Theodore had administered to Gavino in his squalid room. This assault was just as professional and equally without remorse. Twice more I was hit, first in the face, then in the gut. Flashes of light exploded in my brain. With my head still wrapped in the cloak, I gasped with pain, then tried to suck in air, not knowing where the next blow would fall. Overcome with dizziness, I let myself go limp. Whoever had been holding me up allowed me to crumple to the ground. I lay wheezing and feeling sick.

Someone must have knelt down on the dirt beside me, and very close to my right ear a voice hissed, 'How did the flagon get here?'

I must have mumbled something unintelligible or waited too long before I gave an answer, because the next moment a fist crashed down, striking me squarely in the face. I felt a gush of blood from my nose. I was finding it difficult to breathe and wondered if I would be smothered.

'How did that flagon get here?' the voice repeated carefully and slowly. The words were Frankish but with a strong accent that I couldn't quite identify.

Once again I remembered Gavino and how he had reacted to his beating. 'What flagon?' I mumbled through swollen lips.

My reward was another punch in the face. Then another.

'Maybe we've picked the wrong man,' said a second voice from above. My interrogator's accomplice was standing over me.

'I don't think so,' said the man who was hitting me. He sounded remarkably calm, and I had the sense that he was enjoying his work. 'The light's not good enough to find out.'

He struck me again. His colleague must have stepped in behind me, for an instant later I felt a powerful kick in my lower back.

'Tell us about the flagon,' snarled the voice beside my ear. The foreign accent had a cadence that I had definitely heard before. I tried to place it as a way of distracting myself from the agony of the battering.

There was a long pause while they waited for me to speak, and when I remained silent, the standing man must have jumped up in the air and struck down on me with both his feet. I felt the double impact and feared he had broken several of my ribs but I was too badly hurt and exhausted even to roll away.

'Let's get this over with,' said the standing man. There was a finality in his voice.

There was a buzzing in my ears, and I waited for the thrust of a blade.

Instead there was a muttered curse and someone grabbed my ankles and began pulling me across the ground. I was being dragged feet-first and luckily the cloak softened the blow as my head banged against a stone. The impact must have cleared my hearing because I caught the sound of singing, raucous and out of tune. Someone was bellowing out the lines of a lewd drinking song and he was not alone. His companion joined in the chorus. I recognized the voices of two of my fellow *milites*, and the lead singer as a boor who regularly made a nuisance of himself coming back to the barracks in the small hours of the morning, clumsy and still intoxicated. He and his companion must be returning late from the banquet.

My kidnappers were standing very still, waiting in silence for the men to pass by. I sucked in a deep breath, gathering my strength to shout a cry for help when a hand was pushed firmly over my mouth and held there.

I made no more than a slight gurgle and then I heard the singer stop his song and announce loudly and drunkenly, 'I need to take a piss.'

There was a loud belch not far away and I guessed he had turned into the alley, proposing to relieve himself against the barracks wall.

The hand over my mouth was lifted quickly, and I heard a soft thud of feet as my attackers ran off.

I was too far gone, bruised and hurt, to do more than reach up and pull the cloak off my head. I heard the splashing sound of my saviour urinating, and then he turned away and moved off, blearily unaware of where I lay, trying to gather enough strength to attract his attention. Then a great black wave of exhaustion and pain swelled up and seemed to fold around me.

When I came back to my senses, I was chilled and stiff. I forced myself to get up on all fours and then onto my feet. Every muscle ached and, with one hand clutching my bruised stomach and the other steadying myself against the barracks wall, I fumbled my way to the barracks' door and pushed my way in. The interior was thick with the fug of sleeping men, none of them yet awake. My cubicle was only a few steps further and I managed to stay on my feet just long enough to reach my bed and flop into it. Lying back, I closed my eyes and drifted into a pain-wracked, troubled sleep.

*

The other *milites* must have thought I was sleeping off a hang-over for no one disturbed me, and it was mid-afternoon when I awoke. My throat and neck were sore, I had a raging thirst, and my nose was so swollen that I had to breathe through my mouth. I reached up gingerly to feel if my nose was broken and gritted my teeth against the stab of pain from my bruised shoulder. The slightest movement was agony. Very carefully, I levered myself up on one elbow, then swung my legs over the side of the bed and put my feet on the floor. I still had on the shoes I had worn to the banquet, and the same clothes, though they were soiled with mud and dirt. There was a patch of dried blood on my shirt front where my nose had bled. I needed to push down with both hands on the edge of the bed to get myself standing upright. The building was deserted and I presumed that my fellow *milites* had gone off earlier, following the royal hunt. Very gingerly I tottered out into the street and made my way to a nearby oratory where the priests ran a small infirmary. The lay brother who treated me must have presumed that I was the victim of a drunken brawl for he pursed his lips in disapproval as he washed my cuts and smeared them with goose grease. He then advised me to sit outside on the ground, with my face to the sun until I felt better.

For a couple of hours I followed his advice, ignored by passers-by except those who tripped over my feet and cursed me. When the shadows began to length, I judged that Archbishop Arno would be returning from the day's hunt. Moving like an old man,

I hobbled my way to his office, barely able to see with my left eye, so badly was it swollen.

The archbishop's door-keeper took one look at my bruised face and, with the briefest knock at the door, ushered me immediately into his master's presence. I had expected the archbishop still to be dressed in his hunting clothes, but he was seated behind his desk and wearing an everyday working gown, as if he had spent the entire day at paperwork.

'So they got to you as well,' was his opening comment as he looked up and saw my injuries. He seemed neither surprised nor sympathetic.

'I was set upon and beaten up after I left here last night,' I muttered through lips that were split and swollen. 'My attackers wanted to know about the warrior flagon.'

'So do I,' said the archbishop crisply. His face registered annoyance and a certain degree of impatience. 'Last night the flagon was stolen.'

My legs felt wobbly. Without being invited to do so, I sat down on stool. 'Who took it?' I said.

'That is what I was hoping you might be able to tell me,' growled the archbishop. He stood up and came round the desk to stand in front of me, his chin thrust out and glaring down. 'After the banquet, the under-steward, according to his instructions, was to place the flagon in the iron strongbox with the other gold and silver service used at the feast. This morning he was to bring the flagon back to me, in person.'

I waited for Arno to go on.

He turned on his heel and stalked across the room, his back stiff with irritation. His clerk, seated in his usual corner, kept his eyes down and shifted nervously.

Arno swung round and scowled at me. 'The under-steward never showed up and the flagon is missing.'

'The men who attacked me were seeking information, not the flagon itself,' I said.

Arno cut across my words. 'Also, the royal chancery had an intruder. Last night the treasury records were tampered with.'

I struggled to think of any connection between the missing flagon and the treasury records that were carted about in wooden chests wherever the court was located. The clerks and bookkeepers consulted them for written records of taxes, grants and the rest of the paperwork required for the administration of the vast kingdom.

'The Avar inventory has vanished,' the archbishop said, his eyes cold and his expression unreadable.

Abruptly, I saw the link. The treasury staff wrote up lists of plunder that Carolus's armies brought back from campaigns. Besides valuing the booty, they recorded where and when the various items had been obtained, and by whom. This information was consulted if Carolus should decide to reward his troops with special payments.

'So now there's no record of the gold flagon,' I ventured.

'I'm glad the drubbing you received hasn't addled your brain,' Arno snapped. 'The only people here in Paderborn who know of its existence are the two of us.'

'What about the under-steward?'

'His body was found hidden in the pantry. He had been stabbed through the heart.' The flat tone in which the archbishop delivered this news made me wonder if his reaction would have been equally dismissive if he had heard that I had been killed. 'It is imperative to recover the flagon,' he continued, 'and if that fails, I must have proof that the flagon existed and was part of the Avar treasure. Without that evidence there is little chance I can deal with the corruption that is a stain on Mother Church. The king himself wants the matter sorted out.'

I tried to get my thoughts in order and to sound helpful. 'If the person or persons who stole the flagon also removed the Avar inventory, then you're looking for someone who is literate enough to sort through the mass of treasury records and pick out the Avar list.'

'Is that so?' said the archbishop sarcastically. 'It doesn't take a genius to suspect that such a person or persons is most likely to be found amongst Pope Leo's entourage, particularly after the behaviour last night of that treacherous chamberlain of his.'

'Will you interview Albinus?' I asked.

'No,' answered the archbishop sharply. 'That would be showing my hand too early. Before then, I need to get the flagon back. Leo and his entourage leave Paderborn tomorrow, returning to Rome. As you are already aware, I'm travelling with them. On the road I'll have a couple of my men quietly search their baggage.'

I didn't dwell on the thought of an archbishop arranging for the Pope's baggage to be rifled through. 'Surely the thieves will have disposed of the flagon,' I said.

'Not necessarily. Someone sufficiently cultured to pick out the Avar inventory from the rest of the royal archives might be reluctant to destroy such a unique and valuable piece of work or toss it into the river. Equally, a mere burglar – whoever employed him – might decide to sell it on. The piece would fetch a great deal of money.' Arno was regarding me in a calculating way that was beginning to make me feel uncomfortable.

'If I fail to get my hands on that flagon as primary evidence, Sigwulf, I fall back on my less favoured option: replacing the missing inventory of the Avar loot with another document that chronicles the acquisition of that flagon. It will allow me to quote the records if and when I choose to bring charges against the chamberlain and his associates.'

I tensed, knowing that what was coming would involve my participation.

'I've already made arrangements for someone to visit the place where the treasure was looted – the ruins of the Avar Ring,' the archbishop said. He was picking his words carefully. 'His instructions are to interview everyone he can track down who might remember seeing the flagon, or what happened to it. He himself took part in the final assault, and he speaks the language passably well.'

His voice became cold and matter-of-fact.

'Sigwulf, you will accompany this man. You will take notes of what he uncovers. You will prepare for me, as it were, a replacement page for the Avar inventory. Make it as authentic as humanly possible.'

The archbishop had one more unpleasant surprise for me. 'I know it is a very slim possibility, but the master craftsman who made that remarkable gold flagon may still be at work. I also want you to track him down. You've a copy of his mark. Try showing it around and someone might recognize it and lead you to him.'

'He may have been killed during the Avar war, or fled,' I objected feebly.

The archbishop waved aside my objection. 'That does not mean you cannot try to find him.'

My mind was so filled with the enormity of the request that I almost missed the archbishop's next words.

'Should you locate the goldsmith, Sigwulf, you are to commission a replica of that flagon and you will bring it back to me for use as evidence in my case against Albinus.'

My mouth fell open. 'A replica, my lord? But that means the evidence will be false.'

Archbishop Arno looked at me, his eyes flat and hard. 'As long as it produces the right results. You saw the effect the flagon had on the Pope's chamberlain.'

My face must have betrayed my astonishment.

The archbishop gave a sudden bark of laughter. 'If it eases your conscience, Sigwulf, let me tell you that Rome itself is not above deploying fakes if it is to Leo's advantage. You've heard of Constantine's Donation?'

'Only vaguely, my lord. If I am correct, the Donation is a decree signed by the Roman Emperor Constantine. It gives the Pope authority to rule the western part of the ancient Roman empire.'

'And a lot more besides,' the archbishop grunted. 'Leo's people have been waving it in Carolus's face these past few weeks. We know it to be a counterfeit, a forgery prepared by a clever scribe in the papal archives.'

I made no comment, remembering Paul's account of the sly and self-serving ambitions of the papal office-holders. Arno went to his desk and picked up a handwritten note that he held out to me. 'Take this to the Treasury,' he said. 'It's an authority to draw a thousand gold solidi from what remains of the Avar treasure.' He managed a sardonic smile. 'Very appropriate. If you succeed in tracking down the goldsmith, he can melt down the coins to make his duplicate of the flagon.'

I winced as I got up from the stool. Every movement seemed to awake a new source of pain. 'When do I meet this man whom I'm to accompany to Avaria?'

The archbishop treated it as a stupid question. 'On your way out. Both of you will be leaving for Avaria as soon as my secretary has made a fair copy of a letter I've drafted to Margrave Gerold, asking for his cooperation. It's for his eyes only so make sure that it gets to him, no one else.'

For a second time in less than twenty-four hours I had the unsettling impression that I was a pawn in some greater plan that the archbishop did not wish to divulge. Margrave Gerold was a close confidant of the king, a great magnate and married to Carolus's sister. Carolus had given him the task of pacifying and ruling the new frontier province that now included the conquered Avar lands. If Margrave Gerold was being drawn into Archbishop's Arno's scheme, whatever it was, then I was caught up in a matter of major importance to the state.

As I limped towards the door, I wondered if I should have told the archbishop that the leader of my attackers spoke Frankish with a distinctive foreign accent. Admittedly, the man's accent was not much of a clue to his identity; half of Paderborn spoke with regional accents and I was still unable to place where the man came from by the way he spoke. But I had deliberately withheld that information, not wanting to admit that I had been smug and stupid in believing that I was being clever enough to avoid the dangers that my friend the ex-Nomenculator in Rome had warned me about. I had realized my error only when I was on the ground with my head swaddled in a cloak and being kicked with carefully judged and vicious accuracy. My attacker had told his accomplice that the light was not good enough to confirm my identity: he was referring to the mismatched colour of my eyes; one is pale blue, the other greenish hazel. It is an accident of birth and the contrast between them is less than when I was young, but Chamberlain Albinus had noted the difference when I first met him in the monastery. He had spotted it again when I sat opposite him at table in the banquet, and immediately deduced that I had something to do with the warrior flagon. I had been an over-confident fool. Albinus was neither innocuous nor timid, but alert and ruthless; so too were the men he worked with. The spreading throb of my bruises was a reminder that whoever he had sent to interrogate me had enjoyed inflicting such a savage beating. I hobbled out of the archbishop's office, resolved that if Arno had his own unstated agenda, so did I. Simply put, I had a score to settle.

*

There was no mistaking the tall, rangy figure leaning with his back against the wall outside the archbishop's office. The watchful, slightly arrogant gaze, one hand resting on the well-worn hilt of the short sword in his belt while the fingers of the other hand fiddled with a cord almost certainly attached to a hidden dagger hung around his neck – all these spoke of a professional soldier. His thick dirty blond hair was cut in a simple pudding-bowl style, and his moustache and beard were closely trimmed. The plain grey tunic was devoid of any decoration and worn over loose-fitting dark trousers tucked into boots. I put him at between thirty and forty years old, and there was a wariness as well as a chill indifference on the face he turned towards me as I approached him.

'I believe we are to travel together into Avaria on Archbishop Arno's instructions,' I said.

The eyes that regarded me were the very palest blue, and slightly protruding. They were also unwelcoming. I realized that the archbishop had not told me the name of my future companion.

'I'm Sigwulf,' I added.

'Beorthric,' he replied. His voice was guttural and came from deep in his throat. He made no attempt to sound pleased, nor did he bother to straighten up, but remained propped against the wall. His unusual name was a clue. Furtively, I stole a glance at the weapon at his belt. It was not the standard issue army sword forged by Carolus's armourers. The wooden handle was longer, and Beorthric was carrying it horizontally. The scabbard of well-worn oiled leather was the length of my forearm and revealed the shape of the blade. I was looking at a scramseax, the single-edged fighting sword of the northerners that my own people carried into battle. It was also the favoured weapon of Carolus's most implacable enemies – the Saxons.

I studied Beorthric's features again, more closely this time, looking for other signs as to who he was. The skin was ruddy and very slightly freckled, the pale-blue eyes wide set, and a strong jaw and wide mouth made his face seem broader and flatter than most. Now I had no doubt that he was a Saxon, and that caused me a tremor of disquiet. The only Saxons allowed to carry weapons within the wooden ramparts of Paderborn were those who had abandoned their ancient tribal allegiances. They had pledged their allegiance to the Franks instead. For twenty years Carolus had been waging a savage war to break the Saxon tribes and bring them to heel. Small bands of unsubdued rebels still remained, roaming the deep forests. To hunt them down and destroy them, Carolus had recruited the most ferocious of their defeated cousins and formed them into an elite, well-paid force renowned for its brutal efficiency. Their countrymen, surly in defeat, considered them to be turncoats and traitors. I had little doubt that Beorthric was a member of that unit.

'The archbishop has instructed me to write up a report of your findings when we are in Avaria,' I said carefully. As a Saxon whose family had been wiped out by a rival Saxon warlord, I had no reason to trust in tribal loyalties.

Beorthric's cool expression did not change. 'Then we should be on our way. I don't want to have to spend a winter there.'

I bridled at his bluntness. He could see that I was in poor shape to travel. 'There are one or two things I need to arrange before we set out.'

I might as well have been talking to the wall behind his head. 'I'll meet you here at dawn tomorrow, with horses. Keep your baggage light. A single pack animal is enough for both of us.'

It was difficult to keep hold of my temper. 'The earliest I can be ready is in the afternoon,' I snapped.

The way he looked me up and down made it clear that he thought I was a weakling. 'Then don't be late,' he grunted dismissively. He straightened up and walked off with long confident strides, a hand still on the hilt of his scramseax. I watched him go, trying to come to terms with the prospect of travelling hundreds of miles in the company of a mercenary who might decide to kill me for the gold I would be carrying. It added to my existing concern that we would be venturing into a land where the native people had an evil reputation as pagan savages and whose territory had been recently over-run and wrecked by an invading army. And if we ever reached our destination, I saw little likelihood of tracking down a master craftsman who might no longer be alive.

# Chapter Eight

THERE WAS NO shred of compassion from Beorthric, however
shaky and exhausted I must have looked when I came to our ren-
dezvous next afternoon. All I wanted to do was to retreat to the
*milites* barracks and curl up in bed. Already I had dragged myself
to the Treasury, shown the note from Archbishop Arno, and
signed for a thousand gold solidi from what remained of the Avar
treasure. I had then paid a visit to a leatherworker in the artisans'
quarter. When I met Beorthric, the coins were out of sight, neatly
sewn into a money belt of soft calfskin tied tightly around my
waist with tapes. Two saddlebags slung over my shoulder contained a change of clothes and the stock of writing materials that
I had obtained from the chancery clerks. A rolled-up cloak and
a sword completed my baggage. Beorthric was already astride a
sturdy-looking horse and holding the leading rein of a pack pony.
He handed me a letter sealed with Arno's ring and addressed to
Margrave Gerold. 'The archbishop says you are to give this to the
margrave, and no one else,' he informed me curtly. He nodded
towards a second riding horse tied nearby. 'That's yours,' he
announced and, pulling his horse's head around, rode off down
the street without a backwards glance. Hoisting myself into the
saddle was agony and I followed him, cursing under my breath.
The motion of the horse discovered sprains and bruises that I had
not even known before. Every hoof beat sent a stab of pain into
my lower back. To my dismay I saw Beorthric kick his horse

into a trot, and I called out to him to slow down. He ignored me and we trotted out of Paderborn's south gate with me bending forwards in the saddle, tears of pain running down my face. I found myself disliking him intensely.

For the next eight days he gave me little reason to modify my opinion. We were following a well-used merchants' road that ran south through the gently rolling countryside of Hessen and East Frankia. There were many small towns and villages along our route and I would have preferred to find overnight lodgings and sleep in a bed. But Archbishop Arno had not told me who was in charge of our mission and, because Beorthric had previously travelled this route to Avaria, I found myself accepting my companion's inflexible and punishing routine. He insisted that we were on the road soon after dawn, that we put thirty or forty miles behind us each day, and that we stopped for the night wherever we found ourselves. Usually this meant sleeping on the ground, wrapped in a cloak, which was further torment to my bruises as they slowly mended.

Conscious of the gold I was carrying around my waist, I remained wary of my travelling companion, observing him closely during the long hours on the road. The night-time attack on me outside the Paderborn barracks had left me alert to men's accents, and though Beorthric spoke little and then only in short, clipped sentences, I occasionally detected an underlying Saxon intonation in his Frankish. I also noted how awkwardly he rode, long legs dangling down, graceless and out of rhythm with the horse's gait. This fitted my theory that he was a Saxon renegade because the Saxon war bands were indifferent cavalrymen and much preferred to fight on foot. On the other hand, Beorthric showed himself to be meticulous in tending to the well-being of our horses. My guess was that at some stage in his mercenary career he had served with Carolus's mounted expeditionary forces and, while he would never make an accomplished rider, he had learned the importance of looking after his mounts: he would check their hooves at the start and finish of the day, walk and trot the animals to vary the pace, always stop and rest them for a long break at midday, remove saddles and packs whenever we halted, and purchase oats of good quality along the way. In all other respects he was a remarkably prudent traveller. He selected overnight campsites well away from the road where we would escape casual notice, and he built cooking fires that were small and unobtrusive. In the morning he tidied up, leaving scarcely any trace of our presence. Whenever the road lay through thick forest, and the trees pressed in closely on both sides, I saw how he rode bolt upright, his head turning from side to side as he searched for signs of ambush. It occurred to me that these were the ingrained habits of an army scout or, just as likely, a brigand.

We rarely exchanged more than ten sentences throughout the day, and it was only when I asked Beorthric what he knew about the Avars that, finally, I managed to glean a few details about his past. It was on the fifth day of our journey and we found ourselves about to ride down into a fertile valley spreading out before us in the late afternoon sunshine. There was a glint of a river winding through the patchwork of fields, yellowish brown and bare after the harvest, random lines of hedgerows, dark clumps of orchards and, best of all from my point of view, the sight of a small town in the distance where the next range of hills rose. By the time we reached the town, we would have achieved our daily forty miles and I was looking forward to finding a bed to sleep in.

'Archbishop Arno told me that you speak the Avar language,' I said, riding up alongside Beorthric.

He allowed a full minute to go by before he answered. 'I learned the usual way, from a woman.'

'Was that difficult?'

He allowed himself a non-committal grunt. 'Learning Avarish or being with an Avar woman?'

'Either or both.'

'After I'd picked up a couple of hundred words I knew where I was with the language.'

'And the Avar woman?' I coaxed, attempting a light tone.

He turned his face towards me, and there was no trace of amusement in the pale-blue eyes. 'With the Avars, whether men or women or children, you never know where you stand or what they are thinking.'

'I presume you speak from hard-won experience.'

'I was twice in Avaria,' he said, and there was a hard edge to his voice. 'The first time was seven years ago with the big invasion that Carolus launched. We won every fight but there was never a final battle. The Avars kept retreating, dodging us, promising to acknowledge Carolus as their overlord but never doing so.'

'Why couldn't Carolus force them into proper submission?'

The big Saxon leaned forward to pat his horse on the neck. 'Our horses began to die by the hundreds and we had to turn back. It was an unknown sickness. Myself, I think it was an infection that the Avars deliberately introduced. Their overlord, the khagan, sent Carolus a herd of horses as a gift.'

That must have been when Beorthric learned the importance of looking after horses, I thought to myself. 'And what happened the second time you were in Avaria?'

'That was different. I already knew the Avar country so I was hired by the Duke of Friuli to go with the vanguard of his army. The duke finished the job that Carolus started. I was with the troops when they sacked the Avar capital, the Ring, though it turned out to be more of a summer camp than a real town.'

'You make it sound as if the second campaign was straight-forward. The Avars didn't put up much resistance.'

Beorthric rebuked me with a scornful glare. 'The only reason they lost was because they didn't agree amongst themselves. They are as false and treacherous to one another as they are to outsiders.'

I had thought it wiser not to ask him about the Avar woman, but he was pulling up the side of his tunic. A puckered scar began at his left hip and ran diagonally across his ribs until it disappeared from sight.

'That's how loyal my language teacher was,' he growled. 'I saved her life when our troops finally broke their way into the Ring. She was grateful for a few months, but when the chance came to get back to her people, she took it . . . and most of my share of the plunder with her.'

'Let's hope we don't meet up with her or her brothers,' I muttered.

'If we do, we'll have some of Margrave Gerold's troopers with us. Archbishop Arno told me that he's asking the margrave to send a full company of his best cavalry with us to the Ring and to stand guard while we are there.' Beorthric tucked his tunic back inside his belt.

I rode on thoughtfully. Beorthric's words had left me uneasy. When Arno had given me strict instructions that I was to deliver his letter only to Gerold, I had supposed that the letter contained a private request for the margrave to facilitate our short trip to the Ring. Now it turned out that Arno was asking Gerold to devote significant resources to help our mission. A coil of anxiety began to form in my gut as I could not escape the conclusion that our mission into Avaria was far more important to the archbishop than he had chosen to reveal to me. This in turn meant that he would have thought nothing of risking the lives of Beorthric and myself if it furthered his ambition.

Quite what the archbishop was plotting was a question that nagged at me for the remainder of that day and gave me a poor night's rest even though, in response to my suggestion, Beorthric finally agreed that we could spend the night in an inn for travellers. I tossed and turned on the prickly straw mattress, thinking about the Avar Hoard and picturing the moment when Theodore had found the gold warrior flagon hidden in Albinus's house. Without success I tried to find the connections between pagan Avaria, the Pope's chamberlain, and why my former mentor Alcuin should have recommended me to Archbishop Arno. At some point the image floated up into my mind of the gold belt buckle that my friend Paul had shown me in Rome. The buckle modelled a griffin, a creature that was half lion and half eagle. Paul had assured me that the workmanship was Avar, and I found myself wondering where the man who made the buckle had got his inspiration. I decided that if I ever tracked down the master craftsman who made the warrior flagon, I would ask him. Perhaps he would tell me that the griffin was a creature that still roamed beyond the Avar territory in the great grasslands that stretched far to the unknown east. At last, just before dawn, I nodded off and dreamed that the Khagan of the Avars was showing me his menagerie and it contained a griffin and its fledgling cubs.

*

Five days later, everything changed. We reached the north bank of the great river Donau, crossed by ferry and began following the right bank downstream. The road had become a very busy highway, wide enough for two carts to pass one another. There was a constant flow of traffic, drovers with cattle, farmers bringing produce to the market towns along the Donau, beggars and pilgrims, and merchants riding while their servants on foot led pack animals. As a rule, they took one glance at my companion and made the same judgement as I had made when I had first encountered Beorthric. They mumbled a polite greeting and gave us a wide berth. Beorthric ignored them, riding straight ahead as though he owned the track.

I was surprised, therefore, when, in the middle of the morning, he suddenly pulled up his horse and raised a hand. It was my turn to lead our pack pony and, riding close behind him, it was all I could do to stop my horse blundering into his. Looking past him, I saw nothing out of the ordinary. Coming towards us was an empty farm waggon drawn by two oxen. 'What is it?' I asked.

'Listen!'

I could hear nothing except the grinding of the oxcart's wooden wheels on their axle and an occasional thump and creak as the vehicle rolled slowly over the uneven road surface. The driver was seated on the cart, half-asleep in the sunshine, his head under a broad-brimmed straw hat tilted forward, and his chin on his chest.

Then, very faintly in the distance, I heard the single beat of a large drum. After an interval, the drum beat was repeated, deep and mournful.

Beorthric frowned, then, with a jerk of his head, indicated that I should follow him. He turned aside, and soon our horses were scrambling up a narrow side track that climbed through beech forest. We emerged on a low spur of land that overlooked the road. Here we dismounted and tied our horses to the trees. We walked to where we had a clear view ahead. Now we could hear the drum more clearly. It was keeping up its steady, slow, relentless beat.

Below us and half a mile away appeared a column of armed men on horseback. They were approaching along the highway at a slow walking pace. From our vantage point we could see the other road users scuttle to the verges, and wait meekly for the procession to pass by.

'Who do you think they are?' I questioned my companion.

Unconsciously, I dropped my voice for there was something fore-boding about the scene.

'We'll find out at the next town.'

The cavalcade came closer and I counted at least forty riders. The drum, three or four feet across, was carried on a small two-wheel cart at the head of the procession. The drummer, standing upright on the cart, was striking a deep booming note, a signal to clear the way. In the centre of the column, and flanked by riders, rolled a great waggon, a massive vehicle drawn by a team of six draught horses harnessed in pairs. Four stout poles at each corner of waggon held up a canopy striped in red and green. On the flatbed of the waggon was a single item, a boxy shape draped with red and green sheeting. The same colours were repeated on the riders' saddle cloths and on the pennants of their lances.

We waited for fully half an hour until the procession had gone passed, and the drum beat had receded into the distance. Only then did Beorthric untie our horses and we descended the hill and continued on our journey.

The next settlement was a modest halting place where the trickle of a roadside stream had been diverted to fill an enormous hollowed-out log to make a watering trough for animals. There was a tavern, various outbuildings and sheds, and a stall with a display of serviceable-looking clothes and hats. A cobbler was seated on a stool outside the tavern door, stitching the sole back on a riding boot. A man-at-arms, the owner of the boot, was standing waiting, a wooden tankard in hand, one foot bare.

While Beorthric went to find if there were oats for sale, I stood holding our horses and watching the cobbler at his work. The man at arms nodded to me in a friendly sort of way, and I took the chance to ask if he knew anything about the procession we had seen passing.

'That was my lord, Margrave Gerold. He's going home,' he replied.

I felt a quick flash of irritation. Beorthric's caution in making us leave the road meant that we would now have to turn back and catch up with the margrave if we were to deliver Arno's letter.

'The margrave still commands the Avarian March, doesn't he?' I asked.

The man-at-arms wiped road dust from his face with a scarf. Its faded colours were red and green.

'No longer,' he said.

'Why not?' I asked him, trying not to let my disappointment show. It had occurred to me that, unknown to Archbishop Arno, the king had replaced his brother-in-law in his post as governor of the Avarian frontier province. If that was the case, Beorthric and I would have to return to the archbishop in Paderborn and get a letter to the new office holder, whoever he might be.

The man-at-arms was giving me a strange look. 'Because my lord is dead. That procession takes his body back to Vinzgau.'

I stared at him in dismay.

'What happened?' Beorthric had walked up and overheard the last sentence.

The man-at-arms flicked a glance in his direction and must have recognized a fellow soldier, for he said, 'The usual: a last-minute cock-up on the battlefield.'

Beorthric's mouth set in a grim line. 'Not like the margrave to make mistakes. He was a veteran.'

'There's no defence against outright treachery,' observed the soldier sourly.

'Go on,' murmured Beorthric. For the first time, I detected a note of sympathy in his voice.

'A big raiding force of wild Avars came across the border,'

the soldier continued. 'The margrave called out the levies and put together a decent-sized response, enough to see them off.'

Out of the corner of my eye I saw that the cobbler's needle had slowed. He was listening.

'The margrave picked nice, level ground where we could take advantage of our heavier horses in the charge. He had brought his personal guard with him and a couple of squadrons of tame Avar cavalry.'

'I didn't know there was such a thing as a tame Avar,' interrupted Beorthric drily.

'That's what we found out to our cost,' said the solider. 'But they're some of the best horse soldiers in the world, and their job was to pursue the raiders once we had broken up their main force. The margrave made the mistake of thinking it was better to have them on our side, than against us.'

'So what happened next?' said Beorthric.

'Both armies were facing one another, ready to go at it, when my lord decided to ride out in front of our line and make a speech to encourage us. It was the usual sort of blather that you can barely hear through the ear flaps of your helmet.' The man-at-arms shook his head in wonder. 'He finished his speech, turned towards the enemy and raised his arm, about to signal the attack, when a couple of our so-called tame Avars broke ranks. They came galloping out from our line and loosed off a couple of arrows at him and a couple of officers with him. They were good shots, that I'll grant you. The margrave took an arrow between the shoulders and was pitched out of the saddle.'

'What happened to the two Avars?' asked Beorthric.

'They bolted straight past the margrave lying on the ground, and joined their cousins who were facing us.' He turned and spat. 'That's what you get for recruiting the enemy into your ranks.'

Beside me I felt Beorthric go tense. Now I knew for sure that he was a Saxon turncoat.

'And the battle itself? How did that go?' he asked softly.

'Oh, we won all right,' came the answer. 'We were mad for revenge. The margrave had been good to us. We smashed right through the Avar centre. Drove them off the field; lots of corpses. They won't come raiding again, not for a long time.'

He turned to ask the cobbler if he had finished the mend, and I took the chance to draw Beorthric to one side.

'What do you think?' I asked. 'Do we abandon the mission and return to Paderborn?'

The Saxon was dismissive of any such idea. 'You can turn back if you want to. But I go on. That's what I'm paid for.'

I glanced over towards the man-at-arms and made sure that I was not overheard. 'Arno's letter is addressed to the margrave, no one else. You said that we need an escort if we are to enter Avar territory.'

'You heard the man. The Avars have just been thrashed. They won't trouble us if we move quickly.'

I hesitated. I did not fancy appearing before Archbishop Arno and telling him that I had come back empty handed though Beorthric had gone ahead with our mission.

There was insolence as well as contempt in the way that the big Saxon was looking at me, and this irritated me. 'Very well,' I snapped. 'We both continue. But let us try to persuade whoever is now in charge of the frontier to provide us with some soldiers.'

'If it makes you feel easier,' was Beorthric's caustic response and it held more than a trace of condescension.

My hand went to Arno's letter that I had been keeping, safely tucked inside the front of my tunic. I pulled it out and, without taking my eyes off Beorthric, I tore it into shreds in front of him. It was a gesture, partly to show my determination and partly done out of bravado. I saw no need to tell the Saxon that, whatever Arno had written in the letter, I was certain that it would be dangerous for us if anyone but Margrave Gerold knew its contents.

\*

So we rode on, day after day at the same strenuous pace, the yellowish brown flood of the river on our left. The further we progressed, the more signs we saw that the land had been recently fought over. Farmhouses were wrecked, their roofs collapsed or reduced to charred ruins. Cattle sheds and barns lay empty, their doors ripped off, their contents plundered. Hedges and fences beside the road were neglected. All that remained of the fruit orchards were stumps where the trees had been cut down for firewood. There were long stretches of wasteland. Not long after encountering the margrave's funeral cortege, we met another column of men coming along the road towards us. This time they were on foot, unhappy-looking wretches with loads on their backs, shambling along under armed guard. As they drew level with us, Beorthric identified them as prisoners of war. When they had delivered their burdens, he said bluntly, they would be sold into slavery.

On the tenth day, we reached the furthest limit of Carolus's rule. Here a quarter *turma* of mounted troopers, some twenty men, occupied what must have been a posting station long ago. The sergeant in charge was a beefy, pock-marked veteran who spoke broken Frankish with such a thick accent that I had diffi-culty in understanding him. I guessed that he and his soldiers were left-over auxiliaries from Carolus's army who had volun-teered to stay on as a frontier force and settle the newly won lands, taking local wives. Their mud-brick guardhouse was the centre for a cluster of huts and cottages for their families. Judging by the number of toddlers playing in the dust in the afternoon sunshine and the babies on the hips of their mothers, Carolus's policy of resettlement was a success.

'What's your business?' demanded the sergeant gruffly. He had summoned us into an unswept and grimy room in the run-down building. The bare walls lacked plaster, the one small window had no shutters, and the sergeant's chair and battered desk were the only items of furniture. The place smelled of disuse and neglect. The door had been left open because it was too warped to shut properly.

I took it on myself to be spokesman. 'My colleague and I are travelling on the orders of Archbishop Arno of Salzburg.'

From the blank look on the sergeant's face it seemed he had never heard of the archbishop. He leaned back in his chair. 'I've had no word of this.'

'On the archbishop's authority we are to be provided with an escort of soldiers for the next stage of our journey,' I continued. Briefly, I regretted destroying the archbishop's letter to the margrave. The bishop's seal might have impressed the sergeant.

'Where to?' he grunted.

'To the place known as "the Ring",' I told him.

His eyebrows shot up in surprise. 'And why do you want to go to that God-forsaken hole?' he demanded.

'I am not at liberty to say,' I told him. I hoped my reply sounded official and important.

He looked me up and down with open disbelief. 'Nobody goes there. It's too close to Avar territory.'

'I understand that Margrave Gerold recently won a great victory, and the Avars have been pacified.'

He gave a coarse laugh. 'The Avars are never pacified. As the margrave found out to his cost.' He glared past me towards a couple of his troopers who were loitering outside the door, listening in. 'Clear off, you two,' he growled.

They slunk away and the sergeant turned his attention back to me. 'The Avars may have been given a bloody nose, but I'm not sparing any men to go with you, not without a direct order from my superiors.'

I sighed to myself, regretting even more the death of Margrave Gerold. There was a discreet touch on my arm and Beorthric said quietly. 'Sigwulf, you should show the order from the Master of Horse. It must be in your saddlebag.'

Before I could react, the big Saxon was steering me out of the room, my elbow in his grip. I had the good sense not to say anything until we were well outside the guardhouse.

Keeping my voice low, I asked, 'What's all this pretence about the Master of Horse and his written order?'

'I'm sure you can produce something to impress the sergeant. He no more knows how to read than I do,' answered the Saxon blandly. He did not break his stride as he ushered me towards the stable where we had left our horses and baggage.

'He'll notice if the ink is new,' I told Beorthric, 'but I should be able to find something that might suit.'

We reached the stable and from my saddlebag I pulled the package of writing materials the clerks in the chancery in Paderborn had supplied me with. New parchment was expensive and many of the sheets had been used previously. Most of the writing had already been scraped off, and I had a stock of chalk so that I could prepare the surfaces when I was ready to write on them. I remembered that an occasional sheet still carried official-looking lines of script. It did not take me long to find one.

Beorthric stepped up close, right beside me, blocking out the light.

'Why don't you also offer a little of whatever it is you're wearing around your waist,' he said.

Taken aback, I stared at him. He made no effort to move away. Just for a moment I thought he was threatening me.

'You don't think I hadn't noticed,' he added with a touch of exasperation. 'It shouldn't take much.'

Eventually I found my tongue. 'What I am carrying is for making a copy of the missing flagon, if we find a suitable Avar goldsmith.' I feared that I sounded rather pompous.

He shrugged. 'You're not likely to get near any goldsmith if you don't provide the sergeant with a sweetener.'

I realized he had deliberately placed himself so that no one could see into the stable if I chose to get at my money belt, and there seemed little point in rejecting what seemed a sensible suggestion.

'Lend me that little knife you wear around your neck,' I told him. I lifted the hem of my shirt and without removing the belt, used the tip of the blade to unpick a couple of stitches in the soft leather. The slit was just wide enough to squeeze out three gold solidi, each no bigger than a fingernail. I smoothed down my shirt to cover the belt again and returned the knife to the Saxon.

With the coins folded inside the parchment sheet, we made our way back to see the sergeant. He was waiting for us in the same bare room, idly picking his teeth with a dirty fingernail.

'Here's the written order from the Master of Horse,' I said, proffering the folded page. Something in my voice must have alerted him, for he took the parchment carefully and glanced towards the open door. His men were nowhere to be seen. The sergeant half turned away from us as he unfolded the page.

There was silence. 'When my companion and I get back from the Ring, there will be further instructions from the Master of Horse,' I said softly.

The sergeant carefully refolded the parchment and slipped it into his pocket. 'I'll hold on to this, as it's an official document, in case it's required by my superiors.' He treated us to a sly look, full of greedy calculation. 'I can spare two men. They'll ride with you as far as the Ring, and no further.'

'I was hoping for a larger escort—' I began.

He cut me short. 'They'll have orders to return here in five days' time. If you haven't finished by then whatever it is you want to do, it's your look-out.'

He strode out of the room and a moment later was shouting out orders. I paid little attention. I was trying to recall where Beorthric could have spotted that I was wearing a money belt. The only occasion I could think of was when he told me about his run-in with his Avar woman. That evening we had stayed overnight in a tavern, and I remembered the itchy straw mattress. The following morning I had stripped off and washed myself in a tub of cold water, trying to get rid of the rash on my skin. If that was when Beorthric had seen my money belt, he had never spoken of it nor – and that was more to the point – had he attempted to rob me. He was a turncoat, of that I was sure, and a man for hire, and the contents of the money belt were worth far, far more than anything he was being paid as a mercenary. It would have been easy for him to take it and vanish back to his own people. I found myself wondering if I had misjudged my colleague. Now that we were about to embark on the dangerous part of our mission, perhaps it was the moment that I should begin to trust him.

# Chapter Nine

AVAR TERRITORY – SEPTEMBER

The two troopers selected to escort us were the dregs of the *turma*. One was so badly overweight and paunchy that he overflowed his saddle. The other had a wheezing cough repeated every few minutes that quickly became irritating. Neither of them spoke more than basic army Frankish, enough to understand and follow orders, so there was no need for conversation as we set out from the guardhouse the following morning and made our way to the riverbank. We left our pack horse behind as we were expecting a trip of only a few days. The Donau marked the boundary of the Avarian March and, beyond it, according to the sergeant, the Avars had abandoned a swathe of their former territory as a buffer zone, and their khagan had established a new capital much further away, its location unknown. So when a flat-bottomed boat deposited the four of us and our horses on the further shore, we were stepping into no-man's-land.

Nevertheless, our two troopers were uneasy, looking about them nervously as if expecting an ambush at any moment. It was obvious that this was the first time they had crossed the river. By contrast, Beorthric led the way with his usual confidence. He kicked his horse into a trot and soon we were heading along an ill-defined but broad track away from the river and towards a distant line of hills.

'Have you been this way before?' I asked.

'I scouted it for the Duke of Friuli.'

I looked about me. Open grassland was dotted here and there with a few low bushes. The terrain was far from level as there were a number of low rounded hills where the higher ground supported clumps of forest. What struck me immediately was the absence of any evidence of human activity. The countryside had a feeling unlike anything we had travelled previously – a wild emptiness. The tall, pale yellow grasses should have made good pasture for herds of cattle or sheep, even at this late season, and the woods could have provided ample building timber for houses and villages. Yet I could see nothing, not even a column of smoke rising from a village hidden in a dip in the land.

'Where are the people?' I demanded of Beorthric.

He looked at me, his pale-blue eyes cold, waiting for me to remember the grim sight of a column of slave-porters.

'Surely not everyone was carried off as prisoners,' I said.

'Not everyone. Many were killed.'

'What about those who fled? There must be some who returned to their homes and rebuilt their lives once Carolus's troops had withdrawn.'

'The Avars don't think of hearth and home, as we do.'

His tone was so abrupt, it made me wonder if he was thinking about the Avar woman who had left him. Perhaps he had hoped to set up home with her. For several minutes the only sound was the thudding of our horses' hooves on hard-packed earth. The dust they kicked up carried the woody scent of crushed grass stalks.

I swivelled in my saddle and looked back at our so-called escort. The two soldiers were at least thirty yards behind us, riding at a safe distance. I imagined that if we ran into trouble, they would turn round and bolt for home.

'What do you mean?' I prompted, trying to strike up some sort of conversation with Beorthric. The emptiness of the landscape was unsettling, and I was making an effort to see the big Saxon in a more favourable light than before, as someone on whom I could rely.

'They don't have permanent homes. They move with the seasons. Their khagan switches between a summer capital and a winter one.'

'Taking his treasury with him?'

Beorthric pointed to the track ahead of us. 'Look closely and you'll see the grooves left by waggon wheels. This is an ancient Avar road.'

'If we're to provide Archbishop Arno with what he requires, we'll need to interview witnesses about what exactly was in the Avar treasury when it was looted.'

He made no response and I had given up hope of getting any further reaction from him, when suddenly he said, 'If we do find someone, you'll have to hand out more of those gold coins if you want answers to your questions.'

His voice had an edge to it that I had not heard before, and I looked at him sideways, noticing a grimace of distaste.

'Was it so awful?' I asked.

'A massacre. We were ordered to kill everyone inside the Ring.'

'And do you think we'll find anyone who survived?'

'I hope so.'

Nothing more was said for the rest of that day and, towards evening, Beorthric picked a secluded spot for us to camp. It overlooked a small reed-fringed lake. As we watered the horses, ducks and other waterfowl continued to fly in, landing nearby and unafraid. It was another clue that the land was without people. Afterwards, our two troopers sat on their own, chewing on the rations they had brought with them and not offering to share them. Beorthric and I ate dried biscuit and several handfuls of dark purple plums that I found growing wild. As we were finishing the meal, there was a distant trumpeting sound above our heads and a flock of cranes, several hundred of the birds, passed overhead, the shape of their formation etched against the deep red of the sky. It was a sign that autumn had arrived.

*

In the morning, the air had a distinct chill and a thick, clammy fog hung over the land, obscuring the countryside as we rode onwards, with Beorthric again in the lead. Once or twice he missed the trail, and we had to turn back and cast around until he picked up the faint marks of the correct track. We had been riding for almost four hours when there loomed ahead of us the relics of a forest ravaged by a terrible fire. Tall black columns, closely spaced, stood like the teeth of a gigantic black comb. Only when we came closer did I see they were the charred remnants of a huge palisade. Hundreds of massive tree trunks had been erected side by side in the ground to create a barrier, the gaps between them filled with packed earth and woven branches. Even scorched and buckled, the obstacle was forbidding and grim.

It was what remained of the Ring.

'How on earth did Carolus's troops find a way past this?' I asked Beorthric as we rode along the front of the extraordinary defence works. Looking up I could see that the tree trunks were twenty or thirty feet high, impossible to scale without ladders and grappling irons. To knock them down would have required heavy siege equipment.

'The same way we beat the Avars in the field – by treachery.'

It was obvious how the Ring had earned its name: the wall of black, scorched tree trunks continued in a great curve as far as I was able to see into the fog. Presumably, it came back on itself and formed a complete circle. I was awed.

Eventually, we turned in through what must have been some sort of gateway in the palisade. Whatever had closed the gap no longer existed.

'There was room inside for all the khagan's people, their flocks and herds, and that was only where they spent their summers. In winter, they moved to different quarters, taking their possessions with them, even their war engines,' Beorthric explained. He gave a grim laugh. 'We found that they had catapults, stone-throwers and siege engines. Everything mounted on wheels.'

'But why did they need to erect such a fortress? What were they afraid of?' I asked.

'Themselves. Every khagan fears being overthrown by an army of rebels. The Avars are divided into many clans and, given a chance, will fight one another to lord it over the others.'

I sniffed the moist air. Two years after the utter destruction of the Ring by the Duke of Friuli's troops, there was no mistaking the distinctive smell of charred wood. The place reeked of it. 'Who was their traitor, the man who made it possible for the duke's men to take this place?'

'He was called Tugun, though whether that was his name or some sort of Avar title, I don't know. Even before we invaded, he had secretly sent word that he was willing to turn Christian if Carolus would recognize him as khagan.'

'And his men opened the gates for you?'

'They did.' He paused. 'But we still carried out our orders.'

His meaning took a moment to sink in. 'They were massacred along with all the rest?'

Beorthric did not answer.

'What happened to this Tugun, was he also killed?' I demanded.

'His body was never found, though we did not look too hard. We were too busy looting.'

There was a shout behind us: the fat trooper was pointing to one side, into the fog. Indistinct shapes were moving towards us. My stomach gave a sudden lurch of fear, but they were only cattle, half a dozen of them trotting through the fog, curious to investigate our arrival.

'Someone must be living here . . .' I began. The words were scarcely out of my mouth when a human figure appeared behind the cattle, trying to head them off. He was running with a bad limp. He spotted us, spun round and fled. But Beorthric was too quick for him. The Saxon brought his horse into a canter, and in a few strides had wheeled in front of the man, blocking his escape.

When I rode up, the man was standing very still, shivering with fright as he looked up at Beorthric who was questioning him in a rasping language that I supposed was the Avar tongue.

I looked at the man's face and was disappointed. I had expected to see the same high cheek bones, broad features and slightly slanted eyes of the triumphant warrior prince on the flagon. But the man's face, grimy and hollow cheeked, was no different from those of the poorer people we had met on the far side of the Donau. He was dressed as a simple herder; shabby tunic and leggings of homespun, scuffed and well-worn boots. He had a badly crooked left leg.

'He says that he's been living here for the past year,' Beorthric told me.

'He doesn't look like an Avar,' I said.

'He's not. He tells me that his people are Gepids, one of the peoples who lived in this area before the Avars came.'

'Is he the only person living here?'

'Just him.'

The fog was beginning to dissolve, revealing the interior of the Ring. There was very little to see – mounds of rubbish, vague shapes which might be the stubs of house walls, a few charred timbers sticking out of the ground, a fence of salvaged wooden slats to make a rudimentary cattle pen. The rest was emptiness, a bare ground where weeds sprouted through a thin covering of ash and black cinders. The destruction wrought by the Duke of Friuli's troops had been total.

My heart sank. I could not see how I was going to write a replacement page in the inventory of the Avar treasure. There was nothing here for me to learn.

Beorthric broke into my thoughts. 'The man's name is Kunimund. He tells me that before the fall of the Ring he lived here as a servant of the Avars.'

'Ask him if he was here on the day the Ring was stormed.'

The questioning took some time and I saw the man gradually relax as he gave his answers. Then Beorthric raised my spirits by saying, 'I think we're in luck. He was here that day. That's when his leg was smashed, and he can tell us something about the treasure. He's inviting us to his house.'

We got down from our horses, and walked with the Gepid across the wreckage of the Ring, our footsteps crunching on the cinders. He brought us to a shack he had made for himself close to the centre of the abandoned Avar stronghold. Salvaged timbers spanned the broken walls of one of the least damaged houses, and reeds had been used for thatch. Several stools and a rickety-looking bench stood outside.

He pushed aside the rag of curtain that hung across the low doorway and disappeared. When he re-emerged, he was carrying a heavy clay jug and some wooden bowls.

'He invites us to sit with him. We are his guests,' Beorthric translated. The two troopers hung back. They did not trust the Gepid. When he offered them bowls of milk from the jug, they shook their heads. They were left to hold our horses while Beorthric and I sat down. Kunimund filled our bowls, and before we drank, he tipped a small amount of milk on the ground as an offering. Then, with a little prompting from Beorthric, he launched into his account of the day that the duke's army destroyed the Ring.

I could not understand his language but watched his emotion increase as his story progressed. At first he was matter-of-fact, almost casual. Gradually, his voice rose to a pitch, and there was a tremor of the lip as he fought to hold back tears. His knuckles turned white as he held the wooden bowl more tightly. Occasionally, Beorthric interrupted to ask some detail, and the Gepid would gather himself and frown as he tried to remember. Once or twice during his narrative he pointed towards different parts of the compound.

When he finished his tale, Beorthric turned to me. 'Sigwulf, I think you'd better take notes. He's likely to be our only witness.'

I fetched parchment, pen and ink from my saddlebag, Kunimund watching my every move with almost dog-like attention. It crossed my mind that, for the Gepid, having his story written down would enshrine the memory of those who had perished on that day.

'His account agrees with what I recall,' Beorthric began. 'Our army advanced much more swiftly than the Avars expected. It took them by surprise. The khagan was preparing to follow his usual tactics, to withdraw and drag out the negotiations until the invaders lost heart and went home.'

'What about the treasure?' I reminded him.

'According to Kunimund all the gold and silver was loaded on carts, ready to accompany the withdrawal. But Friuli's army appeared in front of the palisade before the evacuation could start. Everyone inside was trapped.'

'Does Kunimund know if there were any special items in the treasure, like the warrior flagon?'

Beorthric put my question to Gepid. 'He says that most of the treasure was in coin, in sacks and boxes. He supposes there were some special items like gold plates and ornaments. On one occasion he was called upon to serve at a banquet for the khagan and his noblemen, and many precious gold objects were on display. But he cannot remember much about them.'

Dutifully, I wrote down what Beorthric had told me, though it was far too vague to satisfy the archbishop's requirement for an inventory of the Hoard.

'What happened next?' I asked.

'When the enemy arrived in front of the Ring, the khagan's servants were ordered to take the treasure off the carts and bury it. But there was too little time to do the job properly.'

Beorthric waited while the Gepid refilled his wooden bowl with milk from the earthenware jug. The Saxon took a sip before continuing.

'I've asked Kunimund to show us where the treasure was buried. He says he knows the spot, because he was one of the squad that dug the trench. Of course there's nothing left. The invaders took everything before they set fire to the Ring.'

'How did Kunimund survive all this?' I asked.

'He was rounded up with the rest of the prisoners, but no one wanted him as a slave because his leg was so badly broken. He slipped away and hid amongst the wrecked buildings. When the troops set fire to the Ring, he crawled away from the flames, and eventually found his way out into the countryside. He lived like a beast for months.'

I noticed that Beorthric had not mentioned anything of his own part in the massacre.

'Does this match with what you yourself remember?' I asked him.

'Mostly. After the Ring fell, I was put with the squad held in readiness in case the Avars launched a counter-attack, so I wasn't involved in sorting out the plunder. That job was left to the King's notaries who travelled with the Duke to make sure everything was accounted for.'

'Ask Kunimund to show us where the treasure was buried,' I suggested.

We got up and Kunimund led us across the barren landscape to a spot close under the southern wall. He stopped and pointed to a dip in the ground.

'He says that is where the treasure was buried, not very deep.'

There was nothing so see. Nevertheless, I drew a sketch of the position of the dip.

We trudged our way back across the cinders and debris to find that the two troopers had put our horses in the cattle pen. The one with the cough was idly poking through the wreckage of one of the huts. Presumably, he was hoping to find some item that had been overlooked during the sack of the Ring.

I tried one more time to dredge up some useful information. 'Ask Kunimund if he saw or heard anything about what was in the treasure when it was dug up by our troops. Did he see anything?'

The Gepid shook his head and Beorthric translated. 'He was lying on the ground with a broken leg. He knows nothing.'

Gloomily I looked down at my notes. There were just a few lines, not enough to recreate a plausible page in the inventory. I would have to use my imagination, perhaps add an extra sketch of the Ring embellished with some credible details. It would at least prove to Arno that Beorthric and I had visited the Ring.

At that moment Kunimund asked a question. From his expression he looked as if he was trying to be helpful.

'What does he say?' I asked Beorthric.

'That he worked as a herder and horse-minder for the khagan. He's sorry that he can't tell us about valuable household items. The only precious items he handled were the saddlery and other horse gear for the Khagan.'

I remembered the buckle I had seen in Rome, the one with the griffin. I had imagined it was for a belt, but now realized it could well have been from a horse harness.

'Did the khagan use very costly horse gear?' I enquired.

'His saddle was decorated with precious stones set into strips of gold, and his horse wore a harness with gold ornaments all over it,' came the reply.

'Were those items buried as well?' I asked.

'Some of them.'

Again I was disappointed.

I took another sheet of parchment and drew the maker's marks that I had copied from the warrior flagon. I held the page up for the Gepid to examine.

'Ask him if he recognizes these?' I said to Beorthric.

Kunimund studied the line of marks for a long moment. Then he looked up at me, a gleam of understanding in his eyes, and gave his answer. 'He thinks he saw these same marks on the khagan's gold breastplate,' Beorthric translated.

I pointed to my own chest, to make sure I had the meaning correctly. The Gepid shook his head. He led me across to where our horses were in the cattle pen. One of them came across, hoping to be fed. He pointed to the centre of the horse's chest. All of a sudden I remembered the picture of the warrior prince on the flagon. He was shown riding in a saddle that had a breast strap across the horse's chest to prevent the saddle sliding back. Decorations were shown dangling from the strap. Doubtless they were in gold, and the one in the centre might be substantial.

I held up my hands, holding them eight inches apart, indicating the possible size of the breastplate.

The Gepid nodded.

I beckoned to Beorthric. 'Does he know who made the breastplate?'

There was another nod from the Gepid as soon as Beorthric had finished translating. 'Kunimund says that on one occasion the plate was badly bent when a horse stepped on it. He was sent to the goldsmith to get it straightened.'

I could scarcely contain my excitement. 'Where was the goldsmith?'

'Less than half a day's ride away, to the south,' came the reply.

The smile that spread across my face must have showed my relief. Here was my chance to find the Avar goldsmith and have him make a copy of the warrior flagon.

Not caring whether or not Kunimund learned about the money belt, I fished out a gold solidi and pressed it into his hand. 'Tomorrow, I want you to take me to see this goldsmith.'

'Maybe he's dead or fled,' Beorthric cautioned. I scarcely heard him. I was already looking forward to asking the goldsmith what he knew about griffins.

*

Our two escort troopers flatly refused to venture deeper into Avar territory. Between coughs, one of them reminded me that they had orders to go no further than the Ring. His overweight colleague took pleasure in adding that they would only stay on for two days. If we had not returned by then, they would head back to their guardhouse. Holding up his hand, the fat one made the universal sign for money and made me understand that he and his colleague expected to be paid for looking after Kunimund's cattle if Beorthric and I decided to press onward. I handed over the bribe without argument. I needed the Gepid as a guide.

Kunimund's shack was too small to accommodate us so we bedded down for the night in a burned-out building, and again kept watches. I wished I had brought a heavier cloak with me for the night was very cold, and the first streaks of dawn revealed a coating of frost on the blackened timbers of the great palisade.

The Gepid brought us more bowls of milk for our breakfast and then fetched himself a sorry-looking nag that he kept stabled in another of the wrecked buildings. The animal's appearance was deceptive. As soon as he had led Beorthric and me out of the Ring and turned south, his horse broke into a flat jolting run that ate up the miles. Beorthric and I had a hard time keeping up.

We travelled under a sky full of scurrying clouds, and the countryside was much the same as before. Expanses of open grassland between low, rounded hills gave way to stretches of bog land dotted with small lakes and reed-fringed ponds wherever the drainage was poor. We were beginning to see evidence of human occupation. We came across groups of burial mounds shaped like over-sized anthills. According to Beorthric they marked the graves of tribal leaders whose peoples had grazed their cattle in the region long before the Avars entered the land.

'People like the Gepids?' I asked. We were passing a cluster of the mounds, six or seven of them, each still taller than a man, though they had badly worn away over time.

'Possibly. The Avars arrived as conquerors.'

His words brought to my mind the image of the warrior prince on the gold flagon, triumphantly dragging along his running captive by his hair.

Beorthric nodded towards Kunimund riding a short distance ahead of us. 'The Avars are a ruling class, lording it over the

Gepids and other peoples they dispossessed . . .' He did not finish his sentence but reined in his horse, swung down out of the saddle, and picked up something from the ground. It was a lump of sheep dung, shiny and fresh.

'I thought so,' he said, holding it up to show me. 'I've been noticing signs of grazing for the past few miles. We're nearing a village.'

It proved to be a straggling hamlet of poor houses, each with its tiny vegetable plot. There was a single street of bare earth, a couple of long open-sided sheds where the livestock could find winter shelter, and little else. Once again I failed to detect any Avar features in the faces of the people who appeared in the doorways to stare at us. They were mostly women and small children dressed in layers of ragged clothing. They looked pinched with hunger. The only men I could see were greybeards and I supposed that the able-bodied adults and youths were somewhere out in the grasslands tending to their flocks. One of the elders greeted Kunimund warmly as he dismounted, though I noted several hostile glances directed towards Beorthric and myself where we sat waiting on our horses.

After a brief conversation with our guide, the greybeard pointed to a building that stood a little apart. Kunimund turned to us and beckoned, smiling. Uncertain what to do, I glanced across at Beorthric. He caught my enquiring look, and gave a slight shrug. He, too, was unsure. Finally, I decided that there was no point in hanging back now that we had come so far. I slid down from my horse and handed over the reins to the old man. Beorthric joined me as we caught up with the Gepid already limping towards the house. I was encouraged to see there was an overhang to its roof where charcoal was stacked and – more puzzling – an even larger pile of dry horse dung.

The plank door was propped open, and I smelled smoke and scorched timber as Kunimund led us across the threshold. The interior was a scene of clutter and disarray. It was a large open space, with a floor of beaten earth and a high ceiling. A screen partitioned off the far end, presumably where the goldsmith lived. His furnace stood on the ground in the centre of the workspace. It resembled a chunky clay pot, about two feet high, with immensely thick walls. The snout of a large, fixed bellows poked into one side. Scattered around the furnace were all manner of tools and waste material – tongs, fire rakes, hammers, cup-shaped crucibles, water bucket, dozens and dozens of fragments of broken clay, broken metal scraps and a pair of low three-legged stools. The metal worker was off to one side, kneeling on the ground. With one hand he was using tongs to hold an odd-shaped lump of clay steady on a thick stone slab. With a hammer in the other hand he was tapping on the clay. As I watched, the clay began to split and crack, falling away in chunks, revealing the shape of a metal axe head at the core.

Kunimund called a greeting. With a final decisive tap of the hammer, the metal worker finished his task, laid down the tongs and hammer, and rose to his feet to face us. He was small and thickset, his heavy tunic specked with burn marks, and he wore a leather apron.

Beside me Beorthric kept up a running translation as Kunimund explained the reason for our visit. 'He's saying that we've heard about his reputation as a master craftsman, and you wish to talk to him about his skill, maybe order some items,' Beorthric murmured.

I was looking about me, puzzled. A large smoke hole in the centre of the roof directly over the furnace let in daylight, and there were narrow unglazed windows in the walls. But the corners of the room were in deep shadow. The place was very dark and gloomy for doing fine or delicate work. The only metalwork I could see were farm tools propped against the wall or casually thrown in a pile.

The craftsman pulled a rag from his pocket. Wiping his hands, he came forward to speak with me. His callused fingers were thick and stubby, the nails encrusted with grime. Trickles of sweat had left streaks on his soot-smeared face.

Beorthric nudged me. 'Say something,' he muttered.

I realized the craftsman was standing in front of me, waiting to hear what I wanted to ask. Distracted by his rough-hewn appearance, I said the first thing that came into my head. 'What's the horse dung for?'

He looked bemused. 'He says he mixes dung with clay to make the moulds, and to repair holes in the furnace,' Beorthric translated.

I fumbled for words. Something was wrong.

'Tell him that we're interested in the items he makes to decorate horse harness,' I suggested.

The man went across to a wooden chest against the wall and brought out several pieces to show me. In shape, they were similar to the harness buckle I had seen in Rome, but they were crudely made, lumpy and rough. I picked one up. Judging by its weight the buckle was made of poor-quality bronze. I ran my thumb over the rough surface, feeling the grit.

'Does he have any buckles that are any smoother?' I asked.

The craftsman showed me a shallow tray filled with sand. 'He says he casts the buckles in sand moulds,' Beorthric translated. 'But if you wished to order better-quality pieces from him, he could use a stone mould.'

I looked around me helplessly. This was not at all what I expected.

'Can he work with silver?' I asked.

This time there was a long pause before he answered. 'He says that he has never worked in silver, but thinks he could learn.'

Finally, I accepted defeat. I was speaking not to a goldsmith but to a village blacksmith. Kunimund had misunderstood what sort of person I was looking for.

I turned to the Gepid to explain the mistake, but Kunimund must have slipped out of the building. He was nowhere to be seen.

'Thank the smith for his time,' I said to Beorthric. 'Say we are sorry to have interrupted his work.'

The blacksmith nodded politely as we made our farewells and headed towards the door.

'That was a dead end,' I said, turning to Beorthric as we ducked out of the building and out into the street. 'Try to make Kunimund understand that we are looking for a skilled gold-worker, someone like the man who repaired the breastplate for the khagan's horse.'

Beorthric had come to an abrupt halt. I looked up to see why.

Confronting us was a half-circle of mounted men. They were sitting quietly; each man had a lance with a pennant, and a sword at his hip. Those not dressed in chain mail were wearing padded over-tunics. Every bearded face under the rims of their metal helmets had the features that marked them as Avars.

Standing in the middle of the semi-circle was Kunimund. He was glaring at us, and I read both triumph and loathing on his face. Too late, I understood the depths of his hatred for the enemy who had destroyed the Ring.

'That bastard betrayed us,' said Beorthric beside me.

# Chapter Ten

THE AVAR PATROL searched us with rough efficiency. They took away all our weapons, including the little knife on its cord around Beorthric's neck. His scramseax aroused their professional interest. They passed it from hand to hand, testing the balance, admiring the sharp edge and commenting on the blade's unusual shape. They also found my money belt and gave me several slaps to the head when I explained I was bringing the gold coins to be melted down and turned into tableware. I stuck with my story and the man I took to be the officer in charge eventually decided that the matter would be more fully investigated after they had delivered us to their commander. Then they lashed our wrists together with rawhide strips, hoisted us up on our horses, and tied our ankles together with a leather strap that passed under the horse's belly to prevent us falling off. As the patrol left the village with troopers holding our lead reins, I twisted round in my saddle to get a last view of Kunimund. He was standing by himself in the middle of the street and, judging by the scowl on his face, he was disappointed that we had not been treated more harshly.

The Avar cavalrymen did not spare us. Their horses were fit and well trained and they rode at the same bone-shattering pace as the Gepid had set. Staying upright in the saddle was agony. When I tried to speak with Beorthric, the trooper holding the leading rein of my horse lashed me across the face with his whip. I sank into a resentful silence as we were hustled onward. The angle of the afternoon sun told me that we were heading south-east. By dusk we had ridden through two more villages, each as shabby as the last, and swum with our horses across a large river. It meant that I was bedraggled and cold when, finally, we stopped for the night in yet another meagre settlement. There we were dragged off our horses and manhandled into a cow byre, both of us so stiff and bruised that we could barely stand. The Avars seated us back to back on the straw-covered earth and tied our arms each side of a stout post. Then they left us alone. It was our first chance to talk.

'Kunimund's a Gepid, forced to be a servant for the Avars. Why would he have betrayed us?' I asked. Our captors had removed our ankle fastenings and I could feel the pain as the blood returned to my feet.

Beorthric sneezed. The straw was old and dusty. 'How would you feel towards people who had killed or enslaved your family and left you half crippled with a broken leg? He knew very well that he was taking us to meet a village blacksmith, not a gold-smith.'

'He couldn't have known that an Avar patrol would be passing by.'

'Maybe not. But sooner or later he would have turned us in.'

Beorthric's remark did nothing to lift my spirits. All after-noon I had been growing increasingly pessimistic about our fate. The two troopers we had left waiting for us at the Ring would ride back to their guardhouse and report to their sergeant that we had disappeared. Their sergeant was unlikely to pass on the infor-mation to his superiors, even if he knew who they were. With Margrave Gerold's death it was not clear who was now in charge of security in Avaria. As for Archbishop Arno, he was a pragma-tist. Hearing nothing more from Beorthric or myself, he would drop the idea of using the warrior flagon to further his schemes.

He might even believe that Beorthric or I – or both of us together – had taken our chance to steal a sizable fortune in gold solidi. Whichever way I looked at our situation, it was obvious that no one knew we were prisoners of the Avars, nor would they care.

My gloomy thoughts were interrupted by a bellow from Beorthric. He continued shouting until finally one of our Avar captors came to the entrance to the byre. The Saxon roared angrily at the man who glared at him, then turned and left.

'What was all that about?' I asked Beorthric.

'I told him we needed food and something to drink.'

All of a sudden I realized how hungry I was. We had not eaten since Kunimund had provided us with milk for breakfast.

'I should never have trusted Kunimund,' I said morosely. 'I was too easily fooled.'

'Be thankful that you didn't tell him about the warrior flagon,' Beorthric answered. 'It would give the Avars something else to question you about, in addition to why you were carrying so much coin.'

The wooden post was pressing into my back and I shifted my position. 'What difference would that make?'

The Saxon gave a sardonic grunt. 'When people think you have something to say of interest to them, they redouble their efforts to make you talk.' His tone of voice left me in no doubt that he was speaking from personal experience.

The Avar returned with some stale bread and a wooden pail of water which he set down on the straw beside us. He unfastened my hands first and stood over me as I wolfed down some of the food and drank some water, scooping it up in the palm of my hand. Then he tied me up again and it was Beorthric's turn. As I watched the big Saxon eat, I wondered where he had been inter-rogated, and by whom. Most likely it was when he was captured by the Franks and before he became a turncoat. There was no way of knowing what the Franks had done to make him switch sides. It could have been a promise of generous pay or, equally, it could have been that he was tortured until he betrayed his own people. After that there would have been no going back. He had to join Carolus's irregular forces. It left me with the worrying thought that Beorthric might be another Kunimund: someone who retained a deep-seated hatred for those who had made him suffer.

\*

The following afternoon our captors brought us into what was evidently the winter headquarters of their ruler, the khagan. A hundred or so wooden houses of varying sizes occupied a patch of level ground halfway up the side of a shallow valley. Clustered around these permanent dwellings was a raggle-taggle assortment of tents, lean-tos and makeshift cabins, as well as a number of waggons with canvas tilts that served as homes. There was no sign of defence works such the great palisade at the Ring, and I presumed the khagan of the Avars had not yet had time to build and fortify a new capital following the disastrous invasion of his territory.

A chill wind carried a fine drift of rain that settled on our faces and on our horses' manes as our escort led us along the muddy paths that criss-crossed the settlement. Looking about me, I saw families going about their daily business, ignoring the dismal weather. The Avars were a sturdy-looking people, burly and vigorous. The women were dressed in heavy shawls and long thick skirts, the hems dragging in the mud, while their children were bundled up against the cold. The men wore fleece caps and heavy capes of dark oily wool. No one paid us the slightest attention. By the time we reached the centre of the settlement the rain had become a downpour. The patrol drew up in front of a single-storey building of massive timbers noticeably larger than the rest. In another country it would have been the home of a prosperous farmer. It dominated an open square of beaten earth which was steadily turning into a quagmire. Here we dismounted, and our escort led away our horses. Their officer pushed Beorthric and me, our hands still bound, towards the double doors guarded by half a dozen heavily armed Avar, presumably the khagan's attendants. Once again we were searched for weapons, and this time I noticed that the officer's sword and dagger were also taken away before we were allowed inside.

We found ourselves in an antechamber, ill-lit and smelling of wet wool and leather. Mud-spattered rugs covered the floor and more rugs, mostly in dark red and brown patterns, hung on the walls. Seated on benches on each side of the antechamber were half a dozen Avars. Apparently they were waiting their turn for an audience with their ruler, Khagan Kaiam. The bands of embroidery on the sleeves and collars of their jackets, the intricately patterned stitching on their soft leather boots, and their ornate belt buckles showed that they were men of substance. Heavily bearded and with luxuriant moustaches, they wore their hair in long braids wound with coloured strips of cloth, then tied in a knot at the nape of the neck and held in place with a metal clasp. These clasps, like their belt buckles, were made of gold or silver.

We stood waiting for perhaps half an hour. The Avars studiously ignored us and I noticed that our escorting officer had brought one of my saddlebags with him. When the door to the inner part of the building finally opened, it was to admit an armed attendant who addressed several sharp questions to our escort. He must have been granted precedence for we were beckoned forward, leaving the other Avars waiting.

As I crossed the threshold, I missed my step and almost fell headlong. The floor was several feet below ground level. A short flight of steps led into a cavernous semi-sunken room where weak autumn light entered through narrow slit windows. We were in an audience chamber, gloomy and full of shadows, which extended almost the entire length of the building. A little off-centre a charcoal fire glowed in a fire pit, the smoke rising to a roof vent. The furnishings were both ordinary and slightly barbaric. There were folding iron stools and low tables of dark wood as well as a number of large storage chests that looked as if they might contain valuables. Rugs were everywhere, on the floor, thrown across the furniture, hanging on the walls. The man I presumed to be the khagan sat at the far end of the chamber on a portable high-backed throne of carved wood. He was too far away for me to read his expression, but he and the score of attendants and councillors standing near him were dressed as richly as the Avars waiting in the anteroom, and they all wore the same distinctive hairstyle.

I was still taking in this unexpected scene when, without warning, the patrol leader beside me dropped to his knees. Then he leaned forward and extended himself flat on the carpet, face down and arms outstretched. For a moment I hesitated, only to hear Beorthric beside me hiss, 'Get down!' A quick glance in his direction confirmed that the Saxon was already halfway to the floor. Awkward with my bound wrists I followed his example. I lay still for several seconds, breathing in the musty smell of the carpet. Then the khagan made a vague grunting sound, the signal for all three of us to get back on our feet. Ignoring Beorthric and myself, the khagan beckoned to our captor to come closer.

'What's being said?' I whispered to Beorthric as the khagan began questioning the officer who gave his answers in a deferential voice.

'The khagan is demanding to know where we were picked up and what we were doing when we were taken prisoner.'

As the questioning continued, I studied the Avar ruler. He had a surprisingly boyish face, round and slightly chubby, with a lighter complexion than his attendants. I put his age at some-where between thirty and forty, and he was unremarkable in every way, being of middling height and build, with small, almost feminine hands. Nor was he wearing any symbols of his rank except, perhaps, for a round fur cap made from some glossy pelt. I would never have singled him out from the rest of the company but for the fact that he was the only seated person in the room.

The patrol leader was reaching into my saddlebag. He pulled out my money belt and held it up for the khagan to inspect. The khagan waved at him to bring the belt forward, felt its weight, poked a finger into the slit that I had made, and extracted a gold coin. Then he looked up, straight at me. Now I understood why he was khagan. His dark brown eyes held a casual cruelty that I had never witnessed before. The hair on my forearms and the back of my neck prickled with fear.

'Speak,' he said coldly. With a shock I realized that he had addressed me in heavily accented Frankish.

'I was bringing the coins to be melted down into ornaments,' I croaked. My throat had gone dry.

There was a long moment of silence as the khagan looked at me, sizing me up. I stumbled on. 'The quality of your Avar crafts-men is renowned,' I blurted. Even as I spoke I sensed that my words had no meaning for the khagan. He knew only a smattering of Frankish and had used a Frankish word so that he could show off to his attendants. I had an uncomfortable feeling that if I said anything more, I risked making him appear ignorant in their eyes. My voice trailed off.

One of his councillors was a Frankish speaker and he provided a quick translation of what I had said. The khagan lifted his chin a fraction, continued to stare at me, then abruptly tossed the money belt back towards the patrol leader, just far enough for him to lunge forward and catch it in mid-air.

The khagan spoke. There was no mistaking that his statement was hostile.

'The great khagan says you are a great liar,' said the interpreter. 'He says you brought the gold to pay his enemies to do him harm.'

'That is not so,' I protested.

The interpreter did not bother to translate.

The khagan turned his attention back to the patrol leader who was now holding out the slender bundle of parchment pages that I had brought with me from Paderborn. I tried anxiously to remember what I had written on them. It was very little. There were only a few notes I had made while looking around the Ring and trying to identify where the Avar treasure had been buried. The rest of the pages were blank. The khagan took the parchment sheets and began turning them over one by one. He checked each side so slowly that I wondered if he knew how to read his own language, let alone the Latin I had used to take my notes. I told myself that even if someone translated the Latin for the khagan's benefit, everything that I had written was harmless. I relaxed.

Then I remembered the page on which I had drawn the runic letters incised on the base of the warrior flagon. It was the Avar goldsmith's mark that I had shown to Kunimund. Unexpectedly, I felt my spirits rise. Perhaps this was the moment when I would learn more about the warrior jug, something useful to add to the report I was preparing for Bishop Arno. The khagan reached that page and paused. He frowned as he puzzled over the letters, then murmured something that sounded like 'Zoltan'.

'What's he saying?' I whispered to Beorthric, standing half a pace behind me.

'Seems to be a name.'

The khagan went on turning the pages. All of a sudden he stopped and inside me something went very cold. The room was filled with tension. His attendants and councillors were gazing at him, half expectant, half fearful. The khagan studied the page in his hand, then turned his gaze on me. There was a dark, angry expression on his chubby face. He no longer looked youthful, only dangerous and unstable.

He held up the parchment sheet so that I could see what was written there, then spat out what had to be a furious accusation.

'He says we're spies,' muttered Beorthric.

Drawn on the page were the simple sketches that I had made at the Ring. Even if the Avar leader was illiterate, he was able to recognize the distinctive outline of the great palisade.

The khagan's youthful face was taut with rage. His voice rose to a shout with his next accusation.

'He says that the gold you brought was payment for a traitor called Zoltan,' translated Beorthric. 'He swears that he will track him down and make sure he suffers a painful death.'

I knew at once that it was futile to try to explain away the drawings and the rune-scratched name. The khagan was beside himself with anger. He turned back to the piece of paper with the goldsmith's marks and his jaw clenched as he began ripping it to tiny shreds as if already tearing the man limb from limb. Then he flung the scraps aside with a gesture of disgust before launching into his next pronouncement. It did not require a word of his language to know he was giving orders for something unpleasant to be done to us. Guards stepped forward, ready to remove us from the chamber. At that moment Beorthric intervened. He addressed the khagan directly, in Avar. The khagan had been leaning across to speak to one of his councillors. Now his head snapped round and he listened until Beorthric had finished speaking. Then he must have countermanded his earlier instructions for I felt a slight slackening in the grip of the guard who had me by the elbow.

'What was all that about?' I demanded of Beorthric as we were hustled up the steps leading back to the antechamber.

'The khagan had given orders for both of us to be taken outside and strangled. It's their punishment for spies,' he replied. 'I pointed out to him that you would be more valuable if kept alive, as a hostage against whoever sent you, and to confront this Zoltan when he is identified.'

It took me a moment to react. 'And what about you? Aren't you a spy as well?'

He bared his teeth in a bleak smile. 'I told him that I don't know how to read or write. So I had no idea what was in your notes. Nor did I know about the money belt because you always kept it hidden. I claimed that you hired me only because I speak Avarish.'

I was stunned. 'And he believed you?'

'Enough to save you from being garrotted with a bowstring.'

'So what's going to happen to me?'

'The Avars don't allow useless mouths, particularly in winter when food is going to be short. I expect you'll be put to work.'

'As a slave?'

He shrugged. 'You'll be better off than some unfortunate who has the name of Zoltan.'

By now the guards had bundled us through the antechamber of the khagan's residence and out into the muddy square. I stood there for a moment, badly disoriented, not knowing whether Beorthric had deliberately abandoned me to save himself or whether he had genuinely prevented my execution.

It was dusk, and the wind had dropped and the rain was turning to snow. Large soft flakes were floating down silently from a smoke-coloured sky. One of the guards cut the leather thong binding Beorthric's wrists. Mine were left in place. Leaving Beorthric, two of the guards marched me across the mire and down a narrow footpath between the wooden houses. My thoughts were in such turmoil that I took no notice of where we were going. Within minutes the snow had increased to a white swirling mass and my escort quickened their pace, until eventually we halted outside a house scarcely larger than a shed. The door of weathered planks was firmly shut but after some shouting and banging, it creaked open to reveal the figure of an old woman, a blanket drawn around her shoulders. A few stringy grey hairs escaped from under the dark shawl framing a wrinkled face. Despite her advanced years and the fact that she stood no taller than my shoulder, she was fully capable of making her irritation known. She looked up at my guards through watery eyes and scolded them in a thin voice full of phlegm.

They stood meekly until a fit of coughing gave them their chance to push me forward with a few words of explanation. One of the men pulled out a knife to slice through my bonds, but a claw-like hand shot out and knocked the blade aside. There was an angry command, and my escort sheepishly unpicked the knots. As soon as this was done, the same hand snatched away the undamaged length of leather thong. The other hand gripped me by the wrist and pulled me in through the doorway. Both my guards turned on their heels and tramped away into the growing blizzard.

*

During the hours of darkness the temperature plummeted. Though it was only early September, a freak blizzard had arrived in Avaria. By daybreak a snow bank, a couple of feet deep, made it difficult to force open the door. That was after the old lady had handed me the empty water bucket for the first time and gestured that I was to descend the slope to the river, fill the bucket and return. Outside everything was white, and the cold was so fierce that it hurt to fill one's lungs with air. I came back chilled to the bone; my hands were blue, and I was shivering uncontrollably. I knew that the clothes I had brought with me were utterly inadequate for the coming winter.

It took me the rest of that day to work out that I had been given as a present to the old lady. Her name was Faranak and, as I later learned, she was the childless widow of the khagan's favourite uncle. By Avar custom, his nephew had the duty of looking after her. The khagan had already provided her with the small house for her winter accommodation and was sending regular deliveries of food. Now he had supplied her with a menial servant.

*

Faranak's dwelling was a smaller, shabbier version of the khagan's audience chamber. The earth floor of the single room was sunk below ground level and a tiny fire pit kept it warm. My servant's duties were repetitive but undemanding. I was expected to tend the fire and prepare meals over the embers. Faranak had lost most of her teeth and ate very sparingly, so cooking amounted to boiling up a few handfuls of millet or some other grain into a gruel. If available, I added some dried fruit or shreds of meat. Afterwards, I scrubbed out the single metal pot, removed ash and cinders from the hearth, and replenished the supply of fuel from the woodpile behind the little house. I was also expected to sweep the floor of beaten earth and generally keep the room tidy. Washing clothes was not called for and, as far as I was aware, the old lady never changed her garments. Like many old people, Faranak never threw anything away. The dark corners of her little room were heaped with items she refused to get rid of. The unfortunate consequence was that her house was infested with fleas and lice, and never before had I found myself itching and scratching so much. The low door at the back of the cabin led to a latrine pit dug inside a tiny lean-to built against the rear wall, so the daily trip to the river for water was almost the only time I was permitted to venture any distance from the little house. If I wandered too far, her neighbours shouted at me angrily. Faranak herself saw almost no visitors.

Naturally, I kept a look out for Beorthric whenever I went outside. I needed to talk with him and try to find out what might happen next. Once or twice I thought I recognized him in the distance, but he had disappeared by the time I reached the spot where I thought I had seen him.

It was mid-winter before I got a definite sighting of him. That morning, Faranak surprised me by hobbling to the door of the house and beckoning to me to follow. Normally, she wore no jewellery or ornaments of any kind, but she had looped several strings of brightly coloured beads around her scrawny neck and was wearing a pair of gold earrings set with purple gemstones. Vaguely aware that something unusual was going on, I hurried to join her out on the footpath. It was one of those rare days when the winter sun, shining from a clear blue sky, overcame the numbing cold, and the entire settlement seemed to have come alive. A stream of people, both men and women and some older children, was making its way in the direction of the khagan's residence. Underfoot it was slippery with hard-packed snow and ice, and Faranak held on to my arm as we accompanied the crowd. When we reached the open space in front of the khagan's headquarters, it was already thronged with people muffled up against the cold. They jostled together, shoulder to shoulder, stamping their boots to warm their feet. Their breath caused a slight fog to form above their heads. Despite her frailty, Faranak pushed her way forward with scant regard for niceties. The crowd parted to allow her through, perhaps because she was a close relative to the khagan, and I found myself standing beside her in the front rank. An open space, some twenty paces across, had been left in the middle of the crowd. In the centre, stood a scarecrow figure. A man was dressed in a tent-like shirt that reached to his ankles. The hem was shredded into rags, and the garment was sewn all over with dozens of loose ribbons and strips of leather that swayed and fluttered as he moved. Tied to the ribbons were dozens upon dozens of trinkets: bells, amulets, pebbles, fragments of bone, feathers. A leather bag hung from a cord around his neck, and he had large, loose slippers on his feet. His conical leather cap was painted white and sprouted a cluster of feathers. His face was only visible from the mouth downward. The rest was obscured by a thick dangling fringe of short strips of coloured cloth and strings of beads.

It was an Avar sorcerer.

I glanced towards the spectators on the far side of the circle. The khagan was there, standing in the front rank, half a pace in advance of his councillors. Without knowing quite why, my attention was drawn to another Avar, well dressed in costly furs and much closer to me. The ugliness of the man marked him out. He was broad shouldered and squat with short legs and long, powerful arms. Under his hat of marten fur his face was blotched and marred with pock marks. With his wide mouth he reminded me of a toad.

A sharp rap, the sound of wood on wood, brought my attention back to the ragged scarecrow. The sorcerer was using a small round shield as a drum, striking it with a short, crooked baton. The low muttering of the crowd died away.

The sorcerer began to rotate on the same spot, revolving slowly, the hanging ribbons and scraps of his garment swirling out. He kept hitting the shield with a regular, rapid beat, then began to wail. It was a high-pitched sound, rising and falling, sometimes from the back of his throat, sometimes from high up in his nose. He repeated the same phrase over and over again as he spun round and round, the skirt of his long shirt flying out. Then, after a slight stumble, he began to trot around the circle of onlookers, almost within touching distance of us. Each time he passed, the crowd swayed back. At random he would stop and thrust his intimidating face with its drool-streaked chin close into the front rank of the onlookers. When he did this close to where Faranak and I were standing, I was impressed that the old lady stood her ground and did not flinch. After several circuits the sorcerer began speed up, beating his shield more rapidly. Soon he was wagging his head from side to side, like a runner in the last stages of exhaustion. As he passed, I heard the gasping intake of breath between his eerie wails.

Finally, he turned back into the middle of the circle, came to a halt, let drop the drumstick and shield on the hard-packed snow, and raised his arms to the sky. Then he threw back his head and let out a long, grating shriek that echoed over the silent crowd.

Lowering his arms, he turned to face the khagan. Reaching into a cloth bag that hung around his neck he took out an object that glinted gold in the sun. Walking across to the khagan he placed it in the man's outstretched hands. I was close enough to see what it was: a human skull, gold plated.

In front of me Faranak let out a small hiss of satisfaction.

Some instinct made me glance towards the toad-like man to my left. He was watching the khagan and his face was set in a cold, vicious mask. He was keeping his hatred under tight control, and it was costing him a great effort. With a sudden lurch in my guts I realized that I knew almost nothing about the people amongst whom I was held captive, least of all about their feuds and rivalries.

The ceremony was over, and people were preparing to go back to their homes. That was when I saw Beorthric. He was standing at the back of the crowd, a little to my right, and perhaps twenty paces away. He was half a head taller than those immediately around him and wearing some sort of hooded cloak. But his pale face with its blond moustache and beard was unmistakable. Our eyes locked. For a long moment he held my gaze, his expression unreadable. I caught my breath, willing him to acknowledge my presence. Then his eyes slid away and he looked off to one side, deliberately ignoring me. A moment later he was walking off, leaving me bewildered, disappointed and angry.

# Chapter Eleven

BEORTHRIC'S REBUFF jolted me. It made me confront the uncomfortable truth that I was deluding myself by hoping that the big Saxon somehow held the key to ending my captivity. My misreading of the situation meant that I had allowed myself to be far too passive. If I did not take action, the routine drudgery as Faranak's serf and my poor diet would eventually reduce me to such a state of apathy that I was likely to remain a prisoner until Kaiam decided I was no longer worth keeping alive. In short, it was essential to get away from Kaiam's clutches, even if it meant turning my back on Beorthric.

I began to plan my escape.

I needed a horse, and preferably a remount as well. My daily trips to the river had shown me that the Avars kept a few horses close at hand even in winter and right in the heart of the settlement. I supposed that these animals were their favourites, and on the rare sunny days I saw them being exercised out on the river flats, usually ridden bareback by youngsters. A stone's throw away from Faranak's house and surrounded by a mud wall was the home of a well-to-do Avar. One bitterly cold morning, as I was on my back from collecting a bucket of water, I noticed that the front gate of wooden planks had been left open. There was no one about, so I stepped aside from my usual path, still with my bucket in hand, and peeked in. The house itself was the usual single-storey wooden building and surrounded by an untidy cluster of sheds, lean-tos, piles of firewood and a parked waggon. Over to one side of the yard was a small square building of mud bricks. The snow had melted from the roof, and in the still air a faint haze of steam oozed from the thatch. I guessed that the building was a winter stable, and the body heat of several horses was causing the steam. My guess was confirmed by the sight of horse droppings and soiled straw thrown onto a nearby midden heap, and a hay pile protected by a canvas sheet.

Thoughtfully, I returned across the lane to Faranak's house, delivered the water, and prepared Faranak's midday meal. As soon as the old lady had nodded off into her usual afternoon sleep, I began to rummage through the piles of Faranak's hoarded possessions. Under a pile of old clothes I found an old saddle that was still serviceable, and tangled in a heap of discarded bedding I came across a couple of damaged bridles that I would be able to repair. Sifting the rubbish at the back of the room I uncovered a bundle of leather straps, and even recognized the one that had tied my wrists when I was first delivered to her. It gave me a moment's satisfaction to imagine plaiting it, with others, into a lead rein for my remount that I proposed to steal.

From what I remembered of the journey when Beorthric and I were brought as captives to the khagan's capital, I could cover the distance to the border with Carolus's domain in a little more than three days. But the countryside was now covered in deep snow and, as a consequence, I would be obliged to stick to the beaten trails, travelling from village to village. In those settlements I was sure to be questioned and I decided that I would pass myself off as a Gepid delivering horses for his master. For the plan to succeed I would have to be able to speak passable Avarish, and my only possible teacher was Faranak. I had learned a smattering of the language from her, enough to carry out my daily chores.

I told myself to be patient as I set about acquiring a better grasp of the language. The task was not easy because Faranak was very hard of hearing and I had to bellow out my questions. If I caught her in a good mood, she was willing to cooperate. Over the next six weeks, my vocabulary expanded, and at the same time I built up a secret cache of the equipment I needed: a couple of threadbare rugs that I sewed edge to edge, leaving a gap for my head, to provide a winter cape, mittens fashioned from strips cut from a discarded blanket, and a cloth bag to contain the scraps of dried food that I put aside from our meagre meals.

Initially, I thought about stealing the horses at night, under cover of darkness. But I abandoned that idea when, returning from the river on another day, I again saw that the neighbour's gate had been left slightly ajar. I went over to confirm my early reconnaissance and this time was greeted by a large and vicious guard dog. The snarling brute flung himself against the gate from the inside, and would have sunk its teeth into me if the gap in the gate had been wide enough to let it pass. That persuaded me that my best course was to wait until the guard dog was absent and take the horses in broad daylight, brazenly pretending that I was a servant.

*

My chance came at the end of January. I went down to the river as usual to fetch the early morning bucket of water. The previous night had been overcast, and the sky was still clouded over. A slight unseasonal thaw had softened the surface of the snow, and meltwater was dripping from the tips of the icicles that hung from the eaves of Faranak's little house. There was no one to be seen in the laneway as I came back up the hill and the grey cheerlessness of the day seemed to be keeping the neighbours indoors. I scratched tentatively on their gate, and when there was no snarling response, I took it that their guard dog was elsewhere. I delivered the water bucket as usual, and when Faranak was settled into her customary routine, muttering to herself as she sifted through her possessions, I slipped quietly out of her front door, clutching my bundle of clothes, the food bag and the makeshift saddlery.

The laneway was still deserted as I quietly walked the few yards to the neighbour's house. I held my breath as I eased open their gate – it was not locked – and stepped into the yard. Everything was quiet. The house itself was shuttered and silent. Best of all, there was no sign of the guard dog. I placed my clothes bundle on the ground by the gate and, carrying only the horse tack, I went quietly over to the stable. It was closed with a simple door, again unlocked, and I held my breath as I dragged it open and slipped inside. Four horses turned their heads to look at me. With their shaggy dark brown winter coats they were typical Avar mounts, barrel chested and sturdy with thick necks and Roman noses. They were crammed together, side by side, filling up all the available space. I worked quickly. Pulling the door closed behind me, I approached the nearest animal. In the semi-darkness the liquid eyes gleamed large. Gently, I stroked the creature's head, not knowing how it would react to a stranger. To my relief the horse stood quietly. I stayed several moments, waiting for all four horses to get used to my presence, then slipped one of the two bridles over its head. There was not enough standing room between the horses to put on the saddle, so I attached a lead rein and then moved on to the next horse and did the same. With the saddle over my arm, I pushed open the stable door and looked out into the yard. The place was still deserted.

Without a backwards glance I stepped out into the open and began to walk towards the gate, towing the horses behind me. There was a bad moment when both animals tried to leave through the stable doorway at the same time. They jostled, jammed in the entrance, and there was the sound of a haunch scraping against the doorpost until one animal pushed ahead of the other. I could feel my heart beating in my chest as I reached the gate to the laneway. There I paused to open it wide enough to let both horses through. Moments later, I was outside with them, and still no one had raised the alarm.

My hands were shaking with nerves as I fumbled to put a saddle on the better-looking of my two horses while still trying to keep hold of the lead reins of both animals for fear they would bolt. I reached down and picked up the bundle of clothes and bag of food. My homemade travel cloak of old rugs would attract attention as I rode out through the settlement, so I prepared to tie it behind the saddle. The horses were creatures of habit and they had moved to stand shoulder to shoulder, taking up the same position they had occupied in the stable all those winter months. I pushed between them, intending to fasten the cloak in place and that was my fatal mistake.

I did not know that Avar horses can only be approached, handled and mounted from their left-hand side. When I walked between them, I nudged my saddled horse on his right side, to get him to move over. It spooked him. He reared up. His companion caught the sense of panic and jerked back. I was pulled off balance and fell, still hanging on to the reins and trying to bring the two animals under control. They were pulling in opposite directions, plunging and kicking. One kick struck the open plank gate with a loud bang. I heard shouts of alarm as the neighbours were aroused, then furious barking. I rose from the ground, only for my remount to rear back and pull me off my feet again. I went down in the slush, knowing that my escape plan had gone disastrously wrong even as the neighbour's guard dog came charging out of the yard and leapt at me, teeth bared. I dropped the reins and threw up an arm. The beast's jaws closed on my wrist, and with deep-throated snarls it began to shake me from side to side. The two horses promptly bolted in a spatter of mud and snow. There was a glimpse of a boy running after them and then a heavy boot kicked me in the ribs. As I struggled to get up, a hard, heavy blow landed on the back of my head, and I was half stunned. The guard dog let go of my arm and fastened its teeth on my leg. I rolled to one side and looked up at an enraged Avar. He was a heavy-set man with a wispy beard, wielding a length of wood as a makeshift club; his face was contorted with anger.

Suddenly there was another attacker, a scuttling shrieking demon who joined the fray. The man landed another blow, this time on my shoulder, and then let out a stream of oaths as he swung at me again and his arm was blocked. I recognized Faranak's voice. The uproar had brought the old lady from her house and she was yelling at my attacker. I recognized the words. She was shrieking at him to stop, that I was her property and that he would have to answer to the khagan if I was injured.

The final blow from the stick was slow enough for me to deflect it with one hand and then the guard dog, still snarling, was being pulled away by the scruff of its neck. Panting, I got to my feet. My forearm was hurting where I had been bitten, I was bruised in several places, and my clothes were cold and soggy from where I had rolled in the lane. Worse, I felt a complete fool for having made such a mess of my escape attempt. I knew that I would not be allowed a second chance. Faranak grabbed me by my wrist and pulled me towards her house. Stumbling, I was dragged to her door and then whisked inside. The door was slammed shut behind me, and I heard the bar shoot into place. Then I was looking into the wrinkled face of my rescuer. A dribble of spittle ran down from one corner of her mouth, and she glared at me. Then, astonishingly, her expression softened. An amused glint appeared in her eyes. She let go of my wrist and turned away with a sniff that conveyed satisfaction at the rescue and derision of my incompetence.

\*

All that week and the next I waited anxiously for my punishment. Every day I expected to be hauled away to appear before Kaiam and hear what he had decided I should suffer for attempting to abscond. But not until early March did one of the khagan's guards finally show up at Faranak's door. He had come to fetch me to the khagan's residence for quite another reason: I was to appear before a foreigner, an ambassador. My heart leapt. I had almost forgotten the role as a hostage that the khagan had assigned me. I could only guess that Carolus had decided to open negotiations with the rebel Avars. In my excitement, I even dared to think that Archbishop Arno had somehow learned of my capture and had a hand in what was happening.

The khagan's audience chamber was much more brightly lit than the previous occasion. Dozens of oil lamps had been placed around the room. Candles as thick as my forearm burned on tall iron stands, adding to the smoky atmosphere of the room that made my eyes water. A feast was in progress. The storage chests and other furniture had been moved back so that a score of guests could be seated in two lines facing one another across a low table in the centre of the room. At the head of the table sat the khagan on his wooden throne. On his left he was flanked by the burly, toad-like Avar, with the wide, almost lipless mouth. Seated on the khagan's right hand was the person I took to be the foreign ambassador. With a sudden thrust of disappointment I saw that he was a complete stranger. Indeed, for a moment, the absurd thought flickered across my mind that he was one of the little folk that many of my Anglo-Saxon people believe in. He was tiny, almost a midget. Seated, his head came no higher than the khagan's shoulder. He was like a ten-year-old child who had become an adult without adding an inch in height. He was wearing an elegant and beautifully cut robe of silk striped in grey and gold, and his dark curls were artfully arranged across his forehead. I suspected that if I were standing closer, I would have caught a whiff of perfume over the rich smells of roast beef and mutton that were making my stomach growl with hunger. I scanned the two rows of guests, seeking a clue to the identity of this ambassador, guessing that he must have come with his own staff.

My sense of disappointment deepened when I saw two obvious foreigners seated amongst the Avar nobles. Both had olive skin and were wearing cloaks of white wool edged with scarlet trim and fastened at the shoulder with jewelled brooches. The older man had short greying hair, but his younger companion had the same neat dark curls as the envoy sitting next to the khagan. I guessed, wrongly as it turned out, that they were Roman aristocrats.

My attention returned to the three men seated at the head of the gathering. The khagan was reaching forward to pick up something from the table in front of him. The khagan lifted the object into my view, and my heart jumped like someone suddenly woken from a deep sleep. He was holding a golden flagon. Even at that distance I could tell that it was exactly the same shape and size as the warrior flagon stolen in Paderborn. I was too far away to see if it was decorated with the image of the victorious horseman, but something told me that it was identical. My mind reeled. I tried to imagine how the gold flagon could possibly have got back to Avaria. Surely it was too much of a coincidence that the thief had sold it to someone who had then traded it back to the Avars instead of melting down the flagon for its gold. It flashed across my mind that the flagon had been stolen to order. But if that was so, then someone had known that the Nomenculator and I had taken the flagon from Albinus – the papal chamberlain – and carried it to Paderborn.

Nothing made sense.

Baffled, I looked along the array of the gold and silver items set out on the low table to impress the ambassador. There was a wealth of costly tableware: goblets and platters, and more than a dozen small bowls of different shapes and designs. Most were plain pieces, with little or no decoration. At the end of the table closest to me was a small gold bowl of very striking design. About the size of my cupped hand, it stood on four short legs and the craftsman had fashioned it so that one side of the bowl became a bull's head, complete with horns. Looking along the table, I saw a second bowl just like it. They were a matching pair. It dawned on me that the golden flagon the khagan was now holding was probably one of a pair.

A sharp prod in my ribs brought my attention back to the room. My escort wanted me to face directly towards the khagan. The Avar ruler was pointing at me and saying something to the ambassador seated beside him. I was impressed to see the little man nod politely. Apparently he could understand Avar. The two of them talked together for several minutes. During the conversation the envoy glanced in my direction several times, his face carefully blank. Meanwhile, I stood where I was, waiting to be called forward.

It never happened. At the end of their conversation, the khagan waved a hand in my direction. I was dismissed. My escort lost no time in ushering me out of the audience chamber and into the street. I could have wept with frustration and the bitter irony of where I now found myself. In my bones I knew that the golden flagon I had just seen was the twin of the one that had been stolen in Paderborn. If I could somehow get my hands on it and deliver it to Archbishop Arno I would accomplish my mission. On the other hand, I could see no prospect of ever regaining my freedom. I was fated to remain a serf to the Avars, forgotten by the outside world.

\*

I was still in a thoroughly black mood when I stepped out of Faranak's house the next morning, empty water bucket in hand, to find the little envoy waiting in the slush outside. He was dressed as fastidiously as at the banquet, this time in a brocade silk cap and a cloak with a fox fur collar. He was alone.

'If you could spare me a few minutes, we should talk,' he said in perfect Frankish, looking me over with more than ordinary interest.

I gaped at him, before gathering my wits. 'Time is something I have plenty of,' I answered sourly, then led him inside.

He bowed politely to Faranak who was regarding him with suspicion mixed with curiosity. My knowledge of Avar was now good enough to understand him as he said, 'My Lady, I would be grateful if you would permit me to interview your servant.'

I doubted whether in her deafness she heard him, for her answer was an incoherent mumble.

He turned to me. 'My name is Nikephorus. I am an ambassador from Her Majesty, the *balissa* Irene, to Kaiam the Khagan of the Avars.' He paused long enough to cast a critical glance around the shabby room. 'Khagan Kaiam tells me that His Majesty King Carolus sent you to make trouble.'

'Khagan Kaiam is wrong,' I answered bluntly. I was suspicious of the ambassador's motive for coming to see me. Irene, the empress in Constantinople and ruler of the Greeks, had no interest in my being set free, and I wanted no more disappointments.

Nikephorus shrugged aside my denial. 'The khagan is convinced otherwise. He says you were caught carrying a large quantity of gold, and with maps of the Avar defences. He believes that the money was to pay for a rebellion against the khagan, even to hire a killer.'

'The khagan's life is not in danger from anything I was doing,' I said, not bothering to conceal my mistrust of the little Greek. 'Judging by the way no one is allowed to carry weapons in his presence, he already has enough enemies without my adding to them.'

The ambassador spread his hands in an apologetic gesture. 'Please don't misunderstand me. Last night Kaiam boasted to me that it was time that he put you to torture. He had been waiting to do so until spring when the outlying tarkans – their sub-chiefs – assemble here. He hopes to learn which of them you were planning to approach with the money. I thought I might get him to change his mind.'

A knot of fear began to form inside me. 'Carolus did not send me. Archbishop Arno gave me my instructions.'

'The Archbishop of Salzburg?'

I nodded, again impressed by the extent of the Greek envoy's knowledge.

'And what did the good archbishop want you to do with all that money?' he enquired gently. 'If I'm to persuade the khagan, he'll need a convincing explanation.'

I hesitated before answering. I knew that Archbishop Arno intended to confront Albinus the papal chamberlain with the warrior flagon, but I did not know why. For whatever reason, men had been killed to get possession of it.

'The money was all in gold coin. It was to be melted down to make gold tableware. As I told the khagan, only an Avar craftsman could to the work,' I said, knowing that my answer sounded weak and implausible.

For the tiniest moment Nikephorus's eyes expressed disbelief, then he recovered himself. 'And why did the archbishop desire such tableware? Not as an altar piece, surely.' A hint of a smile twitched the corner of his small mouth. 'I've heard that the archbishop lacks sensitivity but he wouldn't go as far as to commission from a pagan craftsman.'

'Perhaps it was to be a gift to the khagan,' I suggested. 'The archbishop is in charge of converting the conquered Avars. Maybe he is seeking to establish good relations with the khagan.' I knew the idea was far-fetched, but I had a feeling that the less I said about the warrior flagon, the better.

Nikephorus was not put off. 'What was the tableware to look like?'

'A jug or ewer, decorated with the image of a mounted warrior hauling along his captive by the hair.'

The Greek's eyes narrowed. Again he astonished me with his quickness of thought. 'Then Arno is less intelligent than I supposed. The khagan has at least one of those already, probably two.'

'Two?'

'The Avars have a great love for matching pairs,' he said. 'It's something we learned in Constantinople long ago. We always send them matching gifts, a pair of white horses, identical twin girls trained as musicians and dancers, and so forth.'

He broke off, and the shrewd eyes studied me. 'I presume the coins you were carrying were gold solidi?'

I nodded.

'Now where would Archbishop Arno have laid his hands them, I wonder?' he asked. 'Am I right in thinking that it might have something to do with the Avar Hoard, and that is why you had a drawing of the Ring?'

He had caught me off-guard. My hesitation in replying gave him his answer.

He treated me to a conspiratorial smile. 'If the khagan's people do question you, I suggest you avoid any mention of the place those coins came from.'

He darted a sideways glance at Faranak. 'You know how she lost her husband?'

I shook my head.

'At the storming of the Ring.'

With that he made his way briskly to the door and let himself out, leaving me standing in the half-darkness.

*

A few days later, I had clambered up on the low roof of Faranak's house to mend a leak that had appeared with the spring thaw, when I saw an Avar trooper striding purposefully along the laneway. I recognized him as the officer in charge of the patrol that had captured Beorthric and me four months earlier.

'Come down! You're wanted,' he called up, and when I was back on the ground, he ordered me to accompany him.

I spoke Avar well enough to explain that Faranak's hearth fire was almost out, and first I should have to fetch logs and add more fuel.

'No time for that,' he snapped.

He walked off and as I trailed along behind him, I imagined that Nikephorus's visit had been to warn me that I was about to be interrogated about the gold coins. Desperately I thought what I might say when questioned, and knew that my only real hope was that the Avar interrogators had also summoned Beorthric for questioning and that he would speak up in my support. This seemed highly unlikely. The faithless Saxon had already denied, in the presence of the khagan, that he knew anything about the reason for my mission, and had deliberately avoided contact with me ever since. There was no chance that he would change his story now. Vengefully, I toyed with the idea that if Beorthric was willing to abandon me to my fate, then I could match his betrayal by telling the Avars that Beorthric had taken part in the massacre at the Ring.

The Avar set a brisk pace. The morning was dreary and cheerless, with low, unbroken cloud. The air had lost its winter chill, and the last remnants of the snow banks on each side of the footpath were dissolving into thin streaks of dirty slush. Everything was dripping wet, and the path was full of puddles, forcing passers-by to step around them. I heard Avar being spoken, but also other languages that I did not recognize. I concluded the khagan's winter capital was home not only to Avars, but also to other wandering peoples and tribes. We reached the square in front of the khagan's residence and, to my surprise, carried straight on. I had never been this far from Faranak's house and had no idea where we might be going. The wooden houses soon gave way to a sprawling labyrinth of tents and shacks, and we passed empty stables and cattle pens where the ground was churned up to a slop. I supposed that the Avars had already driven some of their flocks and herds out to spring pasture.

Finally, we arrived at a fenced-off area at the edge of the settlement. Drawn up in neat rows were a number of two-wheeled carts. Loaded on them was equipment that I recognized from my days spent on campaign with Carolus's army. They were devices for throwing rocks and stones and heavy arrows. It was a weapons park.

Squads of men were at work, carrying out repairs, and my escort handed me over to an overseer. With a surge of relief it dawned on me that I was not being brought for interrogation but to help with the annual maintenance of the Avar military machine. This was confirmed by the tall, gangling man, to whom I was assigned as an assistant.

'Several turn-bar sockets are split,' he commented, peering into the winding mechanism of an onager, a stone-launcher. 'Rainwater got in, froze, and cracked the timber. I keep telling them to make sure the sockets are sealed when the machines are laid up for winter.'

'They' were obviously the Avars, and as he didn't look like an Avar himself, I asked him where he came from.

'Lombardy,' he answered. 'I was taken prisoner during the first Avar war. That was nearly ten years ago. Maybe I won't ever go back there. Here they treat engineers with the respect we deserve.'

'I'm a prisoner myself,' I said, 'but I can't say I'm enjoying the experience.'

'Depends how useful you make yourself. The Avars expect every foreigner to be a clever craftsman. That's why they brought you along –' he jerked his head towards the other men busily working on the machines – 'you'll find all sorts: Gepids, Greeks, Slavs, Franks . . . some of them are slaves; others are freemen; a few have married well and think of themselves as Avars.'

He sucked his teeth in disapproval as he found another socket damaged by frost. 'We'll have to take this lot apart.'

'I'm afraid I won't be much use to you. I've no experience of this sort of work,' I admitted.

'You'll pick it up quickly enough.'

We set about dismantling the stone-thrower. For the first time since being taken prisoner, I was enjoying myself. There was satisfaction in the simple tasks of using wedges and levers to prise apart the mechanism without doing further damage. Also my companion liked to talk and, after nearly a decade living amongst the Avars, he was able to answer some of the questions that had been puzzling me. I asked him about the ceremony with the whirling sorcerer.

'Happens at mid-winter every year. The qam – that's what

they call their devil man – invests the khagan for the coming year with his symbol of authority.'

'You mean the golden skull.'

'Handed down through the generations. A long time ago the Avars defeated a people that had been their worst enemy, cut off the head of their supreme chief, and turned the skull into a drinking bowl. The commander of the Avar army on that day was chosen as the first khagan. Whoever is presented with the skull nowadays is recognized as the chief of all Avars for the coming year.'

That, I thought to myself, explained why Faranak had been pleased to see her nephew confirmed as khagan. It also made me wonder if the triumphant warrior on the golden flagon, with a severed human head dangling from his saddle, had been the first khagan.

'Who selects the khagan for the coming year?'

The engineer shrugged. 'I'm sure something has been agreed beforehand. The qam just makes it formal. Avars believe that all power flows from some mysterious figure up in the sky. During the ceremony the qam calls down some of that power, and directs it into the skull. Then he hands it to the chosen leader. The ruler drinks from that skull at banquets. Nasty habit.'

I hadn't seen Khagan Kaiam drinking from the skull at the banquet, and said so.

'He only brings out the gold skull for feasts when all the tarkans, the clan leaders, get together. It lets them know who the boss is.'

I recalled the toad-like Avar's look of controlled hatred as he watched Kaiam receive the gold skull. Toad Face was probably a rival.

'Do you know a surly-looking Avar with a mouth like a great frog? He's some sort of chieftain?'

'That's the tudun,' the engineer replied at once. 'His title means that he's responsible for defence of the western frontier, and it makes him second to the khagan.'

'He doesn't seem to have much liking for Kaiam.'

'He's from a different clan,' said the Lombard, passing me one of the long wooden bars used for tensioning the onager's windlass. 'Put the end of that bar in that gap between the frame and the windlass drum, and give it a good heave while I give the rim a belt with this mallet.'

I did as I was told, and the drum moved along its axle a fraction.

'I met the Greek ambassador the other day,' I said, wanting to keep the conversation flowing. After months of virtual solitude it was good to talk, especially in Frankish.

The Lombard gestured at me to keep pressure on the turn bar, and he gave the drum a couple more heavy blows with the mallet before he answered. 'He usually shows up about this time of year. We call him the Poison Dwarf.'

'Why's that?' I asked, shifting my grip and again throwing my weight on the turn bar.

'Always stirring trouble. It's probably why we've been told to hurry up with fixing these war machines. Someone's planning a campaign.'

The engineer stood back and wiped his brow. 'I wouldn't be surprised if that crafty little so-and-so is busily encouraging Kaiam to move back into his old capital at the Ring.'

I was taken aback. 'But that risks starting another war with Carolus. Surely the Greeks wouldn't encourage an attack on the Franks. They are both Christian, while the Avars are out-and-out pagans.'

'Religion has nothing to do with it,' said the engineer. 'If the Avars are tied up fighting the Franks, they can't trouble the

Greeks. And should the Franks win, then the Avars are weakened. Either way, the Poison Dwarf goes back to Constantinople well pleased with his meddling.'

'And what if the Avars are victorious?' I asked.

'Then the Greeks are almost as happy.' The Lombard smiled sardonically. 'They don't want to see Carolus any more powerful than he is already. They'd do anything to cut him down to size.'

He dropped his voice so as not to be overheard. 'There's a lot of grumbling amongst the Avars. Something's brewing, and if it bubbles over, all of us foreigners best keep out of sight.'

I would have paid more attention to his warning, but my mind was elsewhere: over his shoulder I had just caught sight of a tall figure in the distance, someone who looked like Beorthric. He was directing a squad of men as they lifted a stone-thrower back on its cart.

'Have you come across another Frankish prisoner,' I asked, 'a big fellow, blond, with eyes that are very pale blue? He speaks Avarish.'

'I know who you mean,' said the Lombard. 'But he's not a prisoner. He lives with an Avar woman, a wealthy one. She's first cousin to the tudun. He's done well for himself.'

The tall man in the distance had moved away from the work squad, and I could see him more clearly. He was not Beorthric.

In a strange way I felt relieved. I wasn't sure I wanted to meet the Saxon face to face and to endure another rebuff. I had a more immediate worry: if the Avars provoked a war with Carolus, it would destroy any hope that they would grant me my freedom.

*

Work on the war machines went on all that month. Each day was sunnier and warmer than the last, and the whole of the khagan's winter capital was coming alive. The narrow laneways were bustling as families prepared to shift from winter quarters. Winter clothes, rugs and bedding were brought out into the sunshine and hung up to air, doors and windows left open, tent flaps unlaced and peeled back. Horses were being given extra food and exercised, ready for the spring migration. On the way to the weapons park, I encountered small groups of Avar men riding in from the countryside. Their fine clothes and the fancy decoration on their saddles and bridles marked them as minor chiefs. My Lombard foreman told me that they were arriving for the grand council that immediately preceded the spring migration. During that day-long assembly the qam would be called upon to invoke his powers of divination and look into the future. His responsibility was to foretell the weather for the coming year, the amount of pasture available, and to predict whether there was to be peace with other tribes and nations, or war. In view of the solemnity and importance of the meeting, all work in the weapons park would be suspended.

The following morning, I had just finished cleaning out the ashes from the fire pit when the door was flung open with a tremendous crash. Two Avar troopers half stumbled, half fell into the room. Faranak gave a shriek of outrage, but they ignored her. They grabbed me by the elbows and bundled me outside. It was useless to resist, and I was too shocked to try. The men were drunk. I could smell it on their breath and they had the unpredictable belligerence of the intoxicated.

They hurried me along the laneway. We lurched and slithered down the same track that I took to fetch water from the river and one of them tripped over his own feet. If he hadn't clutched me, he would have gone sprawling. We veered to our right and cut across the slope towards a low grassy knoll overlooking the river. Here a large pavilion had been erected. The sides were open, and a meeting was in progress under the canopy. I was hustled forward into a scene that reminded me of the mid-winter festival. Once again the qam was at the centre of a circle of onlookers, though this time most were seated on the ground. The Khagan sat in the front rank, the tudun beside him. There was no sign of Nikephorus, nor were there any women or children. Evidently, this was the council meeting of the leaders of the Avar clans that the Lombard had told me about. He had omitted to mention the heavy drinking. Every tarkan had a cup or bowl in his hand or on the ground before him. Kaiam himself was drinking from the golden skull. As I watched, he took a long draught, then held it up to be refilled. I was dumbfounded to see that the attendant who leaned forward over his shoulder to pour more wine was Beorthric. The Saxon mercenary had shaved off his blond hair and was dressed as a well-to-do Avar in long soft boots, loose trousers and a thigh-length jerkin with a collar of black lamb's wool. As he stepped back to take his place amongst the small group of servitors standing behind their masters, he made no attempt to look at me, though I stood directly opposite him, not twenty yards away.

Beorthric had poured the wine from the warrior flagon.

The attention of every tarkan was fixed on their sorcerer. The qam was kneeling on the ground, hunched over, his face on his knees. He was rocking back and forth rhythmically, and chanting, his voice muffled. After a while he sat up. He was dressed in the same ragged costume as before and, once again, his face was hidden behind the heavy fringe of tassels dangling from his feathered hat. He shook his head from side to side, like a horse dislodging a fly, and the tassels lashed from side to side. Next, he rose to his feet and from a pouch at his waist produced a fist-sized stone, smooth and mottled bluish-white. He held it out with one hand while he caressed it with the other as he turned in a slow circle. His chant became a monotonous drone that gradually died away until eventually there was silence. He belched. I realized that he, too, had been drinking. Facing Kaiam, he delivered his prophesy in a high-pitched voice and my Avarish was good enough to understand that he was promising a fine summer and that the flocks and herds of all the Avars would multiply and grow fat.

Once or twice he slurred his words. There was no longer any doubt. He was very drunk.

My two guards had moved away, leaving me facing the Avar chiefs, alone and fearful. I could think of no reason why I had been dragged so roughly before the council.

Kaiam asked the sorcerer a question. He wanted to know whether the time was ripe for the Avars to drive back their foes from their ancestral lands and restore the khaganate to its former glory.

In answer, the qam wheeled round and, with a clatter and rattle of the amulets on his gown, came running directly at me. I froze in place. He came to a stop less than an arm's length away, staring into my face. Behind the tasselled fringe, I saw glittering eyes, furious but unfocused. The mouth spat a stream of gibberish, and then a claw-like hand was raised, two fingers extended. They jabbed towards my eyes like a snake's tongue. I shrank back in fright. At the same time the qam's other hand seized me by the shoulder, grasping me so that I could not back way.

The two fingers kept weaving and stabbing back and forth, the qam shrieking with venom. Through my fog of fright I heard that my eyes marked me as the forerunner of great evil. After me would come those who wished to bring harm on the Avar people. I felt a strange tingling as the blood left my cheeks, and knew I had gone white.

The qam's sinewy grip on my shoulder tightened. Long, dirty nails dug in painfully, and a fine spray of spittle struck my face.

There was a waft of a minty, oily smell from some herb that the sorcerer must have been chewing.

Then I realized that the qam was a woman.

She was not so different from Faranak, a few years younger, perhaps, and certainly stronger and more vigorous. Nevertheless, for all her frenzy, she was just that: a ranting crone dressed in rags.

Perhaps she saw my expression change as understanding dawned, or maybe her store of abuse was spent. She let go of my shoulder and stepped back. I stayed where I was, shaking and taking deep gulps of air. I suspected that I had been hauled before the assembly as an exhibit, something to do with Kaiam's plans for war. The qam had returned to the centre of the circle of the assembly. Now she was reaching up towards the sky with both arms, and calling for strength to flow down into the hearts, minds and weapons of the Avar warriors. She finished her appeal and, lowering her arms, let her head slump forward on her chest. Then her knees gave way, and she sank to the ground and lay still, a heap of amulets.

Kaiam held up the golden skull, the symbol of his rule. In a voice loud enough for all to hear, he called on the assembly to bear witness that the omens were favourable and that the Avar nation was to prepare for war under his command.

A deep hush fell on the assembly. It was as if each person in the assembly was afraid to take another breath. Something had happened that I was not aware of. Some of the chiefs were looking at the ground, others across the circle. No one spoke. No one responded to Kaiam's announcement. Raising my eyes, I saw with a shock that Beorthric was staring directly at me. He held my glance for the merest second, and then, with a very slight movement, he gave a tiny jerk of this head. The message was clear: I was to leave.

Before I could act, Kaiam angrily flung down the golden skull and jumped to his feet. Swaying, he faced towards the tudun and let out a tirade of drunken invective. He abused his second-in-command, his voice crackling with anger. Red in the face, he mangled his words badly. I was only able to understand that he was accusing the tudun of cowardice. In response, the tudun rose slowly and carefully from where he had been sitting. He was nowhere near as drunk as the khagan. He paused for a moment, steadying himself. The muscles of his jaw worked as he controlled himself, his wide mouth shut in a thin line. Then his right hand slid down to his boot and reappeared with a blade. There was a brief glint of steel, and the tudun slashed the knife expertly across the Khagan's throat. The blood spurted, even as other tarkans were scrambling to their feet, some more quickly and less drunkenly than the others. The swift ones held knives. The council dissolved into chaos as the Avars with weapons pounced on their chosen victims. Those who supported the tudun had come armed. Their opponents were defenceless.

I spun on my heel and fled. I ran all the way to Faranak's house, arriving out of breath, closed the door, and slid the locking bar across. My heart was still pounding, and I almost jumped out of my skin when a shape stirred in a dark corner of the room. It was Faranak getting up from a pile of bedding. Like a stiff-jointed elderly cat the old lady had several places where she liked to curl up comfortably on the piles of hoarded rubbish. For a moment I was unsure whether or not I should tell her what had happened at the assembly, then decided that there was no point in keeping the truth from her. I had seen enough to know that the tudun and his allies would be pitiless in executing their plan to overthrow the khagan. What I did not know was whether or not the slaughter of Kaiam and his supporters would extend to members of his family. If so, the tudun's accomplices would soon arrive, hunting for Faranak.

She took the news of the massacre so calmly that I thought either she had misunderstood me or she was too deaf to have heard my words. I repeated myself, stepping closer and raising my voice until I was shouting. Before I got beyond a couple of sentences, she silenced me with a gesture.

'Keep the door locked for three days. Don't make any more noise,' she wheezed.

She must have noticed me glance towards the water bucket. It had not been touched since I had filled it earlier that morning. 'There's enough to last,' she added.

'And after three days?' I ventured to ask.

'There will be a new khagan and the old one will be in the ground.'

'You don't fear for your own safety after what was done to your nephew?'

Red-rimmed watery eyes looked at me as though I was a dimwit. 'That's how Kaiam became khagan.'

It took me a moment to understand. 'You mean Kaiam killed his predecessor?'

'The man showed weakness,' she said, then added as if it explained and excused everything, 'He was of a different clan.'

She shuffled off, muttering to herself.

Half an hour later, I heard shouts. They were too far away to know exactly where they came from, but they were harsh and insistent. Then I caught the sound of running feet. Someone was racing towards us along the laneway outside the house. He ran past the doorway without slackening pace, and there was desperation and panic in his grunting breaths. Scarcely a minute later came the sound of his pursuit, several men this time, running as a pack. They, too, passed our door without stopping, and there was a terrible purposefulness about the silence in which they ran. There was no talking, just the thud of their feet that came and passed, and faded away in the distance.

When they were gone, I pressed my face against a crack between the weathered planks of the door, and squinted out. But all I saw was the mud wall of the house across the laneway. I wondered if Faranak's neighbours were also hiding in their homes. It was eerily quiet.

# Chapter Twelve

FARANAK AND I cowered like hunted foxes in their earth for those three days. They seemed like an age. We lived in semi-darkness and increasing stench. We ate cold food, fearing that the smoke from a cooking fire would attract attention. Four cupfuls each day was our water ration and whenever we visited the privy, we trod softly, fearing to make the slightest sound. Faranak slept for much of the time while I positioned myself close to the door, straining to hear what was going on outside. Cooped up in the darkness, it was the only way of knowing what was going on. The near-silence was unsettling. Even the children and dogs were subdued, and at times it was as if the settlement had been abandoned and the people had moved away. With little else to occupy my mind, I puzzled why Beorthric had given me the guarded signal just before the tudun drew his knife. It was clear to me that the Saxon had been actively involved in the murder plot, for he had been topping up the golden skull with wine, ensuring that the Kaiam had the opportunity to get drunk. But why he had chosen to warn me when previously he had ignored my presence, remained a mystery.

I had fallen asleep, seated on the steps leading down into the room when a loud, insistent rapping on the door woke me. My head was lolling back against the door so the knocking seemed to go right through my skull. Startled and groggy, I got up, narrowly avoiding falling down the steps. Daylight filtered through the cracks around the door frame. My mouth felt dry and foul. It was long after sunrise on the third day in hiding.

'Sigwulf, are you in there?' It was Beorthric's voice.

I glanced over my shoulder. Faranak was still asleep, too deaf to have heard the knocking.

I eased back the bar and cautiously pushed open the door, uncertain what to expect. I had to hold an arm to shield my eyes, the sunshine was blinding after so long in the darkened house. Beorthric was standing in the laneway, as well dressed as I had seen him last. He was on his own.

'I've come to collect you,' he announced.

I scanned his face for some indication of how he felt about having abandoned me six months earlier. There was no sign of remorse. He looked relaxed and self-assured.

'Where are you taking me?' I was aware that I sounded petulant and resentful. 'To a burial,' he said.

'There's an old lady in there. I'm meant to look after her,' I said, indicating the room behind me.

'She's no longer your worry,' he answered bluntly.

I was finding it difficult to place any trust in him. I was unsure just how deeply the Saxon was mixed up in Avar tribal rivalries, and whether he had turned his coat yet again, and become one of the murderous tudun's new henchmen. For a moment I considered ignoring him altogether, but this was my first opportunity to discover why he had not acknowledged me at the mid-winter festival, and what he had been doing during the winter months.

Beorthric was already walking away up the footpath and I hurried to catch up with him, the questions chasing one another through my mind. But he seemed in no mood to talk, and there was an awkward silence between us as we walked. We crossed the settlement, heading away from the river, and I kept glancing furtively down the various side alleys that we passed. Nothing much had changed though there seemed to be fewer people than normal in the streets and laneways. Clearly the spring migration had not yet begun.

Finally, I could no longer contain my curiosity. 'Has anything been heard from Carolus or from Archbishop Arno?' I asked.

He shook his head. 'Not while Kaiam was in charge. He detested all Franks.'

I couldn't resist saying, 'You seem to be an exception.'

My remark hit home for he said, 'I took good care to steer clear of Kaiam.'

'Very wise of you,' I responded drily. 'I'm told you found favour with another Avar woman.'

'She's not from Kaiam's clan,' the Saxon retorted with more than a touch of irritation, ending our conversation.

Not another word passed between us as he led me beyond the northern fringe of the settlement. A crowd of Avars was gathered where a dip in the ground formed a natural amphitheatre. They had their backs to us and were looking down to where two pits had been dug in the soft earth. The smaller was the size of a normal grave; the other was longer, broader and deeper. The spoil was heaped nearby. The mood of the onlookers was subdued, and their faces sombre. A few women were present, but no children. Beorthric pushed his way confidently through the crowd who made way for him. When we reached the front rank, I found myself standing elbow to elbow with one of the Greeks on Nikephorus's staff; the older, grey-haired man whom I had seen at Kaiam's banquet.

'Greetings,' he said in accented Frankish. 'Let's hope this doesn't take too long.'

I looked to my right. Not far away was the toad-faced tudun. Beorthric had moved to stand close behind his shoulder. I got the distinct impression that the Saxon had become one of the tudun's inner circle.

The Greek noticed the direction of my glance. 'Kajd will be declared khagan before the day is out.'

I was close enough to see down into the pits. The larger one was empty, and in the other lay Kaiam. He was on his back, dressed in full-length chain mail. Around his waist was a broad belt of worked leather with a massive gold buckle and studded with what looked like large, semi-precious stones. On his head was a gold-embossed iron helmet. A sky-blue scarf wrapped around his neck concealed the wound that had killed him.

At the far side of the grave was a group of about a dozen Avar men. They held themselves stiffly and looked nervous and tense. I guessed that they were surviving senior members of Kaiam's clan. I was surprised to see that some had been allowed to carry weapons – a bow, a quiver with its arrows, a sword, a lance with a pennant attached.

A low murmur of appreciation went up from the waiting crowd and heads turned. A groom was bringing forward a fine-looking chestnut stallion, a far nobler creature than the workaday Avar mounts. The horse was saddled and bridled, but there was no rider. The coat had been brushed to a shine, mane and tail combed and plaited, the hooves oiled until they glistened. The decorations of the harness gleamed in the spring sunshine. Every buckle and strap end was made of gold, so too was the clip that held the nodding white plume on the headband. My eye was drawn to the gold breastplate on the animal's chest. Kunimund had claimed that he had taken one like it to the goldsmith for repair. Gently, the groom led the stallion to the edge of the larger open grave, untied the lead rope, and moved away. The horse remained on the exact same spot, lifted its splendid head, ears alert.

The qam stepped out from the watching crowd. The sorcerer was wearing the now-familiar long shirt hung with amulets. The same high peaked cap with its dangling fringe of beads hid the face but I knew at once that this was not the wrinkled crone who had screamed threats at me three days earlier. This qam was at least a head taller, and the walk was different; no longer a shuffle, but younger and energetic. I was sure it was a man hidden beneath the costume.

He was holding a short spear, its shaft decorated with red feathers. He approached to within an arm's length of the horse as it stood trustingly between the two grooms. He raised the spear and, without any hesitation, drove it expertly through the animal's left eye. He must have struck into the brain for the horse dropped instantly, falling sideways into the pit, the spear shaft sticking out from its head, the feathers fluttering. The crowd let out a low, collective moan of sadness mingled with approval.

'What a waste,' said the Greek beside me. 'Takes years to train an animal like that. It's why the Avar cavalry are so dangerous. They school their horses to perfection.'

Silently I wished to myself that I had witnessed such training and known that all their horses were accustomed to being handled only from their left-hand side.

Kaiam's clansmen came forward. They tossed into Kaiam's open grave the weapons they carried – bow, the quiver, the lance with its pennant. Last of all was Kaiam's sword. When they had finished, the qam turned to face the crowd. 'We are the Avar people,' he called out to them. 'We offer sacrifice to fire, water and the sword, and honour our departed.'

Then he walked across to where the tudun was waiting in the front rank. As had been done at the mid-winter festival, the qam took the golden skull from a leather pouch, held it up high and called down the sacred power from the sky. Then he placed the skull in the tudun's outstretched hands.

'Ten times quicker than a coronation in Constantinople,' muttered the Greek beside me with a satisfied sigh, 'and that's with a funeral included.'

'What do you think Kajd will be like as khagan?' I asked him, wondering if the new ruler of the Avars would treat me more kindly than his predecessor.

The Greek treated me to a sly glance. 'At home we have a proverb – "a serpent, unless it devours another serpent, will not become a dragon." I'd say Kajd's made a good start.'

*

The ceremony over, Beorthric walked back with me into the settlement. The atmosphere between us was far from cordial and neither of us spoke. He brought me into the central square, and I was about to turn down the laneway leading to Faranak's house when he nodded towards one of the timber houses across from the khagan's residence.

'There's someone over there who wants to have a chat with you,' he said. 'I'll come back to collect you an hour before dusk.'

He walked off without giving me an opportunity to ask who wanted to speak with me, or why.

The presence of two Avar guards standing at the door of the house made me wonder if I was about to meet a fellow captive. The guards eyed me with interest as I approached, and after a moment's hesitation one of them stood aside and waved at me to go in. I was unprepared for the sight that greeted me. Someone had transformed the gloomy, dank interior of an Avar house. Extra windows had been cut in the wooden walls and their shutters were open to the air and sunlight. The sunken floor had been raised, boarded over and covered with stretched canvas cleverly painted to resemble mosaic. Panel screens served as partitions to divide off small side-alcoves from the main room. There were upholstered chairs, several small tables, a couch with cushions, and a portable writing desk. From the ceiling hung delicate glass lamps. Oddly, one or two of them were lit. Then I smelled perfume in the air and realized they were for burning scented oils.

The curtain to one of the alcoves parted, and out stepped the diminutive figure of Nikephorus, the Greek ambassador. His clothes were a match for the quality of the furnishings – a long tunic of fine wool, dyed lemon-yellow, that reached down to where the toes of his pale green slippers poked out beneath the hem. I was reminded of an expensively dressed doll.

'Do we have a new khagan?' he asked without any preamble.

'The qam presented Kajd with the golden skull.' It struck me as odd that the ambassador had not gone to see the ceremony for himself.

As usual he seemed to be able to read my thoughts. 'I try to avoid public ceremonies. Standing with a crowd makes me look out of place.'

I hesitated, still only a couple of paces into the room. 'I was told that someone wanted to speak with me.'

'That's right. I asked your friend, the tall Saxon, to bring you here after the burial ceremony.'

I wanted to say that Beorthric was not really my friend, but the ambassador was already waving me forward.

'You must be hungry after all that standing around. I was just about to have my meal. I hope you will join me.'

His courteous manner was making me feel grubby and uncomfortable. 'Perhaps, if I could wash first . . .' I suggested.

'Of course.' There was a flash of jewelled rings on his fingers as he pointed. 'In that alcove over there you'll find a basin, soap and towel.'

After I had washed the grime off my face and hands, I picked up a small mirror placed beside the basin and examined my reflection. I looked as if I had been living all winter in a cave. My hair was matted and filthy. My beard had streaks of grey. My eyes were so sunken that it was difficult to see that their colours differed.

Nikephorus was waiting beside a table set with plates of food when I re-emerged. After months of Faranak's plain gruel, my mouth watered at the sight of sausages and sliced, dried meats. There was cabbage, spinach and several vegetables I did not recognize, and a stack of flat bread.

He waved me to take my place and selected for himself a high stool with an unusually thick cushion. Nevertheless, I still had the feeling that I was seated at table with a meticulously dressed child. There was no one serving us, so presumably this was to be a private conversation.

'You have created a very comfortable residence for yourself,' I complimented him.

'Put it down to experience,' he said. 'This is the fourth time I've been sent as ambassador to the Avars.'

That explained how he came to speak Avarish so fluently. It also reminded me that he had earned a nickname for himself amongst the foreigners living amongst the Avars: the Poison Dwarf. It made me wonder why he was going to such lengths to charm me.

'Try starting with this,' he suggested, pushing across a small earthenware bowl of what looked like soft curds. 'I've finally succeeded in training the cook to make it.'

'What is it?'

'Chopped chicken mixed into beaten egg white, then cooked in wine, and topped with honey.'

Faranak and I had used our fingers or – occasionally –

cow-horn spoons. Here the spoons were of silver. I took a taste. It was delicious.

'Each visit teaches me what to bring with me the next time,' he went on, reaching for the wine jug and filling our two glasses to the brim. 'The better furniture can be taken to pieces easily for transport. Some of the larger pieces I left behind from previous stays, knowing that I was likely to be sent back here.'

Nikephorus raised his glass. Like the rest of the tableware the glasses were stylish, swirling colours of sea-green and orange. 'I think we should celebrate the achievement of a shared objective.'

I took a sip of wine, trying to guess what on earth he was talking about.

Nikephorus put his glass back down on the table. 'Now that Kaiam is safely disposed of, Kajd should be more biddable.'

'Kaiam did seem to be dangerously unstable,' I agreed cautiously.

He leaned forward as if taking me into his confidence. 'Was it bad luck or poor judgement that you ran into that Avar patrol?'

My mind ran in circles. I was utterly mystified.

He allowed himself a ghost of a chuckle. 'With the Avars it always comes down to gold solidi in the end. It's either bribe or reward.'

His knowing look was an admission that he had been involved in the plot to murder Kaiam and install Kajd as the new khagan. I wondered how much of his own gold he had spent on achieving his aim.

Then it dawned on me that he believed that the gold I was carrying when I rode into Avaria really had been intended as payment for Kaiam's enemies. My claim that I had been in search of a goldsmith was a flimsy cover story. The money was to encourage the overthrow of the khagan. Nikephorus was so steeped in the arts of deception and conspiracy that he took it for granted that everyone else thought and acted in the same way. Little wonder that he was known as the Poison Dwarf.

'You succeeded in distracting our unlamented friend Kaiam, and that was important,' he said. 'After you showed up, he was blind to where the real danger lay. He was too busy hunting down every tarkan who was called Zoltan. Fortunately, there were very few.'

The depth of his knowledge was impressive. His informants had provided a full account of all that had taken place when I was first brought before Kaiam. The little Greek must have kept a permanent spy ring in place even when he was back in Constantinople.

'So now all sides can relax.' I kept my tone neutral.

'It'll be at least twelve months before Kajd feels secure enough as khagan to launch a major war, and maybe not even then.' He made it sound as if he would use the time to devise another stratagem to keep the Avar clans at one another's throats.

'Surely Kajd will be more alert than his predecessor to the risk of being overthrown.'

'It takes just one man with a dagger to make a change at the top,' the ambassador assured me. 'The Avars are vulnerable because they make up a ruling class, nothing more. It wouldn't be difficult to find someone who resents being lorded over.'

'Pick your man carefully,' I advised him. 'I made the mistake of thinking the same about a Gepid, a groom at the Ring. But he proved loyal to his new masters. That's how I came to be captured.'

'Along with your Saxon friend. Tell me about him.' Nikephorus fastidiously dipped a piece of flat bread into a saucer of pungent fish sauce, and sucked on it as he listened to my reply.

'I know little about him. He was assigned as my guide and escort for my mission.'

'Are you sure that he wasn't the one who betrayed you to the Avars? Perhaps for a reward?'

It was a shrewd remark. It fed my resentment of Beorthric and the way he had abandoned me. Thinking back to the day of our capture, I remembered how I had depended entirely on Beorthric as our interpreter. I had no idea what was being said when he was talking with Kunimund, and he could have been in collusion with the Gepid. Beorthric was now living far better amongst the Avars that he would have done in Paderborn. Perhaps that had been his reward.

'I don't have any direct evidence of treachery,' I said defensively.

Nikephorus gave an elegant little shrug and dropped the subject. I judged the ambassador to be a born mischief maker and no doubt he had amused himself by planting a seed of doubt in my mind. If I was not careful, I would find myself being manipulated to suit whatever scheme his fertile mind was hatching.

Not wanting to appear rude, I cast about for a less controversial topic. The splendid trappings of the sacrificed stallion had reminded me of the large gold buckle that my friend Paul in Rome had recovered from the dealer in stolen goods. Paul had identified it as Avar workmanship and from the hoard. It was very possible that Nikephorus, with his knowledge of the Avars and their way of life, could provide some extra information. I was very wary of disclosing to the Greek why Archbishop Arno had sent me to Avaria, but saw a way of broaching the subject while saying nothing of the gold buckle itself.

'Do the Avars believe in griffins?' I asked.

For a moment he looked startled by the unexpected question. 'Why do you ask?'

'On the way here I visited a village blacksmith. He had been casting bronze buckles in the shape of griffins.' I paused, then added, 'Some years ago, I travelled to Baghdad with a shipment of unusual animals from Carolus's menagerie. They were a gift to the Caliph. I've retained an interest in exotic beasts ever since.'

He looked at me with renewed interest. My remark had confirmed his opinion that I was an agent of the Frankish king.

'I'd like to hear about that trip someday,' he said. 'As for griffins, my guess is that the Avars learned about them from us.'

'There are griffins in the imperial menagerie at Constantinople?'

He laughed openly. 'Not at all. Griffins are a favourite motif with our artists. They represent vigilant strength. Have done so for centuries. But I doubt they exist in real life.'

I felt a twinge of disappointment. My mission to Baghdad had nourished a faint hope that one day I would be privileged to see a griffin. In the Caliph's zoo I had seen extraordinary creatures that defied the imagination: enormous cats with black and yellow stripes and frighteningly ferocious yellow eyes that the keepers said would devour human flesh, and a cameleopard standing twenty feet tall with a patterned skin, stumps of tiny horns on his head and a cow's tail. If a cameleopard appeared to be the offspring of a long-necked deer and a spotted leopard, why could not a griffin be the result of a mating between a lion and an eagle?

Nikephorus was smirking at my naivety. 'Avar metalworkers are good at copying.'

'But how did they know what a griffin looks like?'

'We've been giving expensive and eye-catching presents to the Avar rulers for as long as anyone can remember – jewellery, expensive fabrics, fancy tableware. There'll have been plenty of items decorated with images of griffins.'

I thought back to the display of gold tableware set out on Kaiam's banquet table. It was more than possible that many of those golden plates and bowls had been made by the craftsmen in Constantinople and sent as gifts.

The Greek had not finished. 'It's now got so bad that every Avar khagan expects to receive lavish gifts from the hand of any ambassador who arrives from Constantinople. I've brought several of them myself.'

He treated me to a malicious grin. 'Not all were pure gold. Our craftsman have found a way of adulterating the metal so that you wouldn't notice the difference.'

The rest of the meal passed largely in silence, and by the time Beorthric came to collect me I still had not succeeded in working out why the Greek had asked to speak with me. It was a question I put to Beorthric as we left the house.

'He wants to get to know you better,' he answered casually, making it clear that Nikephorus was of no interest to him.

'But why? I count for nothing.'

He shrugged. 'Isn't that what ambassadors are meant to do, keep themselves well informed about everyone and everything?'

We were crossing the square towards the khagan's residence and I realized that was where the Saxon was taking me.

'Nikephorus was involved with the plot to overthrow Kaiam,' I said, hoping the remark would prompt Beorthric to explain his own role in the murder. After months of near-isolation living in Faranak's hovel, I felt uneasy at being so out of touch.

It was as if he had not heard me.

Frustrated, I tried another line of questioning. 'Am I still a prisoner?'

'That's for Kajd to decide,' he grunted.

He came with me into the waiting room to the khagan's audience chamber. There, as before, we were searched for weapons. Then we were shown into the audience chamber itself. Little was different from my first visit except that toad-faced Kajd now sat on the khagan's carved wooden throne. I presumed that the tarkans standing each side of him were those who had helped him murder Kaiam. Everything else was the same. The same profusion of rugs and storage chests, the same poor lighting and the air heavy with the smoke from the thick candles guttering on their massive iron stands and the charcoal glowing in the fire pit. I stretched myself out beside Beorthric on the floor rugs and made my obeisance, and wondered if the transition of power had gone so smoothly because it occurred so frequently.

The new khagan addressed me directly as we got back on our feet. 'I am returning you to your master. Tell him that I wish to establish good relations between us.' Kajd's harsh and gravelly voice suited his ill-favoured appearance.

It was a struggle for me to hold back the surge of excitement. My captivity was over. Instead of fleeing on a stolen horse, I would be sent on my way with official encouragement. I arranged my features in what I hoped was a suitably respectful expression.

'No more war between the Avar nation and the Franks,' Kajd continued. He reached a hand inside his loose jacket and scratched an armpit. Fleas and lice troubled even the most high-ranking Avars.

'Tomorrow my people move to fresh pastures. We've already delayed too long. One of my tarkans will travel with you. You will bring him to King Carolus.'

I bowed my head politely and waited for him to go on.

Kajd had stopped speaking and seemed to be waiting for me to respond.

'I shall carry out your orders,' was all I managed to mumble. My mind was still reeling at the sudden and unexpected change in my circumstances. The khagan's rasping voice cut through my daze. 'Repeat my orders.'

I guessed that he was checking that I spoke Avarish well

enough to have understood him properly. I repeated his instructions.

He gave a little grunt of satisfaction, sat back on his wooden throne, and looked round at his advisors, seeking any further suggestions.

One of them, I thought it was the man who spoke Frankish at my first interview, suggested that perhaps the khagan would wish to send presents to his fellow monarch.

Kajd's head twisted round to face me again. The toad mouth opened in a smile that was meant to encourage but succeeded in being alarming. He showed wide gaps between stubs of brown teeth. 'What will please your king?' he asked me. 'Fine horses? Furs?'

'A good choice, Your Excellency,' I said tactfully. Then I took a deep breath as a bold new idea jumped into my head. My luck had turned. I might as well ride it to the end.

Kajd had sensed that I had something more to say, and he did not wish to be kept waiting. The smile vanished as quickly as it had appeared.

'My lord,' I said carefully, 'you will remember that I came to Avaria, bringing gold coins with me.'

At the word 'gold' his eyebrows came down in a scowl. He was expecting me to request the return of the solidi to Carolus.

I hurried on, 'Those coins were meant for Avar goldsmiths to melt down and turn into beautiful ornaments. My king had heard about the skill of Avar craftsmen.'

Kajd's face clouded over with suspicion as he tried to fathom if there was another meaning behind my words. I held my breath, fearing that I had gone too far, and he was about to change his mind, no longer trusting me to escort his envoy. Then his face cleared and he turned to the councillor who had suggested the gifts. 'Kuber, pick out some items.'

He snapped his fingers and an attendant came forward from the shadows holding a bunch of heavy iron keys. The attendant unlocked one of the larger storage chests and lifted the lid so that the tarkan Kuber could rummage inside.

He brought out a pair of gold goblets and an ornate wine bowl with twin handles in the shape of vine leaves and laid them on the carpet at the khagan's feet. There was no sign of the warrior flagon. I did not have the courage to suggest adding anything to the selection of gifts.

Against all my expectations Beorthric came to my rescue. 'My lord, Carolus should be reminded of the prowess of the Avar people.'

The khagan tilted back his head and squinted at the Saxon. 'Are you suggesting I send him a fine sword, or a suit of chain mail?'

'No, my lord. That might be taken as a provocation that suggests warfare.'

'What then?' demanded Kajd.

'Something that informs him of the great victories of your ancestors.'

It was Kuber, the Avar tarkan, who thought quickest. He turned back to the storage chest and brought out the warrior flagon. He carried it across to Kajd who took it from him and turned it over in his hand. Kuber moved closer to murmur a few words in confidence.

There was a long, thoughtful pause as Kajd examined the image of the warrior horsemen. Clearly he was very reluctant to part with the flagon. Eventually, he nodded towards the gold wine bowl still on the carpet in front of him. Kuber picked it up and gave it to him. Kajd held it in one hand while he weighed the flagon in the other. Apparently the ornate wine bowl was heavier.

'Put the bowl back and make sure the flagon gets safely to

King Carolus,' he said passing them to his councillor. 'You speak their language, so you will travel as my ambassador and explain my wishes so that there is no misunderstanding. Bring back his answer swiftly.'

The interview was over. Beorthric and I made our way out of the audience chamber and back into the last of the spring sunshine outside.

I was light-headed with relief. 'What now?' I asked the Saxon.

'I expect Kuber will be ready to set out tomorrow. We meet here mid-morning.'

'Thank you for speaking up when you did,' I said.

Beorthric responded with a thin smile. 'I see now why Archbishop Arno picked you. You're a quick thinker.'

It was the first time since I had known him that Beorthric had paid me a compliment.

# Chapter Thirteen

THAT NIGHT WAS the last I spent in Faranak's cluttered house. By the harsh standards of Avar life she had behaved fairly to me as her servant. She had never shown me any kindness but neither had she treated me badly. So before setting out the next morning, I went down to the river and filled the bucket with water one last time. I was bringing in an armful of firewood to stack by the fire when she stopped me, telling me sharply not to be wasteful. Now that her nephew was dead, she was moving to live with members of her own clan in one of the outlying villages. It appeared that my usefulness was at an end, and she did not enquire about my own future.

Beorthric was waiting for me in front of the khagan's residence. The embassy to the King of the Franks was getting ready to depart. It consisted of Kuber and his escort of three mounted troopers. A mule was surrounded by attendants busily tightening ropes and checking its load. I presumed that the bundle contained some furs that Kajd was sending as gifts to Carolus. Another of the presents was a chestnut stallion with a white blaze. The animal could well have been the half-brother to the fine creature that had been sacrificed at Kaiam's grave. It was equally well-schooled and was standing quietly with a groom holding its halter. On its back was a fine saddle of tooled leather with matching saddlebags and I noted that the buckles and strap ends of the harness were bronze. Kajd's generosity only went so far. Kuber, who was already mounted, rode across and leaned over to double-check that the two saddlebags were securely strapped in place. Doubtless, they contained the warrior flagon and the other gold tableware that had been entrusted to him.

As we stood waiting for the preparations to be completed, I saw that Nikephorus had appeared at the doorway of his house across the square and was watching us.

'He won't be happy when he finds out that Kajd is seeking peace with Carolus,' I muttered to Beorthric.

'The Poison Dwarf probably knows already,' Beorthric grunted. He was wearing his scramseax sheathed at his belt.

A groom brought forward the horse that was to be my own mount. As I checked that the girth strap was tight, I recalled how uncommunicative Beorthric had been on the day we set out from Paderborn. Now we were retracing our steps, I was unsure how I should deal with him over the coming days.

'Are you pleased to be returning to Frankia?' I asked the Saxon. 'When you spoke up yesterday in Kajd's presence, you threw away the chance to stay here amongst the Avars.'

'It's time for me to leave.' His voice was flat and without emotion.

'What about the woman you've been living with? Will you miss her?'

'She's Kajd's sister-in-law. Now that Kajd is khagan, he'll marry her off to a tarkan from another clan, a political marriage. I'm disposable.' He swung himself up into the saddle of his own horse. 'We'd better get going,' he added, cutting our discussion short.

We rode out of the settlement against the flow of carts, pedestrians and riders already leaving the sheltered valley where winter had been spent and starting on their journey towards Kajd's summer capital. Our little party was the only group heading north so we soon found ourselves alone on the ancient track that would lead to the burned-out ruins of the Ring. It was a fine spring day and there were splashes of colour everywhere I looked. Meadow flowers made specks of yellow and purple against the vivid green of new grass. Hawthorn bushes and wild cherry trees carried their snow-white blossoms. The first few pink roses were appearing on briars where small song birds flitted and darted amongst the branches and the air was full of their twittering and chirps.

Kuber set an easy pace. At every hamlet along the road we paused so that he could exchange courtesies with the local headman. Usually we were invited to share a simple meal and several hours would pass while the villagers were assembled to be told about their new khagan. Thus a journey that had taken no more than three days when Beorthric and I were brought south as prisoners tied to our horses, stretched out into a week and more. I was in no hurry. Relaxed and in good spirits, I was enjoying the change from Faranak's cramped winter home to a landscape where the horizon was defined by distant low rolling hills, their crests smudged with stands of oak, hornbeam and beech. On most days the sky was cloudless and a glorious pale blue, and there were long spells of warm sunshine without a breath of wind. One daybreak we rode early out of the Avar village where we had spent the night and into a ghostly white mist. It clung as tiny droplets on everything it touched – our clothes, the horses' manes and ears, even our eyebrows. An hour later, a very slight breeze sprang up and the mist oozed away in long undulating streamers and we found that the road was taking us around the rim of a great soggy wetland. At regular intervals, grey herons stood hunched in the shallows, standing over their reflections and patiently watching for their meals to swim closer.

There was little conversation amongst us. Our little column

rode in silence, hearing only the jingle and creak of harness and the hoof falls of our mounts in the soft earth. One of our mounted escorts took it in turns to be in the lead, wearing his mail shirt and helmet, a pennon fluttering from his lance, his war bow slung across his back, and his sword at his belt. Next came Kuber, then a second trooper holding the lead rope of the gift stallion. The third man-at-arms had the task of leading the laden mule. Beorthric and I brought up the rear. I was light-headed at the notion that the liberty I had longed for during those months as a captive was now an effortless reality. My luck had turned, or so I thought.

By the fifth day of our journey, I was beginning to recognize a few landmarks – a cluster of boulders beside the track, a mis-shapen tree, a ford I remembered crossing on the way to being brought before Kaiam as a captive and suspected spy. At the village where Kunimund had betrayed us, there was the familiar shape of the blacksmith's workshop and I half expected to lay eyes on Kunimund himself. But the Gepid was nowhere to be seen and, though we shared a meal of hard-boiled eggs and sheep's milk curds with the village headman, he gave no sign that he had ever met Beorthric or myself before.

We left the village in the early afternoon. I calculated that another three or four days at our leisurely progress should bring us to the Donau, the river frontier with Carolus's domain. On the way we would pass the ruins of the Ring some fifteen or twenty miles ahead of us. As best as I could remember, we would first cross an uninhabited stretch of scrubby grassland. It was open countryside criss-crossed by narrow gullies carved out by the small streams that drained into ponds and small lakes.

Our small party had been ambling along for the best part of two hours when I began to have serious doubts that we would reach the Ring by nightfall and find some sort of shelter. There was no point in mentioning this to Beorthric. I had long since given up any hope of engaging him in any conversation. So I rode quietly along at the rear of our group, turning over in my mind what I would say to the first Frankish patrol we encountered on the great river and looking about me at the wildlife. A pair of buzzards was circling over the plain to our left, and I had seen a number of small birds with bright red patches on their heads that looked like woodpeckers. Oddly, for it was full daylight, I was sure that I kept hearing the hoots of an owl. I was straining my ears trying to detect where the sound was coming from when three deer sprang out of the ground, as if by magic. They had been feeding in the bed of a gully close to the path. They went bounding off, weaving their way between clumps of scrub and willow. Following the direction of their flight, I saw, less than a mile away, a low mound, a man-made earthwork. It was one of the ancient burial tombs we had seen when coming south with Kunimund.

I urged my horse forward so that I rode knee to knee with Beorthric, and pointed. 'Not so far to go now.'

He held up his hand to silence me, and was looking intently towards the spot where the deer had appeared. I waited.

He gave a low whistle to attract the attention of the trooper leading our little group. The man looked back, and Beorthric pointed off to our right.

'What do you see?' I asked.

The trooper had already wheeled his horse around and, lance in hand, was riding back to speak with the Saxon. There was an enquiring look on his face.

He was twenty yards away from us when an arrow took him in the ribs.

The trooper was knocked sideways. His chain mail jacket must have stopped the arrowhead penetrating too far, because he swayed momentarily, then, letting drop his lance, grabbed his saddle and managed to stay on his horse. The shaft of the arrow remained, dangling from his body.

Several more arrows hissed around us. They came from a clump of small trees close to where the deer had been feeding. All passed harmlessly except the one that struck the haunch of the pack mule. The animal threw up its head, ripping the lead rope out of the hand of another trooper, then bolted, running with a peculiar twisted gait.

Kuber was bellowing a warning to the rest of us. He wrenched his horse's head around to face the direction of the ambush. He had neither chain mail nor helmet, and was reaching for the sword that hung from his belt.

The two unwounded troopers were scrambling to put on their helmets and unsling the war bows that they carried on their backs.

We had been taken completely by surprise.

Half a dozen mounted men burst out from cover, forty yards to our right. They had been sheltering in a gully and now came charging at us, yelling. Four of them brandished short lances, while the others wielded swords.

At that moment I realized that I had no weapons and wore no armour.

Beorthric pulled his scramseax from its sheath. He was very calm.

'Sigwulf, we're going to have to fall back. Ride for the tomb.'

I heaved on the reins, trying to turn my mount. But the animal refused to shift. Frustrated and angry, I kicked with both heels and, using the loose ends of the reins as a whip, slashed the animal across the shoulder. It shot forward, luckily behind Beorthric's mount, just as the first of the charging riders arrived, lance levelled. Beorthric calmly leaned to one side, and made a low, controlled sweep with his scramseax. The blade struck the shaft of the lance, deflecting it upward. As the rider rode past, Beorthric reversed the scramseax and with a sideways blow smashed the hilt of the weapon into the man's shoulder.

Yards away, the rest of our party was in difficulty. The trooper with the arrow in his side was under attack from two riders and resisting feebly, trying to ward off their sword cuts as they closed in on him. The trooper who had been leading the stallion, must have taken a lance thrust in the initial charge and been unhorsed. He lay curled on the ground. One of our attackers was already dismounting, sword in hand, about to finish him off.

Kuber was proving to be their toughest target. He had his horse under firm control and was fighting off two of the attackers. There was a ringing clash of steel on steel as he blocked one man's sword as it cut downward towards his head. With a turn of his wrist, the tarkan then slid his weapon under his opponent's guard, and thrust the point into the exposed armpit. His victim was jolted backwards even as Kuber forced his horse sideways, barging into his second opponent's mount, causing it to stagger.

'Get going!' Beorthric snapped at me.

A rider came at me from nowhere and hacked at my head. I ducked and heard the blade slice through the air just inches away. The next moment I was past him and galloping for the burial mound. I heard shouts and the drumming of hooves behind me. I threw a quick glance over my shoulder and saw that the surviving members of our little group were also in full flight. Right behind me was the trooper who had been hit by an arrow. He was doubled over, out of control. I reined in slightly so that his mount drew level and our two horses ran side by side, close enough for me to reach out and grab the bridle of his horse. I clung on as the two animals raced for the burial mound.

The men who had attacked us were not professional fighting

men. They wore no armour, their horses were scrubby and unexceptional, and their marksmanship had been indifferent. The flight of arrows should have done more damage than it did, and they had sprung their ambush too soon.

I could only suppose that they were common brigands eager to waylay a group of travellers, or an undisciplined band of outlaws operating in the no-man's-land on the fringes of Avaria.

The burial mound was much closer now. Formerly, it would have been an imposing monument and dominated its surroundings. Weather and the passage of time had reduced it to a grass-covered heap of earth some fifteen feet high and forty paces across. Yet it still offered some hope of protection if we made a stand against our enemies, with our backs against the slope. Our attackers had been slow to take up the pursuit, and we had enough time to regroup as we reached the base of the mound and pulled up our lathered horses. I dismounted immediately. My mount was going lame, favouring his front offside leg. The injured trooper next to me toppled sideways out of his saddle and I was just able to catch him and ease his fall to the ground. He huddled there, his face twisted in pain and one hand clutching at the arrow. I watched Kuber dismount and walk across to him. Taking a firm grip on the shaft of the arrow, the tarkan tugged. The shaft snapped. Kuber flung it aside and turned to look back at our enemies. I followed the direction of his gaze and felt a cold wash of fear as I saw why the attack against us was delayed. Our attackers had been waiting for reinforcements to join them. Now there were at least a dozen riders. As I watched they began to organize themselves, spreading out into a line. At any moment they would begin to advance.

Beorthric came up to me. He was on foot and holding the lead rope of the chestnut stallion. The well-trained animal had not run with the other horses despite the confusion, keeping company with us as we retreated. 'Take this one and get out of here.' He thrust the lead rope of the stallion into my hand.

I hesitated. 'What about you?'

'I'll catch up with you later.' He gestured over his shoulder towards the enemy. 'They're a bunch of amateurs. They'll lose heart soon enough.'

'Who do you think they are?'

'Too ineffectual to be Avars. They could be any of the subject tribes, Gepids or Slavs, someone with a spirit of rebellion.'

My reluctance to abandon the others must have shown because Beorthric gave a snort of exasperation. 'Sigwulf, this is not your fight.'

Kuber was kneeling by the injured trooper, stuffing some sort of wadding under the man's mail shirt to stop the bleeding.

'As soon as Kuber and his troopers are able to look after themselves, I'll slip away.' Beorthric assured me.

'You should come with me now.'

The Saxon was brimming with elation, a strange expression in his pale-blue eyes, both confident and vigilant. He was enjoying the fight. 'If two of us leave at the same time, it will send the wrong message to those clods over there. They'll think they have us beaten.' He summoned a dangerous smile. 'If you go now, they might decide we're sending you to fetch help.'

He flicked a finger against the saddlebag containing the warrior flagon. 'You've got what you came for. I'll meet you at that posting station beyond the river, if not before.'

I climbed up on the stallion's back, Beorthric slapped it on its rump, and I rode off at a steady canter. After a hundred yards I twisted round to see that Kuber had helped the wounded Avar to get back on his feet. He still had an arm around the trooper's shoulder for the man could barely stand.

The advancing line of attackers saw me leave. One rider broke away and came chasing after me. I touched my heels to my horse, and the stallion's canter changed smoothly to a powerful gallop. The stallion was fit and fresh, and there was no chance that he would be caught. Very quickly my pursuer gave up the fruitless chase. When I next turned round, he had vanished.

I slowed the stallion to a steady trot and rode north-west. The afternoon sun gave me my approximate direction towards the great river and safety.

Try as I might, I could not shake off a heavy sense of unease. Kuber and his men-at-arms with Beorthric's help might succeed in repelling a second onslaught. But the embassy was too heavily outnumbered for their attackers to be discouraged and give up the fight. They would continue to harass Kuber and his men wherever they retreated, picking them off one by one. In my mind's eye I could picture the first to go: the wounded trooper. He was too badly hurt to last much longer and would fall back. Beorthric would be next. He had miscalculated, if he thought he could ride away unscathed. I remembered how clumsy he was on horseback. His weapons skill would not save him. He was a big, heavy man, and his horse would tire under his weight. Compared to the Avars who were bred to the saddle, the tall Saxon would be easy meat. Eventually his lighter, faster enemies would isolate and surround him, cut him down.

I pulled up the stallion.

It was difficult to define precisely why I could not abandon Beorthric. Partly it was to do with my self-respect. I knew that if I rode away when he was in grave danger, the knowledge would trouble me far into the future. But there was another reason, vague and ill-defined and just as compelling. In some fashion a bond existed between us. The nature of that bond, and how it had arisen, was unclear to me, though it hovered in the back of my mind. It might have come from the long hours we had spent together on the road, or have arisen through mutual respect. At our very first meeting outside Archbishop Arno's office in Paderborn I had recognized him as a skilled fighter, and later he had acknowledged that I had a quick and subtle mind. Somehow we had succeeded in supporting one another. Nor was I able to forget that secret nod of warning he had given me just before Kaiam's murder. It had saved me from the ensuing bloodbath. Now was my opportunity to repay that debt.

Of all the half-formed ideas that ran through my head, the only one that made any sense was that I should find myself some weapons and join the fight. I had trained as a cavalryman with Carolus's household troops. I knew how to wield lance and sword. Long hours on the practice ground had taught me the tricks of close-quarters combat. The wounded Avar trooper was already lost to the battle. With his sword in my hand, my presence would tip the balance.

I turned and began to head back towards the burial mound. I had gone little more than a couple of miles from the scene of the fighting and took care to approach from the side away from where I had left the others. When I came close enough, I halted and quietly got down from the saddle. I left the reins dangling. As I had expected, the well-trained animal dropped its head and began to crop the grass, waiting for my return. Keeping low, I scrambled on hands and knees to the crest of the mound and looked down on the far side.

With an awful, sick sensation, I saw that I had left it too late. The fighting was over. Kuber was kneeling on the trampled ground, his arms bound behind his back. He had been badly knocked about. A deep wound on his head was leaking blood, and his Avar hairstyle had come undone, the long braids hanging to the ground. A few steps away lay the bodies of our three Avar troopers. The corpses had been stripped of their armour.

I looked around anxiously for Beorthric and was dismayed not to see him. The final stages of the fight had taken place at the foot of the burial mound. There the bushes and undergrowth had been trampled down, the grass flattened. I counted four more bodies laid out in a neat row. The men who had attacked us had paid a heavy price for their victory. Most of the survivors were now occupied in sorting through a bundle of furs that had been dumped on the ground. Someone must have recaptured the runaway pack mule.

A movement close to where the attackers had tethered their horses caught my attention. Beorthric was standing there, his left arm in a sling. He had only two men guarding him.

I had seen enough. I slithered back down the slope of the burial mound with a plan of action already clear in my mind.

The stallion was waiting exactly where I had left him. I mounted up, and rode around the end of the burial mound at a controlled walk. As I emerged within sight of the attackers, I pressed my heels into the stallion's ribs and the animal surged forward into the charge. I rode straight into the group of tethered horses and crashed right through them. Panicked by the sudden appearance of the snorting stallion, they bolted in all directions. One of the men beside Beorthric was knocked off his feet. The second man I simply rode over. Sweeping up to Beorthric I shouted at him to hang on. He hesitated, then gave a great roar, part triumph, part astonishment. Moments later I was riding away with him clinging onto the stirrup leather with his good arm, bounding along at my side. No one was close enough to stop us, and no one made a move to do so. The men who had been sorting through the furs were gaping at us, too startled to move. We got clear away.

After another hundred yards I slowed the stallion to a walk. 'Reach up with your good arm,' I told the Saxon. He did as he was told. I leaned sideways. 'Now hold me by the wrist,' I took a firm grip. 'Up you come!' I grunted as I swayed back upright. The stallion knew exactly what I was doing. I felt his left shoulder droop at just the right moment, then rise. In one scrambling movement the big Saxon was lifted off his feet and able to swing one leg behind the saddle and over the horse's back.

'Where did you learn to do that?' he gasped as he put his arms around my waist and clung on as the stallion moved back into a steady canter.

'Lots of practice with Carolus's household squadrons,' I told him. 'But it helps to have a properly trained horse when you're hoisting up a great lout of a foot soldier.'

'The rescue was masterly,' he said. Then, to my astonishment, he burst into laughter, adding, 'Everything is now back to front.'

\*

It was not until nightfall that he explained. By then we must have covered half the distance to the frontier. There had never been any sign of pursuit and though the stallion was more than capable of bearing our combined weight, we had been taking turns to ride while the other person walked alongside. The many streams and ponds had provided plenty of water for the horse and ourselves but we were ravenously hungry. The last glow of the sun was a faint pink stain on the western horizon when we came across a suitable place to spend night, a sheltered spot below the slope of a wooded hill. I unsaddled the stallion and made hobbles from its reins just in case it decided to stray. Then I was glad to flop down on the ground, and let my tired muscles relax. I lay on my back, gazing up at the sky, counting the stars as they began to appear. Beorthric was seated on the ground close by, arms clasped around his knees. His expression had turned very sombre. The only sound was the regular tearing of grass as the stallion grazed. It was going to be a cool night. Just as I was about to drop off into an exhausted sleep, I heard Beorthric's voice, low and serious.

'Thank you for what you did for me today.'

For a moment I failed to understand his words. I was too startled. Beorthric had addressed me in Saxon, my mother tongue. He spoke it like a native. When I had first met him in Paderborn, I had guessed he came from Saxony. But he had concealed the fact and always insisted on speaking to me in Frankish. I wondered what had made him change his mind.

'Nikephorus arranged it,' he said. 'You were right in thinking he wasn't happy about Kajd's cosying up to Carolus. He knew about it almost from the start.'

It hit me like a blow that he was referring to the attack on the embassy. I sat up. 'How did he get to know?' I began, then stopped. The answer was obvious. 'You told him.'

'He pays extremely well.'

'So you knew that we would be attacked?'

'Yes, but not where. I was beginning to think that it would never happen.'

'So who attacked us?'

'I think they were Slavs. They're moving into the area that the Avars abandoned when they withdrew from the Ring. Nikephorus keeps in touch with all the incomers – whether Slavs or Bulgars or another tribe, it doesn't matter – he gives them gold and uses them.'

He was still speaking to me in Saxon. I shook my head trying to clear it. 'How long has Nikephorus been paying you?'

'Ever since I moved in with that Avar noblewoman as her partner. In the beginning he paid me for the scraps of information I passed on. Later I acted as his go-between.'

'So that was how you knew about the plot to kill Kaiam,' I said slowly. I was beginning to grasp the extent of Beorthric's involvement in the murder. 'I noticed how you refilled the golden skull that day in the assembly. It was to make him drunk.'

'That was Nikephorus's suggestion. From the moment he arrived in Kaiam's capital he had been encouraging Kajd to do away with Kaiam and become khagan himself.'

I recalled Nikephorus himself telling me that he preferred to see the Avars kept in turmoil. If they were too busy fighting amongst themselves, they were unable to launch any attacks on Constantinople. The Poison Dwarf must have been alarmed by the unintended consequence of his scheme when Kajd decided to open negotiations with Carolus.

'No wonder he arranged to have our embassy ambushed,' I said. 'A peace treaty between Kajd and Carolus isn't in the best interests of Constantinople. I'm lucky to be alive.'

The Saxon let out a long sigh. There was bitterness in it. 'You're wrong there. You may think that I am a mercenary, ready to take anyone's gold. But I wouldn't have allowed you to be killed.'

'I'm glad to hear it,' I commented sourly. 'I presume that is why you told me to ride away from the ambush.'

'Sigwulf, let me explain.' There was a pleading note to Beorthric's voice. It was almost as unexpected as hearing him speaking Saxon. 'Nikephorus knows that he can only delay a pact between Kajd and Carolus. It will happen sooner or later; another embassy will be sent. He has a deeper, more serious plan.'

There was a long silence while Beorthric gathered his thoughts. 'I was to help you escape from the ambush. Not the other way around. Later, I was to have re-joined you, taken the credit for rescuing you, and gained your trust.'

By now I was completely baffled. 'But that makes no sense. The last time I spoke with Nikephorus he insinuated that you had betrayed me by arranging with Kunimund to hand me over to the Avars.'

There was just enough starlight to see the Saxon's mouth set in a grim line. 'Nikephorus plays with people. That's the sort of misinformation he deals in. It keeps his victims off-balance. I've seen it dozens of times.'

'And what about our mission to obtain the warrior flagon? Nikephorus is fully aware that Archbishop Arno sent us. I told him.'

'Nikephorus sees this whole business of the Avar gold and the warrior flagon as an opportunity. If he can find out why the gold flagon is so important to Archbishop Arno, he gets an insight into the plans of Carolus and his councillors.'

'And he suspects that Carolus is preparing some sort of masterstroke that may be against the interests of Constantinople?'

'That's exactly what he thinks.'

I recalled my own suspicions of Arno and his reasons for wanting to get his hands on the warrior flagon. I also remembered the evening in Paderborn when I suggested that the attack on Pope Leo had not been an attempt to kill him. Arno had as good as dismissed me on the spot. He had been hiding something.

'Then Nikephorus will be disappointed,' I told Beorthric. 'Neither of us will ever get to know why the warrior flagon is so important. Once I hand it over to Arno, that will be the end of the matter.'

'You misjudge Nikephorus. He believes that what we are doing also allows him to place his agent close to Arno and the others who advise Carolus.'

'His agent—' I began, then stopped. 'You're still his agent.'

'Or his informer, if you prefer that description. That's how Nikephorus sees me, and why I was told to gain your complete trust by "rescuing" you from the ambush.'

I sat shocked. I had been utterly wrong to think that Beorthric had been taken prisoner when I saw him after the fight. The men standing close to him were not his guards, but in charge of the horses.

'That wound of yours. How did that happen?' I asked

'Nikephorus hadn't given the men who attacked us a precise description of who his agent was. It took a bit of swordplay before I cleared enough space to be able to identify myself.' He gave a mirthless laugh. 'It cost one of them his life.'

'Why are you telling me all this?'

Beorthric reached down and must have picked up a twig from the grass. There was a slight snap as he fiddled with it. 'It's something I decided less than an hour ago.'

'You're speaking in riddles.'

He cleared his throat. 'It's a matter of loyalty.'

'Loyalty to me? Surely not.' I knew I sounded sarcastic and I meant it.

He took his time in replying. The twig snapped several more times as Beorthric broke it into smaller and smaller pieces. I sensed that he was about to expose something deep within his feelings. Finally, he spoke, 'Sigwulf, there comes a time when one has to decide where to place one's trust.'

I could not stop myself from remarking, 'Real trust, I hope, not something arranged through deceit.'

There was a sudden movement in the darkness as he flung aside the broken twigs angrily. 'I admit I sold my services, first to Carolus, then to Nikephorus. Afterwards, with both of them, I witnessed too many acts of treachery and double-dealing.'

'You should have thought about that earlier.' I saw no reason to be sympathetic.

Beorthric ploughed on, speaking as much to himself as to me. 'This winter I thought a lot about where my life was headed. It was a bad prospect. Then today you rode back, risking your own life because you believed you had to save me.'

I said nothing, waiting for him to go on. His next words made matters no clearer. 'When Kaiam was murdered, his family and clansmen came forward to claim his body and give him a proper burial. They stood by him.'

At last the truth sank into my muzzy brain. Beorthric had decided to place his trust in me because we shared a distant common ancestry. We were both Saxons. My decision to go back and help him had touched upon what he believed to be an ancient bond between us. Despite my misgivings, I felt more than a twinge of sympathy.

'I had just turned sixteen when I was made an outcast,' I told him, 'I was sent into exile by a vindictive warlord as a *wineleas guma*.'

There was a low grunt of understanding. Throughout the Saxon world *wineleas guma* describes a 'friendless man'.

'But I've managed to find a way, thanks to those who became my friends or were willing to assist me, and partly to luck,' I added. 'My origins, neither tribe nor clan, had nothing to do with it.'

Beorthric's voice had been starting to go husky with emotion. Now he cleared his throat. 'Sigwulf, you live by your intelligence. I sell my fighting skills. We are very different. For me the values of the Avars make good sense.'

Despite my misgivings I could not ignore the sincerity in his words. 'If our roles had been reversed, and I had been held captive by the Slavs, would you have ridden back to help me?' I asked.

'Now I would.'

The statement was so flat and definite that I found myself believing him.

'Then let us leave it there,' I said warily. 'We'll find Arno and hand over the warrior flagon.'

I was about to settle back down to sleep when it occurred to me to ask, 'If Nikephorus is paying you to act as his spy, how were you to pass on the information you learned?'

'Nikephorus said that someone would contact me.'

'No idea who that would be?'

'None. Nikephorus stressed that my contact would decide on the value of the information and act.'

It took a few heartbeats for the meaning of his words to sink in. 'That sounds very much as if it could lead to another plot. Like the one that removed Kaiam as khagan.'

Beorthric's silence told me that he agreed.

# Chapter Fourteen

Archbishop Arno had installed himself in the Lateran Palace. Compared to Rome's down-at-heel buildings, Pope Leo's official residence was in remarkably good condition. A team of masons and stone polishers was putting the finishing touches to a lavish new wing that added a grand banqueting hall, its gable wall faced in alternating bands of russet and white marble. At the opposite end of the palace a labouring gang was unloading bricks from a cart and stacking them ready to hoist up to where a section of the parapet was being refurbished. The square in front of the palace had been re-laid with fresh paving slabs, and the copper sheeting on the sloping roof of St John's Basilica that loomed in the background had been neatly patched.

Beorthric and I had left our hired horses at a stable after riding into the city soon after dawn, and walked up the gentle slope of the Caelian Hill intending to meet Archbishop Arno. It was more than a month since we had crossed the Donau and re-entered Carolus's domain. We had paid a visit to the field headquarters of the new Margrave of the Avarian March and I had spoken to him about Kajd's wish for a peace treaty. But I had chosen to reveal nothing about the warrior flagon I carried with me. Instinct told me that I should place it directly into Arno's hands, and I told the margrave that my immediate duty was to report to the archbishop. He was to be found in Rome, I was informed. He had stayed on there after accompanying Pope Leo back from Paderborn, and was still conducting his inquiries into the disgraceful attack on the Holy Father.

'No expense being spared,' Beorthric commented, watching two gilders, father and son by the look of them, apply gold leaf to the letters in a rubric carved in the marble above the entrance to the new banqueting hall.

'Probably paying the bills with some of the Avar Hoard that Carolus sent,' I answered. The saddlebag with the warrior flagon was slung over my shoulder. The heat of the spring sunshine had warmed the leather and I could distinctly smell the horse sweat. Tactfully, I had left the stallion and his splendid harness to the new margrave, asking him only for enough money to pay our expenses on the road to Rome.

The palace was certainly impressive. I counted more than thirty windows in the long brick façade and there were three separate entrances, each with its own portico, through which bustled priests and papal messengers. In their long black gowns, they reminded me of diligent ants entering and leaving their colony. The central doorway appeared to be the main one, so we made our way to where half a dozen armed men were loitering outside. With their tanned complexions and big-boned hands holding short pikes, they looked more like farmers than city-dwellers. They wore no uniform but were identified with black armbands tied around their upper arms. They stopped us from entering and one of them, apparently their leader, as he also wore a black sash, demanded to know who we were, and whom we wished to see.

'Archbishop Arno of Salzburg,' I replied. 'My name is Sigwulf, and my companion is Beorthric.'

'Is the archbishop expecting you?' The question was abrupt.

'If you send a message to the archbishop, he will receive us.'

'Wait here.'

After a suspicious glance directed at Beorthric, Black Sash despatched one of his men inside.

'Who are that lot?' Beorthric asked me as we withdrew out of earshot.

'The Pope's militia. I think they call themselves the Family of Saint Peter. They act as his bodyguards,' I said.

'If that's the best the Pope can do, then he doesn't have much protection.'

'In theory, a man of the Church doesn't need protection,' I said.

The Saxon allowed himself a derisive snort.

After a few minutes the messenger returned with a young lad dressed in brightly coloured and expensive clothes cut in the latest style. I supposed he was one of the youngsters whose aristocratic Roman families placed them in papal service as the first step on a lucrative and influential career.

'The archbishop says he will receive the man called Sigwulf.'

Leaving Beorthric to wait outside, I followed the youngster into the building. Passing through a lobby, we turned right and proceeded down a long corridor, the heels of my guide's smart scarlet shoes rapping on the tiled floor. The passageway was lined with doors, and where they stood open, I caught a glimpse of clerks and scribes at work, bent over their desks. The palace sheltered a vast sprawling bureaucracy of functionaries and office-holders, as well as the members of the Pope's private household staff.

We made another right turn, came into an antechamber, and then I was escorted into a large, high-ceilinged room where tall windows gave a view over the city. The furnishings were simple but refined: a crucifix of enamel and silver on an immaculately whitewashed wall, book shelves of dark, fine-grained wood, matching carved chairs with embroidered cushions, and a mosaic floor. The place smelled of beeswax. Seated behind a broad-topped desk very different to the rough campaign table when I had last seen him was Archbishop Arno. Dressed in a fine planeta, the long clerical gown, he looked more of a priest than when I had previously seen him. He had shaved off his beard but his jowls were left shadowed with dark stubble, and with his blunt-fingered hands and barrel chest there was still a strong resemblance to a sturdy bricklayer.

'I didn't expect to see you again,' was his curt greeting. He scowled at the lad. 'Go away, close the door, and make sure we are not disturbed.'

He waited till we were alone in the room, then turned his bleak gaze on me. 'Well?' he demanded.

I opened the flap of the satchel, produced the Avar warrior flagon, and laid it on the desk in front of him.

Arno looked at it for several heartbeats, his expression unreadable. Then he picked it up, and held it up to the light so that he could examine the image of the warrior prince more closely.

Apparently he was satisfied, for he put the flagon back on the table, and – still without expression – announced, 'If you had brought it to me earlier, it would have been some use.'

I felt a surge of resentment. The thought that I had endured a miserable winter as Faranak's serf for so little thanks, made me angry.

The archbishop looked at me under heavy brows. 'I'm nearly done with the culprits for the theft. They still deny direct responsibility, but the panel of investigators will find them guilty.'

He was talking about Campulus and Paschal, the two senior members of the papal hierarchy who had organized the assault on the Pope.

The archbishop picked up the flagon again and examined the decoration a second time. 'Still, this may come in useful at a later stage.'

To my chagrin he did not even ask how I had managed to obtain the warrior flagon and, in my disgruntled mood, I saw no reason to tell him that it was the twin of the one I had been sent to find. Nor did it seem to matter. Apparently, now the flagon was in his possession, he wanted no discussion on the subject.

'There is something you should know,' I said, struggling not to let my irritation show. I was being treated like an errand boy.

'And what is that?' he sounded distracted, almost bored. He had not even asked me to be seated.

'You remember the mercenary soldier you sent with me to Avaria?'

'His name is Beorthric, if I recall correctly.'

'He has been recruited by the Greek envoy to the Avar khagan.'

'I'm sure his loyalty has its price.' Arno's attention turned towards a pile of documents lying on the desk beside him. He reached out and picked up the nearest one. He made it clear that he wanted to put an end to our brief meeting.

'Beorthric was instructed to find out why you want that flagon so badly, and then pass that information on to a Byzantine agent here in Rome.'

That shook him.

The archbishop's hand stopped in mid-air. He slowly returned the document to the pile and carefully placed both hands, thick fingers interlaced, on the desk in front of him.

'And what was this Byzantine agent to do with this information?' His gaze from under bushy eyebrows was intimidating. Without moving a muscle, he waited for my answer.

'Beorthric was not told. The agent would decide for himself what action to take.'

A faint flicker of unease mingled with impatience in the clever grey eyes. 'You had better tell me exactly what happened on your mission to Avaria,' he conceded.

After I had described all that had taken place, Arno sat silent for several minutes. Finally, he said, 'Campulus and Paschal insist that they did not instigate the attack on Leo. And I must admit that neither man seems capable of organizing the attack on their own. So one has to presume they had associates, and these might make another attempt.'

He rubbed the bristles on his chin. 'It is fortunate that Pope Leo is well protected.'

I thought about Beorthric's recent comment on the poor quality of the guards at the gate to the palace, but said nothing.

The archbishop was speaking again. 'Nevertheless, it would be prudent to learn the identity of this mysterious Byzantine agent here in Rome.' He gave a sour smile. 'I don't suppose Beorthric was given any hint about who it might be?'

I shook my head. 'He was only told to gather the information and wait to be contacted.'

Arno's voice hardened. 'In that case, Sigwulf, you stay at Beorthric's side and report back to me the moment he hears from the agent.'

This might have been the moment to point out that I had fulfilled my original mission. But the archbishop was acting as though he still had Carolus's full authority, and he seemed to take it for granted that he could command my cooperation.

'Of course, Your Excellency.'

'While you're at it, I also want you to find out what you can about a man called Maurus of Nepi.'

'I'm a stranger to Rome . . .' I began to protest.

He cut me short. 'Speak to that friend of yours, the man who was so useful on your last visit.'

'Paul, formerly the papal Nomenculator. Is there anything I should tell him about this Maurus from Nepi?'

'Indeed there is,' Arno rasped. 'Campulus and Paschal have both claimed that Maurus was involved with setting up the attack on the Pope. Maurus has vanished. Learn where he is, and then I'll have him picked up for questioning.'

'I'll ask Paul what he knows,' I assured the archbishop.

'Yes, do that. We can't have Leo done to death by some unknown killer. Don't come back here until you have something useful to tell me, something on which I can take action.'

As I made for the door, the thought struck me that the archbishop had been remarkably quick to assume that Pope Leo's life was still in danger and he had still not revealed why he needed to have the warrior flagon in his possession. Somehow the two were linked, and I had a suspicion that being despatched to search for a Byzantine agent and this man Maurus was a misdirection.

*

It was less than an hour's walk to Paul's villa on the slopes of the Viminal Hill, and on the way I told Beorthric what Arno expected of us. When we reached Paul's home he was standing on the porch of his house and deep in conversation with a stocky middle-aged man dressed in a dusty smock, whom I took to be a gardener. Beorthric and I hung back until the man had left, then came forward and were greeted with genuine warmth.

'Sigwulf, you've a knack of choosing a good time of year to visit Rome. When did you arrive?'

'Just this morning. I'd like to introduce Beorthric. He and I have recently come from Avaria, where we were sent by Archbishop Arno.'

Paul turned towards the big Saxon, and the side of his face twitched in a conspiratorial wink. For a brief moment Beorthric looked disconcerted. Then he realized that Paul suffered from an uncontrollable facial tic.

'Your archbishop is a hard taskmaster,' Paul told the Saxon mercenary. 'For the past winter he's been turning Rome upside down, trying to unravel the mystery of who tried to do away with Pope Leo.'

'And he's nearly reached a conclusion,' I said. 'Though something else has come up that needs urgent attention, and you may be able to help.'

Paul rubbed his hands with anticipation. Not for the first time I thought to myself that he was a true Roman: he loved intrigue. 'Tell me more while we sit where we can enjoy the afternoon sunshine,' he said.

He led us off the porch and into his garden where two stone benches were placed to give a view of his display of salvaged statuary.

'Now, how I may assist?' he asked.

'Campulus and Paschal have admitted to Arno that they were party to the assault on Pope Leo.'

Paul waved a dismissive hand. 'I know that already. It's the gossip of all Rome. Has the archbishop been able to link that rascal Albinus to the conspiracy?'

'If he has, he didn't tell me.'

Paul made a wry face. 'What about that magnificent flagon we recovered from Albinus's house. Did you show it to him?'

'When I brought it to him in Paderborn, the flagon was promptly stolen.'

I gave an account of the theft and then proceeded to describe what had happened in Avaria afterwards. 'So Arno now has the twin of the flagon, not the original,' I concluded.

'Let's hope he takes better care this time,' said Paul. He gave a wicked grin. 'As you and I know, the Lateran has its share of thieves.'

'It's not theft that concerns the archbishop now. It's murder.'

Paul cocked his head on one side, his curiosity very apparent. 'And who's to be the victim?'

I explained how Nikephorus had hired Beorthric to discover the importance of the flagon, then report to an unknown Greek agent in Rome. 'For whatever reason, Arno thinks that Leo's life is once again threatened.'

Paul glanced across at the big Saxon, sitting quietly on the marble bench and listening. 'So now you're the bait that will bring this mysterious Greek agent out into the open before blood is spilt.'

Beorthric gave a barely perceptible nod.

Paul turned to me. 'And what about you, Sigwulf? The last time you were in Rome, you were lucky not to have been killed when you ventured into the slums with Theodore. Have you considered the risks?'

'I find it hard to believe that a scheme hatched by Nikephorus in Avaria can be played out here in Rome.'

Paul clicked his tongue in reproof. 'Nikephorus will have sent despatches to Constantinople, reporting on the change of Avar leadership and the new policy towards Carolus, as well as outlining his own scheme, whatever it is. While you've been on the road, his masters in Constantinople have had ample time to pass on instructions to their supporters in Rome. Heaven knows, there are enough of them.'

'That's as may be,' I said, 'but right now Arno has given us a more immediate task than finding this Byzantine agent: he wants to trace a man whom Paschal and Campulus claim set up the attack on Leo. He's gone missing.'

'Does this man have a name?'

'Mauro of Nepi.'

Paul's eyes widened in surprise.

'You know this Maurus?' I asked, startled.

'Not personally. But I am aware of his family background. He's minor gentry and his people have a small palazzo in the city.'

'So it should be easy enough for Arno to have him picked up for questioning.'

'Quite the opposite. Maurus must know that he's a wanted man and he'll have fled to his family properties in Nepi. That's a town about two hours north of Rome.'

'So he could be arrested and brought before Arno for questioning.'

Paul grimaced. 'Only if Arno sends a small army to collect him. Nepi and similar provincial towns are independent. They are ruled by local lords who resent outsiders interfering their affairs, least of all those from Rome.'

'If Maurus stays in Nepi, then at least he can't get up to any more mischief.'

Paul gave me a patient look. 'That shows how little you know of Italy, Sigwulf. I wouldn't be surprised if a lot more trouble comes from the same direction.'

I was about to scoff at Paul's gloomy prediction when I was stopped by the glum look on his face. 'Surely you're not serious.'

Paul raised an eyebrow. 'Should I remind you about Pope Constantine the Second?'

'I've scarcely heard of him,' I admitted.

Paul pulled a face. 'Not surprising. No one likes to mention him, though it wasn't that long ago. I was still working my way up through the ranks in the Lateran at the time.'

'What did Constantine the Second do that makes him such an embarrassment?'

'He got himself elected Pope by violence and subterfuge.'

I laughed aloud. 'But surely that's routine. You told me how Pope Leo spread enough money around to get himself elected within twenty-four hours of the death of Pope Paul. Purchasing St Peter's throne is hardly honourable.'

Paul did not join in my mirth. 'Constantine broke his solemn word, used armed force, and made a complete mockery of established procedure.'

I had the impression that this last transgression mattered most to the former Nomenculator.

He settled back on the bench and closed his eyes for a moment while he ordered his thoughts.

'Any candidate for election as Pope must already be a senior priest, at the very least a deacon. That's the time-honoured custom.' He opened his eyes and leaned forward. 'But Constantine was a layman, though he had good political connections in the Lateran. When Pope Paul lay dying, he came into Rome with a band of armed men at his back. He bullied a local bishop into ordaining him as a monk. The very next day the same bishop was forced to elevate him to the rank of sub-deacon, and within hours Constantine was promoted deacon. A week later, when Paul was dead, Constantine used his contacts and influence to have himself appointed Bishop of Rome and presented before the people as their Pope and head of the Church.'

I glanced across at Beorthric. Judging from his sardonic expression, Paul's tale confirmed his low opinion of the Christian faith.

'What happened then?' I asked.

'He sent a letter to the King of the Franks, Carolus's grandfather, asking him to approve the appointment. He received no answer. A few months later a group of his opponents got together in the city, raised an armed mob and there was bloody fighting in the streets. Constantine's supporters lost, he was arrested and imprisoned. Taken into St John's Basilica at the Lateran, his Pope's gown was ceremoniously ripped off him, he was thrown on the ground and his papal shoes cut from his feet. Later again, he was put on public show, mocked by the mob, his eyes put out, and left lying in the gutter.' Paul paused.

'That sounds familiar,' I said sourly. 'The same treatment was intended for Leo not so long ago. That's what got this whole business started for me.'

Paul sighed. 'Constantine survived his beating and was returned to prison. Summoned before a tribunal, he refused to acknowledge his sins and was shut up in a monastery. He's not been heard of since.'

Beorthric spoke up. 'What has this got to do with Maurus?'

Paul treated us to a level stare. 'Constantine was one of four brothers. All were active in the plot to seize the papacy. His oldest brother styled himself "Duke of Nepi" and was the ring leader. It was his soldiers who marched into Rome to place Constantine on St Peter's throne. Nepi remains the family's seat of power. Little wonder it's also where Maurus comes from.'

My head was spinning. 'So you think that there is another plot to overthrow Leo and it is being directed from Nepi?'

'The town is a hotbed of opposition to the Roman Church, and there are others.' He gripped me by the arm. I had never seen Paul so serious. 'In Italy the Pope is much more than a churchman. He's a great prince who ranks alongside sovereigns and kings. Whatever your Archbishop Arno has in mind, this meeting with the Greek agent is high politics and very dangerous.'

I took a deep breath and looked at Beorthric. 'Do you still want to meet him?'

'Of course.'

His certainty took me by surprise. 'Why?'

'I told you: I sell my fighting skills to make a living.'

'But this is different: you'll be exposing yourself to an unknown danger that strikes without warning.'

'As does a scout who rides through enemy territory at the head of a company of soldiers. He's the man who will draw the ambush.'

A vivid picture came to me of Beorthric on our way to Avaria, riding through the forest, his head turning from side to side, always on his guard. 'And when this Greek agent contacts you, what will you tell him? Neither of us know why Arno went to such lengths to get hold of that flagon.'

Beorthric was already getting to his feet. 'My mind's made up.'

As I rose to follow him from the garden, Paul said, 'If you really do want to go through with this, I suggest you take lodgings at the Schola Anglorum. It's the first place the Greek agent will look for you when he wishes to make contact.'

Beorthric looked at me enquiringly, and I explained to him that the Schola Anglorum was where English pilgrims usually stayed on their visits to Rome. 'It's a church and hostel on the far side of the river, just by St Peter's Basilica. I've stayed there before.'

'And about as far away from the Lateran as possible,' Paul added meaningfully.

*

The Schola had grown much larger since my first visit to Rome nearly ten years earlier. Then it had been a small church with an adjoining hostel for pilgrims. Both hostel and church were still there, but now they were part of a walled compound with a refectory, two or three shops, a tavern, and a long building that served as a dormitory. Beorthric and I were able to rent a couple of sleeping cubicles at a very reasonable price because the Schola was subsidized by grants from the English kings. Ironically, King Offa of Mercia, now dead, had been an important benefactor. It was Offa who had sent me into exile at Carolus's court, hoping to be rid of me. I wondered what he would have thought had he known that twenty-three years later I was benefitting from his generosity.

Beorthric and I settled in to wait. There must have been at least another thirty guests in residence, mostly devout pilgrims and their families with a sprinkling of priests and itinerant merchants. We took our meals in the refectory where the kitchen prepared porridge and boiled meats to remind the visitors of their homeland cooking. Beorthric fitted in well because the conversation was in Saxon. He was also pleased to come across someone who sold him a scramseax to replace the one that had been left behind at the ambush in Avaria.

'I can't face seeing any more sacred relics,' Beorthric complained to me on the eighth day of our stay. We were the last people left sitting at table after the plates from the midday meal had been cleared, and still the mysterious agent who reportedly represented the Greeks had made no attempt to contact the Saxon. The whole afternoon stretched before us.

'We'll draw attention to ourselves if we fail to keep up a pretence of piety,' I told Beorthric. All that week we had trudged around the various churches, oratories and shrines dotted throughout the city. It had been difficult for Beorthric as an Old Believer to hide his ignorance of Christianity. For my own part, I had toured many of the sites before and was indifferent to their religious significance.

'What will you do if all this comes to nothing?' I asked. With each passing day I was more doubtful that Nikephorus or his masters in Constantinople had managed to get word to their man in Rome.

'I'll hire myself out as an escort to some wealthy band of pilgrims making their way back home.'

'And until then?'

'I'll take a temporary job as a door guard at the Schola.' A swarm of unscrupulous rogues always hovered around the entry to the compound. They harassed any foreigners who appeared to be suitably gullible. They plucked at their sleeves, offering to bring them to money changers who, they swore, were honest traders but in fact gave atrociously bad rates and frequently palmed off counterfeit coins. Others tried to sell over-priced tours of the holy sites, fake relics, shoddy keepsakes and other dross. The Schola was obliged to hire guards to prevent these pests from getting further inside and making greater nuisances of themselves.

'I can't see you making a career of chasing away urchins and hucksters,' I said.

'Well, somebody's not doing the job properly,' said Beorthric looking over my shoulder.

I turned to see a round-faced, smiling man with shifty pebbly eyes advancing across the refectory towards us. I recognized him as one of the more imaginative guides who had a lucrative sideline in selling little packets of iron filings. He claimed they were rasped from the iron chains that had bound St Peter. It was remarkable how many of his innocent clients parted with their money.

It crossed my mind that he had paid someone a bribe to be allowed in through the compound's gate.

'Sirs!' he called out. 'Today I can offer a very special tour.'

'Go away,' Beorthric growled. 'We've done all the tours.'

'No, no, I swear to you. This is entirely fresh and new. To explore a holy tomb opened to visitors for the first time only yesterday.'

'Leave us alone,' I snapped. I didn't believe a word of his pitch, and he had come close enough for me to smell the garlic on his breath.

'I have special permission to show the saint's remains. He was a man of such surpassing holiness that when his bones were located, the skull had turned to gold.'

Beorthric and I exchanged glances. 'Where is this place?' I asked warily.

'Not far, sir,' the guide wheedled. 'An hour on foot, no more.'

'I'll meet you at the gate,' Beorthric said to me.

The guide and I left the refectory and walked across the compound. When Beorthric joined us, I noticed that he had gone to fetch his scramseax and was carrying it slung on his hip. The guide noticed it too.

'No need for alarm, sirs,' he cried. 'Where I'm taking you is quite safe. I swear it.'

We followed him down from St Peter's and across the Tiber by the St Angelo bridge. He set a brisk pace, plunging into the tangle of alleys that were an uncomfortable reminder of my narrow escape from Gavino's gang. Every so often he turned to ask us to hurry, assuring us that we would be pleased with what we would see. Eventually, we emerged on the Via Lata not far from the spot where Pope Leo had been attacked, and from there crossed into the more open areas of the disabitato with its ruined buildings and overgrown monuments. It was more than the hour's walk he'd promised when, eventually, we found ourselves passing under the arch of the Salarian Gate with its crumbling twin towers and leaving behind us the ancient city wall, its plaster flaking away from the rotting bricks.

'Where are you taking us?' I demanded. It was mid-week and there was very little traffic on the Salarian Way, only a few carts returning to the nearby farms after delivering produce to the city markets.

'Come, sirs, it's not much further.'

Finally, we came to a small knoll on the left-hand side of the road, about a half a mile out of the city. The side of the knoll had been cut back into what appeared to be a small quarry. Our guide turned off the road towards it and led us along a footpath that threaded between small boulders and loose stones overgrown with grass and weeds. As we got closer it became evident that what I had mistaken for a quarry was the remains of an ancient burial site, the original facing slabs long since removed or fallen away. In the centre was its entrance, a low doorway cut in the living rock.

'Here it is, sirs,' explained the guide. 'The doorway to the holy tomb of the blessed St Pamphilus.'

I had never heard of St Pamphilus nor, I was sure, had Beorthric. In the weak afternoon sunshine the place looked unthreatening and tranquil.

'Lead on,' I said to the guide.

'Sirs, I can only show one person at a time. Further inside, the passageway is very narrow.'

I glanced at Beorthric. He appeared composed and had shifted the scramseax to hang close by his right hand. 'I'll wait for you just inside the entrance,' I said.

The doorway was so low that Beorthric had to duck his head as the three of us went in. We were in a cave, some eight feet across and twice as deep, with a roof close enough to reach with an outstretched arm. The light from behind us showed that the cave was natural, its walls uneven, but the roof had been heightened. The chisel marks were plain.

The guide bent down and opened a sack lying on the floor just inside the entrance. He took out two torches made of tow soaked in oil and wrapped around wood shafts. It occurred to me that the sack must have been placed there very recently, and the little clay lamp in a niche in the cave wall also. The lamp was lit.

The guide used the lamp's flame to light both torches and handed one to Beorthric. He kept the other for himself. 'One person at a time,' he repeated, giving me a sharp look. 'We should not be long. Then you may have your turn.' I watched as he walked to the back of the cave where a flight of steps led downward into the darkness. With Beorthric following him, he disappeared.

I counted to one hundred, went to the head of the steps, and stood listening. I could hear nothing. Very quietly and slowly I began to descend, feeling my way with one hand on each side against the rock face, treading cautiously. Very soon I was in complete darkness and unable to see anything. I continued downward, far deeper than I had expected, sixty-four steps in all until, on my left, the rock wall came to an end and my hand was in empty space. I presumed I was in an ancient catacomb and had reached a gallery leading sideways. Very cautiously, I reached out directly in front of me: more empty space. I tested with an outstretched foot: the steps continued downward. I listened again, holding my breath, and thought I heard a faint sound to my left.

I made the decision to follow the gallery and turned into it. The air was cool and had a musty, damp smell. I paced forward, arms still spread wide, setting down each foot forward carefully, fearful that I might step into empty air. The galley was no more than five feet in breadth, and my outstretched arms spanned it easily. My fingertips brushed against different surfaces, sometimes it felt like rock, and sometimes it had a gritty texture. I guessed that I was feeling my way past rows of *cubicula*, the little chambers cut in the rock to receive the bones of the dead, then sealed with stones and mortar. Underfoot there was a soft crunching as I trod on a thick layer of dust and chippings.

I must have advanced some thirty or forty yards when I detected a faint flicker of light ahead of me. My eyes had grown accustomed to the darkness so the light was enough to show me that I was approaching a section in the gallery where it had been enlarged to form a small chamber. Beyond it the underground passageway continued into darkness. It seemed that I had guessed correctly when I had turned down the gallery: the guide was standing off to one side in the chamber, holding a torch and waiting.

Inch by inch I moved closer, staying pressed against the wall, remaining in the shadow. I halted when I could go no further without being spotted, and listened. From the darkness beyond the guide came the sound of a voice, someone speaking slow, careful Frankish. The shape of the gallery and the rocky walls carried the sound clearly, though the speaker was too far away to be seen. My spine tingled. I did not know the voice but I recognized the distinctive accent. It was the same accent I had heard from the men who had waylaid me in Paderborn and who had given me a beating as they demanded to know about the golden flagon.

I stayed for a couple of minutes at most. I had no wish to be discovered, and Beorthric would be able to tell me about the man he was meeting. So I turned around and crept back down the gallery until I reached the steps and mounted them back into the entrance chamber. I was waiting there when the guide and Beorthric reappeared not long afterwards.

'You next,' said the guide to me. Beorthric held out his torch for me to take.

'No thank you,' I said. 'I have a fear of enclosed spaces.'

The guide made no attempt to make me change my mind. He took Beorthric's torch and extinguished it as well as his own, put them back in the sack, and led us out into the daylight.

'We can find our own way back,' I told him firmly.

He must have been well paid already because the fee he demanded for guiding us was less than outrageous. Nor did he argue when I told him I would only pay half. 'You failed to warn me that the saint's tomb is deep underground. I have a fear of confined spaces, so only one of us is satisfied with your services.'

In response he pulled from his pocket a small clay ampoule. 'Sir, even if you did not see the saint's tomb for yourself, you should bring this home with you. It contains holy oil from the lamp that burns in front of the saint's shrine and has miraculous qualities. The flame never goes out, yet the lamp is never replenished.'

'Then that's even more of a miracle if you keep stealing the lamp's oil,' I said.

'I can let you have it for a very reasonable price.'

When I declined his offer he shrugged, turned on his heel and headed back towards the city.

I waited until he was well out of earshot before asking Beorthric, 'Did you get a good look at who set up this meeting? I followed you down, but only near enough to listen in for a couple of minutes.'

'I didn't get close enough to be able to identify him again. He's tall. He stayed in the shadows and was wearing a fur hat with the flaps down and tied under his chin. It didn't leave much of his face visible.'

'Did he question you about the warrior flagon?'

'I told him that I hadn't been able to learn anything about it. Then he asked a question that I thought was strange: he wanted to know whether I had ever laid eyes on the Pope in person, or on King Carolus. I told him that I'd seen the king at a distance several times but never the Pope. Then he dropped the subject.'

'And how did your conversation end?'

'He said that he might have a job for me. But it was not his decision. He would contact me again very soon and I should be ready to leave Rome for a day or so.'

Beorthric's words left me baffled and more than a little uneasy. With Carolus far away in Frankia, I could not see an immediate connection between him and Pope Leo in Rome. Nor had I got any nearer to establishing the identity of the mysterious Greek agent. The only fresh information that I could bring to Archbishop Arno was what Paul had told me about Maurus of Nepi.

\*

'So you never saw the man's face?' Paul asked. Our route back to the Schola had taken us close to Paul's villa on the Viminal Hill and I had decided that we should call again on the retired Nomenculator. Just possibly, he might be able to tease out more from our visit to St Pamphilus's shrine.

The three of us were gathered in the room where Paul kept his collection of scrolls and Beorthric had finished describing his conversation in the catacomb.

'He spoke Frankish with a very distinctive accent,' I told him.

'What does it sound like?'

I imitated the accent as best I could, and must have done it accurately because Paul immediately said, 'That's someone from Benevento. They have their own way of speaking, from high up at the back of the nose.'

Benevento, he explained, was a city four or five days' distance by horseback to the south-east of Rome. It was ruled by a powerful family of aristocrats much as Nepi had its duke.

'There the comparison ends,' he said and there was an undertone of respect in his voice. 'The lords of Benevento take the title of Prince, and have good reason to do so. They own vast swathes of land, hold their own court, even strike their own coinage. If

Benevento is involved with whatever is going on in Rome, then you need to be very, very careful.'

I recalled his earlier warning that the Pope ranked alongside princes and kings and that papal politics was fraught with risk. 'Why would the Beneventans be interested in Beorthric?'

Paul treated me to a long slow stare, encouraging me to think for myself. 'What does our mysterious man in the fur hat know about Beorthric and why would he ask if he had ever laid eyes on the Pope?' he prompted.

'So that Beorthric would recognize the Pope when he saw him . . .' My voice trailed away and my throat went dry with fear as I realized the enormity of what Paul implied.

Calmly Paul continued with his bleak assessment. 'Beorthric is unknown here in Rome. He arrives from the scene of a successful killing of a foreign ruler, and if I may say so,' he gave a slight nod towards the Saxon, 'he looks like a man who can use a weapon effectively.'

Beorthric, who had been silent up to this point, interrupted with a typically practical question. 'Are the Beneventans capable of setting up a similar attack to the one that Kajd arranged?'

'If the Beneventans can't do it for themselves, they'll find help inside Rome,' Paul assured him. 'There are plenty of others who would be glad to be rid of Leo, and willing to arrange the practical details.'

'Then I must warn Archbishop Arno immediately,' I said.

Paul frowned at me. 'It might be more profitable to make sure that Beorthric is taken on as a killer for hire.'

'And if he is?'

'Then you'll be in a position to thwart any attack that's being planned.' He saw that I was reluctant to accept his suggestion. 'You're forgetting that Fur Hat also asked if Beorthric knew Carolus by sight.'

I was finding it difficult to keep up with Paul's reasoning. He seemed capable of finding plots and conspiracies where none might exist. 'Surely you don't think that the Beneventans and their allies might strike against Carolus too?'

He shrugged. 'It's a possibility. It's better to have Beorthric at the heart of any conspiracy than for the Beneventans and their allies to turn to some unknown cut-throat whom we cannot watch.'

Still I hesitated. 'If this goes wrong and Beorthric is exposed, he'll be killed. I know these people. They're ruthless.'

'I can take care of myself,' Beorthric put in sharply and I hoped it was not his pride that made him do so.

Paul treated me to a wintry smile. 'I'm sure Arno would approve. Wasn't he the one who proposed that Beorthric lured the Greek agent from hiding?'

There was little point in reminding Paul that Arno's scheme had not produced the result the archbishop had been hoping for. 'I don't see how all this ties in with the warrior flagon,' I said.

'Neither do I,' Paul admitted.

He glanced out of the window. There was a little more than an hour to sunset. 'If you intend to get back to your lodgings before dark, you should set out now.'

# Chapter Fifteen

IN THE DAYS that followed, Beorthric made it very clear to me that he intended to carry out Paul's scheme for him to be chosen by the Beneventans as a killer for hire. However, I was still apprehensive about its outcome. More than once, I decided to go back to the Lateran and report to Archbishop Arno, only to change my mind at the last moment. The archbishop had asked for information on which he could act, and I had none. But every time I tried to talk to Beorthric about the dangers of what Paul had proposed the Saxon flatly refused to consider any alternatives. The most I could get him to accept was that, as far as possible, he would include me in whatever developed. It left me uncomfortably aware that if anything went wrong I too was likely to suffer the consequences. Both of us could finish up being arrested by the authorities if they got wind of the Beneventan conspiracy. Worse, if the Beneventans discovered that that Beorthric was a double agent, he and I would be done away with. Yet in the end I managed to persuade myself, perhaps naively, that it was preferable that I share the same risks as Beorthric as he would have a better chance of success if I stood by him, and that should he find himself in trouble I might be able to help him out. With all this bickering between us, Boerthric must have found me to be irresolute. Certainly I found him stubborn, and as a result we became irritable with one another as we waited at the Schola for contact to be made.

A full month went by, each day hotter than the previous one as spring turned into summer, and the compound of the Schola felt increasingly cramped and confined. I wasted many hours trying to puzzle out, unsuccessfully, if there was a connection between the Avar flagon and the threat to Pope Leo.

Beorthric, bored by the inactivity, began frequenting the taverns in the neighbourhood. He also took to eating his meals in them, loudly announcing one day in the Schola's refectory that he could no longer put up with the mumbling of prayers before being allowed to eat the food already set out on the table. He was also annoyed by the singing of devotees on their way to services in the great basilica of St Peter. Our lodgings lay on the processional route so it was impossible to escape their hymns and anthems and ecstatic cries that floated in across the compound wall. If he was in a sour mood, Beorthric would mock their fervour by imitating their songs in a deliberately tuneless, squawky voice or calling out to them to stop their racket.

One day in mid-June, just when I was beginning to think that Beorthric's graceless behaviour would get us evicted from the Schola, he returned from his evening tavern meal to say that our wait was over. A stranger had approached him as he was entering the gate of the Schola and told him to gather together his belongings and be ready to leave next morning at daybreak.

'Was he the same man you spoke with in the catacomb?' I asked hopefully.

'No. He was not tall enough but he had the same sort of accent. There was a badge stitched to his sleeve. Some sort of livery mark. I'd say he was a manservant.'

'Any hint where he was taking you?'

'None. His Frankish was very limited. I think he was saying that I would be away for several days and might not be coming back here.'

'I presume you told him that I would be coming with you.'

'With sign language, but I got the point across. He didn't look pleased.'

To my relief the swarthy, sullen-faced man who met us at the gate in the half-light of the following dawn was holding the reins of three horses. He gave me a mistrustful look as I adjusted my saddlebags on the crupper of the animal allotted to me. As soon as we were mounted, he took us at a brisk trot through the empty city streets so that we were already clear of Rome and riding out into the countryside while the morning's mist still lay on the fields. It was evident that the highway we were following dated back many centuries. In the first mile we passed one grandiose tomb after another, each close beside the roadside and erected to house the noble dead from imperial times. The majority of these mausoleums were badly dilapidated, and those still in fair condition were now being used as barns and cattle shelters by the local farmers. From the direction of the morning sun I could tell that we were heading south-east, but our escort made no attempt to explain where we were going or whom he was taking us to meet. Tight-lipped, he ignored us and I suspected that if I tried to speak to him he wouldn't respond, and so I didn't bother. At noon, when we stopped at a posting station to water and feed the horses, I asked a stable boy if he recognized the boar emblem stitched on our guide's sleeve. The lad looked at me as if I was a dolt. The boar was the badge of the Princes of Benevento. It was the answer I half expected.

According to Paul, the city of Benevento lay at four or five days' distance from Rome so it came as a surprise when our escort turned off from the main highway on the third day of the journey. The landscape had scarcely changed since leaving Rome. It was the same pleasantly wooded hilly countryside where olive groves and fruit orchards outnumbered fields under the plough. Most of the inhabitants chose to live in small towns on the tops of the steeper hills whose lower slopes they planted with vines.

'Where's he taking us now?' Beorthric asked. The guide was riding ahead along a track that led through an olive grove. The ground was soft enough to absorb the sound of our horses' hooves, and the air was full of the buzzing and creaking of insects enlivened by the warm afternoon sunshine.

'I've no idea,' I said. 'We must be getting close to Beneventan territory. At the inn where we stopped last night he didn't pay. He just showed his badge.'

'No wonder the innkeeper had a sulky face.'

The track began to climb and the olive trees gave way to a thick beech forest where the horses had to scrabble for purchase on the crumbly surface of the path that looped ever higher. Eventually, we came clear of the trees and found ourselves on a level hill crest where a lad watched over a few sheep grazing on the meagre upland pasture. Looking back the way we had come, I could see far below me the line of the road we had left. Beorthric was a few yards ahead of me and I heard him utter a slight groan of dismay. I rode up to join him. He was gazing ahead to where the track would take us. The end of the ridge rose to a peak and on it stood a cluster of buildings dominated by a bell tower.

'Not another monastery,' he growled.

Our reception was efficient and wary. The porter in the monastery gatehouse made us wait while he sent an assistant to summon two men-at-arms dressed in the Beneventan livery. They took delivery of us from our escort and searched us for hidden weapons. They removed Beorthric's scramseax and handed it to the porter for safe-keeping. They then brought us in through the monastery double doors and up a long flight of steps that led to a broad raised forecourt. It was clear that they had orders to make sure we were not seen by the monks, for we were hurried around the rear of a building which smelled like a bakery and, a few steps further on, we turned into the first doorway we came to.

'Nice to know we had a place reserved for us,' said Beorthric sarcastically as he let drop his saddlebags on the floor of the cell-like room into which we were shown. Behind us was the sound of the stout door being barred, shutting us in.

I looked around. The room contained two cots, a three-legged stool, and a table with a bowl and an earthen water jug. Someone had left a loaf of bread and a large chunk of cheese beside the water jug.

'No point in staying hungry,' said Beorthric, reaching for the loaf and tearing it in half. He broke the cheese into two pieces and took a bite. 'Sheep's cheese and good too. You should try it.'

A single small window, high up, allowed in light and air. Hearing a very faint whistling sound from beyond a curtain closing off a recess in one wall, I went across and drew it back. The alcove served as a privy, and there was a hole in the floor. The sound was the wind whistling past the aperture. Looking down the hole, I saw an open forty-foot drop to a near-vertical hillside. Coming back into the room, I placed the stool under the window and climbed up so that I could peer out. As I suspected, the monastery was perched on the edge of a steep scarp. Our room faced outward over the void and below us stretched an expanse of wooded hills and shadowed valleys as far as the eye could see.

I went across to the door and listened. I could hear nothing. Nevertheless, I was worried that somehow our conversation might be overheard.

'Stop fretting,' Beorthric told me. He sounded relaxed and unworried. 'They'll come and fetch us when they're ready.'

'When do you think that will be?'

He shrugged and ran his fingers through his hair which had

grown back, long and blond, since the days with the Avars. 'Probably after dark.'

He stretched out on one of the cots, laid back his head, closed his eyes, and promptly fell asleep, leaving me to pace up and down the room, worrying.

The silence was numbing. The outer wall of our room was four feet thick, and the solid interior walls not much less. They blocked out noise so that all I could hear were my footsteps on the floorboards, Beorthric's breathing and the faint, hollow whistle of the wind next door. The dead, empty feeling reminded me of the derelict tombs we had ridden past on leaving Rome. With a shiver of fear I thought back to another monastery, the one in the foothills of the Alps. It was where I had my first encounter with Albinus, the Pope's chamberlain. I wondered if I was about to see him again. If so, he was sure to recognize me. Then both Beorthric and I would not be allowed to live.

My anxiety increased as the hours dragged by. I felt exposed and helpless, not knowing where we were or why we had not been taken to Benevento. Clearly, the Beneventans were not the only people who wanted to meet Beorthric, and it was impossible to guess who their allies might be. I found myself wishing that Paul had been more informative about Italian politics. The uncertainty weighed on my thoughts and I lost track of time. We were buried too deep within the monastery to hear the bell in the church tower marking the hours and calling the monks to service, or perhaps they did not require their belfry to measure out their day.

It was long after the light from the little window had faded that I heard the sound of the door bolts being drawn back. Beorthric opened his eyes and sat up. Two men-at-arms in Beneventan livery entered. A third man stood in the corridor outside holding up a torch. They were not the same men who had escorted us before. Once again we were searched for hidden weapons, then taken from the room and out into the open air. We turned to our right and followed the line of the monastery's perimeter wall, always keeping away from the more public areas. A sliver of moon showed the bulky outline of a large basilica on our right, its high roof black against the stars. Then a short flight of stone steps brought us to an upper level and the entrance to a small building that filled the space between the basilica and outer wall. The flickering light from the escort's torch fell on small, narrow bricks like those used in the city walls of Rome. The building we were entering was very old.

Our escort knocked on a closed door, and the moment it opened, we slipped inside before it was shut behind us. We were in some sort of a vestibule, not large, which smelled of mildew. It was badly lit by three or four torches in wall brackets. The floor was paved with large buff-coloured clay tiles so worn that their centres were slightly dished. Plain benches, dark with age, stood arranged against the walls, and pale patches in the plaster showed where pictures had once hung. I was fairly sure that we were in the antechamber to the monastery's original chapel.

Beorthric was remarkably self-possessed. Ignoring our escorts, he walked across to one of the benches and sat down, arms folded. I followed him. 'I wonder how long we'll be kept waiting,' I said in an undertone, taking care to address him in Saxon. One of the guards promptly stepped up to me and snarled angrily, 'Silence!' – or something to that effect, for he spoke in the local dialect. Meekly, I settled back in my seat, careful not to make eye contact with him or his two comrades.

We waited for perhaps half an hour and I caught snatches of argument from raised voices on the far side of the door that led deeper into the building. Eventually, that door opened and the same sour-faced man who had brought us from Rome looked out and beckoned to us to enter. Careful to walk a couple of steps behind Beorthric in the role of his assistant, I followed him into a spacious high-vaulted room. Most of it was in deep shadow though I could make out a line of window embrasures along each side. Directly ahead of us on the end wall was a fresco. It was a crucifixion scene in which a bearded man in an abbot's dress and with a nimbus around his head knelt at the foot of the cross. Patches of the original paint had peeled away, the remaining colours were faded, and there were streaks across the picture where water had leaked from above. A name was written underneath the kneeling abbot, and though I strained my eyes to read what it was, the script was too blurred to be legible, and several letters were missing. To my mind there was no longer any doubt that we were in an abandoned oratory, disused now that the monks had built themselves a large basilica immediately adjacent.

All original furniture had been removed and where an altar once stood, a group of four men sat at a table. My eye was drawn at once to the man directly facing us. Between forty and fifty years of age, his long dark hair hung loose to his shoulders, framing a bony, narrow face with an expression that managed to be both calculating and jaded at the same time. He was beautifully dressed in an over-gown of brocaded red and gold silk trimmed with fur at the collar and cuffs, and held together at the throat with a gold brooch studded with precious stones. The candlelight from twin candelabra placed at each end of the table struck a deep red glow from the fat ruby he wore on a ring on the index finger of his right hand. Even before he spoke, it was clear that he was in charge of the meeting.

'Your name is Beorthric?' There was the slightest hint of a Beneventan accent in his slow, careful Frankish. I judged him to be a high official of the prince's court rather than a member of the ruling family.

'It is, my lord,' Beorthric answered firmly.

The official turned his gaze towards me where I stood a couple of paces behind the big Saxon. 'And you are?'

Beorthric replied for me. 'My associate, my lord.'

'What sort of an associate?'

'He was with me when the khagan of the Avars enjoyed his final meal,' Beorthric told him.

The hint of a grim smile stretched the corners of the official's mouth. 'Tell me about it,' he said.

While Beorthric recounted the plot against Kaiam, I had a chance to study the other men seated at the table. Richly dressed, they all had that indefinable air of those who are accustomed to giving orders, not receiving them. Also I detected that there was some tension between them. The stout man with the meaty shoulders and the grizzled beard sitting on the left of the Beneventan official appeared to be his deputy. A sour-faced, stooped old man with hooded eyes and thin wisps of white hair scraped across his nearly bald scalp was unhappy with what was being considered. He was chewing on a fingernail and treating the company to a suspicious scowl. Facing him was a priest. Thin-faced and not particularly tall, the gaunt cheeks above the greying beard were covered with a network of broken veins. I put his age at fifty and he seemed to be uncomfortable, shifting in his seat. Instead of looking at the others, he studied a point in the empty air above their heads. He appeared to be having difficulty in understanding what Beorthric was saying.

When Beorthric had finished giving his account of how Kaiam had been overthrown, it was the old man who spoke up. 'How do you know he's telling the truth?' he rasped, taking his hand from his mouth and spitting out a morsel of fingernail. He put the question in Latin to the senior Beneventan, presuming, I supposed, that neither Beorthric nor I would understand him. His arrogance and the pallor of his skin, contrasting with the swarthy

Beneventans, led me to believe that he was a nobleman who had come from Rome.

'We agreed not to employ your gutter scum this time,' answered the Beneventan evenly, confirming my guess. He too spoke in Latin.

The old man was insistent. 'And if this also goes wrong? What then?'

'We'll be even more ambitious next time.'

The old man turned his scowl in my direction. His eyes were pale blue and a dark wart-like growth showed on his upper lip, at the corner of his mouth. 'Get him out of here. One butcher is enough.'

I had the good sense to keep my face blank, pretending not to understand, and also to look startled when the Beneventan man-servant took me roughly by the arm and marched me out of the room and back into the antechamber.

Under the hostile gaze of the guards I found myself a seat and tried to commit to memory what the men at the table had looked like. None of them had been tall enough to be the agent in Rome for the Greeks, and for that I was both disappointed and thankful – disappointed that I could not get a proper look at his face, and thankful that he had not been there to recognize me from the beating in Paderborn. The haughty old man at the meeting, I suspected, was from the aristocratic faction in Rome who wished to get rid of the upstart Pope Leo whom they regarded as an ill-bred commoner. The priest was an enigma. If he was the abbot of the monastery, or a very senior monk, he could have been at the meeting because he was the host for the visitors. On the other hand, he might be someone from the Lateran and actively engaged in the conspiracy against the Pope.

Beorthric reappeared not long afterwards. In one hand he had a soft leather pouch dangling from its drawstring. Without a word, he jerked his head for me to follow him as he brushed past the guards and strode towards the outside door. Both of us remained silent while we were escorted back to our cell-like room, and locked in again for the night. Only when the noise of their footsteps had died away, did I dare to speak, and then only in a whisper.

'What did you learn?' I asked.

'That they are serious about getting rid of Leo,' he said. 'They gave me a down payment of a hundred solidi'– he held up the pouch – 'and promised four times as much again when he's in his coffin.'

'And how are you supposed to carry out the killing?'

'On my own. They were most insistent that it has to be a solo attack, without accomplices.'

'That's because they employed a gang of city cut-throats last time and it was bungled.'

'I told them that if the attack was to be successful, I had to be provided with detailed knowledge of my target's movements and how well he is protected.'

'What did they suggest?'

'They had already picked a location where I can get close to the Pope when he's unguarded.'

'And where is this place?'

'It goes by the name of the Forum of Nerva, and I presume it's somewhere in the centre of the city. Naturally, I insisted that I had to scout it for myself.'

'And what about the timing?'

'They didn't say. Only that I would be contacted when all the other arrangements were in place.'

Beorthric hefted the pouch and I heard the chink of coins while I thought about what he had said. It appeared that the attack on Leo was part of a much wider plan.

'What did you make of that bad-tempered, balding old fellow, the one with the wart on his lip?' I asked.

'He always spoke to the others in Latin, and I know only a couple of phrases but I think he was demanding that the Pope was dealt with by October at latest.'

'And what was the response?'

'The man with the ruby ring gave him an answer but I couldn't understand what it was. I did notice that afterwards he looked to the old monk with the staff as if to check with him that he'd said the right thing.'

'What old monk with a staff?' I said, surprised. 'I didn't see anyone.'

'He shuffled in through a side door not long after you had left. I've a feeling that he turned up to the meeting earlier than he was meant to, and I was not meant to have seen him. He stood in the shadows, listening.'

'Shuffled?'

'He had difficulty in walking. Either he was very old and his joints were stiff, or his eyesight was nearly gone. It was too dark for me to see much more.'

I found myself wishing that I had been allowed to stay in the room to get a glimpse of this elderly priest. With a sudden lurch in my stomach I recalled Paul's tale of the last time that armed violence had been used to place someone on St Peter's Chair. The Duke of Nepi had successfully installed his own brother as Pope Constantine II and he had held the office until driven from the Lateran by an opposing faction. Though publicly humiliated and beaten up, Constantine had refused to admit any wrong doing, claiming that he was still the true Pope. Eventually, he had been sent away from Rome . . . to live in a monastery. Hurriedly, I did the calculation in my head. All this had taken place when Paul was a young official in the Lateran so it was certainly possible that

Constantine was still alive. Now this new plot also involved someone from Nepi – Maurus. Like a thunderbolt it struck me that the shuffling old monk listening in to the conspiracy to remove Leo might well be Constantine himself, former and false Pope.

Finally, I had something of solid value to report to Archbishop Arno, and the sooner I did so the better it would be.

# Chapter Sixteen

BEORTHRIC AND I got back to Rome four days later. Our escort, another silent Beneventan retainer, left us off at a lodging house in the Trastevere quarter. Its location had been carefully chosen. The Trastevere was across the river from the main city, an out-of-the-way area frequented by bargemen and itinerant workers. The lodging house was small and discreet and we were told to remain there without drawing attention to ourselves until Beorthric received further instructions. Our rent was paid in advance.

Naturally, as soon as I was sure that the house was not being watched, I slipped away to seek out Archbishop Arno. I was annoyed with myself that I had not worked out earlier that if the conspirators intended to dispose of Pope Leo, they had to have a successor ready to replace him. The day was blisteringly hot and when I got to the Lateran Palace shortly before noon it was to find that the half-dozen members of the Family of St Peter who were meant to be on guard had retreated into the shade of one of the porticoes. They were chatting amongst themselves and casually waved me through. Making my own way along the corridors I noted that many of the small writing rooms were empty and silent, the clerks and copyists finding an excuse to abandon their desks during the oppressive heat. Even the archbishop's secretary looked half-asleep when I walked in on him and asked to see Arno on an urgent matter. The secretary was one of the *scriniarii* on loan from the regular Lateran bureaucracy, and there was a patronizing look on his face as he informed me smugly that I would have to wait, probably for weeks. The archbishop as well as the Pope and the senior members of the papal administration had all left Rome and dispersed to various summer retreats in the countryside. They would only return when the weather was cooler.

That explained why the Family of St Peter were so slack.

I badly needed to discuss the events at the monastery with someone who could help me understand them. The obvious candidate was my friend Paul, so I set out on the long walk across the city towards his villa. The sun-scorched streets were almost deserted and the glare reflecting off the broken paving stones was blinding so I stopped at a stall on my way past the Colosseum and bought a broad-brimmed straw hat from the rogue selling keepsakes and tokens to foreign visitors. Naturally, I had to pay four times what the hat would have cost elsewhere. Along my route most of the ancient public fountains had long since broken down, their basins cracked and filled with rubbish. One or two still ran feebly, trickling into stone troughs. I stopped to splash water over my face and, taking off my shoes, cooled my feet in the run-off. I refrained from drinking the water as it was lukewarm and scummy. By the time I reached Paul's villa I was footsore and very, very thirsty.

Paul had taken refuge from the heat by retreating deep inside his villa. He was dozing on a couch beside the small pool in the centre of the interior courtyard that was fed from rainwater from the roof. All the doors and windows of the villa were open and a faint breath of a breeze was keeping the building cool.

'It's you, Sigwulf,' he said, heaving himself up with a grunt as he heard my footsteps on the mosaic floor. The square of light muslin which had covered his face fluttered to the ground. I had taken off my new hat and used it to fan my sweat-streaked face. 'You really must learn to respect the Roman heat,' he chided me.

'It was a lot hotter in Baghdad,' I told him, 'and I must talk to you about something that cannot wait.'

He sighed and bent down, looking for his sandals where he had left them under the couch. 'All in good time,' he wheezed as he slid his feet into them, adjusted his crumpled gown, then clapped his hands. A servant appeared from the depths of the building. 'A chair for my friend, cups and a flagon of water, as cold as you can find . . . add lemon juice and mint leaves,' he ordered.

The drink arrived in a porous clay jug that must have been stored underground for the surface was beaded with moisture. Greedily, I drank two cups of it while Paul fussed with a basin and towels brought by another servant. Only after he had washed his face and hands, mopped them dry, and insisted that I do the same from a basin of fresh water, did he finally look me at me expectantly.

'You've come to tell me that the Beneventans finally made contact,' he said, sitting up straight on the edge of the couch, his hands on his knees.

'Nine days ago. Beorthric and I were collected from the Schola and brought to a night-time meeting, but not in Benevento.'

'Where, then?' Paul's eyes were bright with interest.

'In a monastery three days' ride from Rome. We arrived in the evening, and left the next day after the meeting. So I don't know much about it.'

'It's not like you to leave your wits behind when travelling.'

I licked my lips to capture the lingering lemon taste. 'I'm sorry. But we saw no one while we were at the monastery except the Beneventan guards and men we were brought to meet. The whole thing was being kept very secret.'

My friend was patient. 'So what do you remember?'

'The monastery is built on the edge of a very steep hill. We entered up a long flight of steps and then across a broad courtyard. There was a bell tower and a fairly new basilica.'

Paul pulled a face. 'That's not much to go on.'

'This one had a disused oratory. It was where the meeting was held. There was a decaying fresco on the end wall, a crucifixion scene—'

Paul held up a hand to stop me. 'And an abbot shown kneeling in front of the Cross.'

I looked at him in astonishment. 'You know the place?'

'I would be a very ignorant priest if I didn't. You're talking about the monastery on Monte Cassino. It's where Saint Benedict spent most of his remaining years.'

'I couldn't decipher the writing on the label over the kneeling man's head, but it could have read Benedict.'

I had Paul's full attention by now, and had never seen him so enthralled. 'Did you see any of the monks?' he asked.

'Only one. A man of about fifty; he had a reddish face, many broken veins. He sat in at the meeting.'

'That will be Pelagius. He's the praepositus, second only to Abbot Gisulf. I met Pelagius seven or eight years ago when he came to Rome with a delegation from the monastery seeking confirmation of a land grant.'

'He wasn't entirely comfortable with the others.'

'And who were they?'

'Two men looked to be Beneventans. One was thin faced, with long hair. He ran the meeting. The other was shorter and burly with a grizzled beard. My guess is that they were officials sent by the prince.'

Paul shook his head. 'Can't place them. I haven't been to Benevento for a long time, and the courtiers change. Who else was there?'

'A much older man. He had just a few strands of white hair

and was bad tempered. Almost certainly from Rome. He had a large wart on his upper lip.'

'That's easy. He's Paschal of Alatri, a senator. He's a good friend of the current Duke of Nepo, and a senior officer in the city militia.'

Paul sat back on his couch and thought for a moment. 'So that's the four of them. What was discussed?'

'Hiring Beorthric to murder the Pope.'

Paul took my statement in his stride. 'No wonder Pelagius looked uncomfortable. Either his abbot doesn't know what is going on or Abbot Gisulf sent Pelagius to the meeting in his place, not wanting to appear directly involved. By the way, Gisulf is himself related to the Princes of Benevento.'

I shifted my shoulders under my shirt. The sweat had dried, and my skin was beginning to itch. 'They insist that Beorthric carries out the attack on his own.'

'They must be very confident in their planning.'

'Apparently he can get very close to the Pope when he is unguarded.'

'And where's that?'

'The Forum of Nerva was mentioned.'

I was astonished to see a broad smile light up Paul's face. 'I knew it!' he exclaimed. 'It's exactly where I would suggest.'

Chuckling to himself he heaved himself up from the couch, and called for a servant to bring him a hat and shoes. 'I want to show you something, Sigwulf,' he said happily. 'Now that it's not so hot outside, we should take a stroll.'

\*

Mystified, I followed Paul out of his villa and downhill across the rough ground of the disabitato. We were heading in the general direction of the great broken drum of the Colosseum, and everywhere the remains of ancient buildings rose up from the scrubland like the bones of battered shipwrecks. Scattered amongst them, seemingly at random, were farmhouses and cottages, some with roofs of mouldy thatch, in which the remaining citizens of this quarter chose to live. The still air carried the smell of their cooking fires, and I could hear the shouts and laughter of children as they played in derelict gardens or amongst the walls of tumbled-down villas. Where the land flattened out at the foot of the hill, the ground was poorly drained, marshy and soft, even on this dry summer day and we veered to the right, passing in front of an ancient colonnaded temple that had been converted into a Christian church. Here the roadway broadened out and brought us into an area crowded with even larger, decrepit buildings, their functions often unrecognizable. Paul identified them for me as former temples, theatres, public baths and courthouses.

'Not everything was quite as grand as these ruins suggest,' he said with a sweeping gesture that took in our surroundings. 'That boggy area we've just passed through was once the red-light district, and where we are standing was the street of the booksellers until an egotistical emperor sought to leave his mark by having it remodelled as the Forum of Nerva.'

I looked about me at what must once have been a remarkable public space. A pillared arcade, two storeys high, extended the full length of the forum on both sides, dominating what had once been a square filled with shopkeepers and their customers, idlers, traders and officials, visitors and citizens of the Republic. Some of the marble columns had lost their carved capitals, others had broken in half, and all were grimy and badly weathered. Yet the effect was still magnificent and made the houses, sheds and shops of more recent times look mean and shabby as if they were leeches stuck to the body of a worn-out host. I thought that in its own way the empty grandeur of the forum mirrored the hollowed-out wreckage of the Avar Ring with the charred uprights of its great palisade.

Paul had halted in front of a sturdy two-storey dwelling of stone and timber backing up against the base of the ancient arcade. It was the most substantial of the newly built structures. It had a covered walkway along the front, a small stable to one side, and a walled garden. I mistook the green roof as made of turf, then realized that it was copper sheeting, stripped from the ancient buildings.

'Who lives there?' I asked, for it was evident that this was the place Paul had brought me to see.

'A branch of the Signorelli family. The grandfather made a fortune in the cloth trade, and his successors are adding to it. Several of them serve on the city council.'

He saw my puzzled expression and his lips twitched in the beginnings of a grin.

'It is also the home of Caecilia Signorelli, a person of interest to the Holy Father.'

He waited for my reaction, his eyes alight with mischief.

It took me several moments to understand what he was implying. Then I recalled my first interview long ago in Archbishop Arno's office in Paderborn when Arno had told me of the letters of complaint he had received about Pope Leo's behaviour. Amongst the many accusations was that the Pope was an adulterer. I had made a joke of it, and been reprimanded.

'She's his mistress?' I blurted.

Paul chuckled. 'Why else would he visit her so often and so discreetly, and always after dark – to hear her confession?'

'Doesn't she have a husband? And what about the servants?'

Paul smirked. 'Paolo Signorelli is most accommodating. It's very advantageous to have such good connections with the Holy Father, and the servants are well trained.'

'But Leo must be aware of the risks he's taking.'

'Look about you, Sigwulf. How many people do you see? Half of Rome is deserted even in the daytime. Leo comes here after dark, with just one attendant who keeps watch outside. Long before dawn, he makes his way back to the Lateran.'

A thought struck me. 'If Leo is so discreet, how do you know about this arrangement?'

'It's been going on for years. Even when I was employed at the Lateran. One thing to be said for Pope Leo: he's a constant adulterer.'

Paul rubbed his hands with glee. He was delighted with himself. 'Can you imagine? The Pope is murdered while paying an adulterous visit to a respectable Roman matron. Even if he survives the thrust of the knife, his reputation will be destroyed. There's no chance that he'll be turned into a martyr.'

He clapped me on the shoulder. 'I suggest you lose no time in bringing Beorthric to the Forum of Nerva so that he can scout the scene of the intended crime. I'm sure the Beneventans and their allies are well aware of Leo's carnal appetite.'

Chuckling to himself he turned on his heel and went striding off. Too late, I remembered I had not told him everything about my visit to the monastery. Paul had been so eager to show me the Signorelli house that I had failed to ask him about the old priest whom I feared might be the former Pope, Constantine.

*

That night a powerful thunderstorm rumbled over the city. In the morning, when I brought Beorthric to the Forum of Nerva, wisps of steam were rising from ancient stone slabs still wet and gleaming from the torrential rain. It was going to be another scorching day.

'When is Archbishop Arno back in Rome?' he asked as we sauntered around the forum, pretending to look at the sights.

Like me, he was worried. It had been Paul's suggestion that we allow ourselves to be drawn into the plot against the Pope and to learn who was involved and what was planned. But how best to use that information was far from clear. Events were moving rather too quickly.

'I have no idea,' I admitted. 'When the weather cools down, I suppose.' I had already told the Saxon of my visit to Paul and he had not been the least surprised to hear that Pope Leo kept a mistress tucked away. It confirmed his opinion that Christians were hypocrites.

A large brown and white dog appeared from the stables attached to the Signorelli house and came forward to investigate us. Beorthric clicked his fingers. The dog advanced stiff-legged with suspicion and Beorthric spoke to it softly until it relaxed and came forward, tail wagging.

He leaned down and fondled it behind its ears. 'There's something not quite right about this whole business,' he murmured.

'As long as Pope Leo is out of Rome and safe from danger, we don't have to worry.'

'We're missing something important.'

A face appeared in the stable doorway, a groom checking to see where the dog had gone.

'What gives you that feeling?'

'Our landlord at the boarding house reports on us daily. He meets up with the neighbourhood watchman.'

'Probably providing information for that bad-tempered old fellow who interviewed us at the monastery.'

There was a sharp whistle from the stable, and the dog trotted away reluctantly.

Beorthric's voice kept its level tone. 'I've been thinking what to do if I'm called upon to earn my killer's fee before you've had a chance to speak with Arno.'

'Find an excuse to delay,' I suggested. 'Pretend a bout of fever. The shaking ague appears in Rome every summer and the Trastevere is worst affected.'

'That's too obvious. It'll be better if I come out to the forum, then postpone at the very last moment, saying that the conditions weren't quite right. That will gain us more time. But I want you to be here.'

He pointed with his chin to the garden beside the Signorelli house. 'You see where the wall juts out, just before the gate. That's a good place for you to hide.'

'But you've been instructed to act on your own. If the hostel is being closely watched, I can't leave the hostel in your company and come here with you,' I said.

He treated me to a grin of encouragement. 'I'm sure you'll think of a way of evading attention.'

We had walked the length of the forum and, rather than turn around and risk drawing attention to ourselves, I suggested that we continue in a loop that would eventually bring us across the bridges over the Tiber and back to our hostel.

I was still mulling over the problem that Beorthric had set me when we passed in front of another of the temples converted into a Christian basilica. The priest was descending the steps in front of the church after conducting a service.

'Excuse me, Father,' I called to him in Latin. He stopped and turned towards me.

'What is it?' he asked irritably. He was young for a priest, just in his twenties, with curly hair cut short, and wide-set innocent-looking eyes.

'I'm a pilgrim,' I said meekly, 'come to see the sights and pray at the tombs of the holy martyrs. I would dearly love to lay eyes on the Holy Father himself. It is something I would be able to tell my children.'

'Then you will have to be patient. His Holiness is not in Rome at this time,' he said, and he started to move away. He had no wish to linger in the blazing sun, chatting.

I put on a pleading tone. 'How long must I wait? I have to set out for my homeland soon, or the mountain passes will be blocked.'

'The date when the Pope returns is not known. Perhaps in another month or six weeks.'

'But that will be too late. Is there no chance that he will come back to the city before then?'

The priest began to sound exasperated at my persistent questioning. 'He may return briefly, to take part in the procession of St Symphorosa. You might be able to get a glimpse of him as he passes.'

'Forgive my ignorance, but I know nothing of St Symphorosa, nor the date of her feast.'

'It falls on the eighteenth day of July. The blessed saint was martyred by the emperor Hadrian for refusing to sacrifice to the pagan gods, so too were her seven sons. Their bodies were buried outside the city by the Via Tiburtina.'

'But you said the Holy Father will come to Rome for the procession.'

'Pope Stephen had the bones dug up and brought to the Church of St Angelo.'

'And where is that?'

'Right beside the fish market; you can't miss it,' he snapped. Without waiting to be thanked, he turned on his heel and marched off.

'What was all that about?' asked Beorthric. The conversation had been entirely in Latin.

'I've found out when the Pope may next be in Rome. On July the eighteenth there's a procession he usually leads. My guess is that he'll come into Rome the previous evening.'

Beorthric smirked. 'Sigwulf, I knew I could rely on you.'

\*

Two days before the Feast of St Symphorosa, I moved out of the lodging house in the Trastevere with my belongings, leaving Beorthric behind. I again rented a cubicle at the pilgrim hostel of Schola Saxonorum where rumour there was that Pope Leo would indeed be taking part in the procession to St Angelo Church. So on the evening of 17 July, I left the hostel's gate at sunset and made my way towards the Forum of Nerva. By the time I arrived it was dark and the forum was already deserted. Unnoticed, I took up my position in the little recess by the Signorelli garden wall that Beorthric had pointed out to me, and began my vigil.

In that part of Rome the working day finished early. No lights showed in the few houses within the ruins of the square. The only sounds were those that I associated with the countryside: the buzz of night insects and the occasional bleat of a goat from one of the lean-to sheds. Behind me, the bricks in the garden wall retained the heat of the sun and I leaned back comfortably, feeling the warmth through my shirt. The night sky was clear of clouds, and a three-quarters moon created deep shadows between the columns of the ancient arcade. At the far end of the forum was an ancient temple which, Paul had told me, had been dedicated to Minerva. The white marble of its facade glimmered in the moonlight. To its right, a monumental archway, locally known as 'Noah's Arch', according to the former Nomenculator, led to the Suburra district and its tenement buildings.

Very soon I was finding that I had to force myself to stay alert. I was all too aware that this could prove to be a long, tedious and ultimately useless watch, and there was no guarantee that Pope Leo would come to visit his mistress. There were occasional rustlings and scratchings in the garden behind me; rats, probably looking for food. Then one of them made me jump as it ran over my sandalled foot. From time to time I shifted my position, resisting the temptation to slide down and sit on the ground. I knew that if I did that, I would certainly nod off. The movement of the stars wheeling through the sky and measured against the forum's columns seemed to be desperately slow.

A low voice, from less than six feet away, startled me. Beorthric had approached from the other end of the forum, treading so softly that I had failed to hear him.

'It's to be tonight,' he murmured. 'I got word from the landlord at midday.'

He was wearing his scramseax at his belt.

I reached down and showed him the cudgel that I had propped against the wall at my feet. 'I was fearful of running into the watch and being questioned, so I brought this hidden under my shirt.'

'With luck it won't be needed,' he said, stepping in beside me. 'Now all we have to do is wait.'

An hour must have passed and then we heard faint sounds, coming from our left. After a few moments the noise stopped, followed by a long silence.

'What's going on?' I whispered.

'There's a small shed back there. If they're who I think they are, that's where they leave their horses,' he answered.

We waited some more, and then two men walked quietly past us. They were dressed in dark clothes and were keeping away from the open area of the forum. They passed no more than ten yards from where we waited in the shadows, and went towards the side door of the Signorelli house.

Beside me, Beorthric chuckled. 'Seems that our friends at the monastery are well informed.'

I wondered about the guard dog we had seen earlier in the week, but there was no barking. Either the dog had been removed or, more likely, it recognized the new arrivals.

Now one of the visitors was at the side door. We saw his hand raised as he scratched gently on the timber. The door opened at once, and both men vanished inside. There was no doubt in my mind that one of them was Pope Leo. The other would be a trusted attendant.

'More waiting,' muttered Beorthric. Suddenly he tapped me on the arm and pointed towards the distant archway that led into the Suburra. There was just time for me to detect a flicker of movement. Someone was entering the forum from that direction, though whoever it was had passed out of sight almost at once.

I kept staring in that direction until, several minutes later, I made out the dark figure of a man keeping in the shadows, stealthily making his way towards the Signorelli house. It was too far to establish anything but a general impression. When the man passed through a bar of moonlight between two of the columns, it was only possible to see that he was thin and very tall.

Beorthric put his mouth close to my ear. 'Our friend from the catacombs, I think.'

'What is he doing here?' I asked, my heart pounding. This was something unforeseen.

'Come to check up on how well I'm doing my job,' said Beorthric sourly.

Again the man vanished, this time disappearing into the dark shadow under the covered walkway that ran the full length of the front of the Signorelli house.

For what seemed like an age we waited. My attention was divided, sometimes checking the side door to the house, more often trying to squint into the gloom under the walkway, seeing nothing but dark shadows.

Then, about an hour before the very first flush of dawn, there was a movement at the side door. The two men emerged from the house and began to walk back along the route they had come. Something about the confident manner of the man on the right and the way his companion lagged deferentially a half-step behind him identified him as Leo.

They had not gone more than a few paces before Beorthric took me completely by surprise by suddenly bursting out from our hiding place.

He raced towards the two men. A heartbeat later I saw the tall dark figure leave the shelter of the covered walkway and also head towards the Pope, moving with long, quick strides.

I was still rooted to the spot as Beorthric barged into Leo, knocking him sideways so that he fell back against his companion and then to the ground.

Beorthric whirled round to face the approaching stranger who was now within an arm's length. He had not had time to draw his scramseax and I saw the glint of a blade in the stranger's grasp. Neither man uttered a sound as they closed and grappled. The tall thin stranger threw an arm around Beorthric's neck and pulled him close, as if hugging him. Beorthric reached up with both hands to grab his opponent's throat, then turned sideways and tried to hook a leg behind his enemy's knee. It was intended as a wrestler's throw, but was too late. The stranger used his free arm to drive home his knife.

I was running forward. As soon as I was close enough, I lashed out with my cudgel. It was a wild blow but by luck I struck the knifeman on the shoulder. It was enough to make him release his grasp of Beorthric and step back. I heard an angry hiss of frustration. Then the attacker spun on his heel and fled. I let him go. Beorthric had one hand pressed against his side and he was breathing through gritted teeth. 'See to the Pope,' he hissed.

The Pope had got back on his feet, so shocked that he was incapable of speech. His companion was making a distraught mewing sound.

'Get out!' I snarled at them fiercely. 'Get out!'

They stumbled away in the direction of the place where they had left their horses.

I turned back to Beorthric. He was unsteady on his feet, his lips drawn back in pain. The pale wash of moonlight made him look deathly white.

'We've got to get you away from here,' I said as I put my arm around his waist to keep him from falling. No one living in the forum had been alerted by the sounds of the brief scuffle or, if they had, they were too cautious to emerge from their homes.

'Where are you taking me?' he grunted.

'I think it's best we go to Paul's villa. Do you think you can make it?'

'Of course,' he gasped. 'I fear that bastard cut me badly. I always knew that something was wrong.'

'Save your breath,' I said, 'we've got a climb ahead of us.'

*

We finally limped through the gate into Paul's garden when the sun was already a hand's breadth above the horizon. Beorthric had been forced to stop and rest several times as we laboured up the slope of the Viminal Hill. He was leaning heavily on my shoulder as we negotiated the last steps into the villa and into the atrium. Each time his right foot trod on the mosaics, it left a bloody imprint. Paul, alerted by a worried-looking servant, brought us to a side room where a cot was hurriedly prepared so that Beorthric could be eased down on a mattress. A red stain had spread down his right side and soaked into his leggings.

'My head gardener's good at dealing with wounds,' Paul said to me. 'He keeps a stock of salves and bandages. I'd trust him to do as well as any doctor. He lives at the back of the house. I've already sent someone to fetch him.'

He looked down at Beorthric. The Saxon lay with his eyes closed and seemed to have fallen into a deep sleep. Paul jerked his head for me to follow him out of the room. Once we were out of Beorthric's hearing, he said to me, 'I hope that blade wasn't poisoned.'

'I've been wondering why Beorthric is in such a bad way.'

Paul grimaced. 'Let's pray that my man can save him. Tell me how it happened.'

My description of the night's events in the forum was interrupted by the arrival of a middle-aged stocky man who I remembered having seen talking with Paul one day on the porch of his house. He had a calm, placid air and a countryman's tan. In his large, capable-looking hands was a wicker basket filled with small clay pots and rolled bandages. He was accompanied by a young lad who seemed to be his son. Paul explained that Beorthric had been stabbed, perhaps with a poisoned dagger and required urgent attention. The gardener took in the details calmly, nodded, and without a word, went into the room where Beorthric lay.

Paul turned back to me. 'Go on with what you were telling me.'

I finished my story by adding, 'Beorthric always suspected that something was not quite right about the manner in which he had been hired.'

'With good reason,' said Paul grimly. 'That man with the dagger was there to tie up the loose ends. He was to kill Beorthric once he had despatched Pope Leo. Very convenient, finding a foreigner's corpse next to the murdered Pope.'

'And it would lay a false trail if it became known that Beorthric served in the Frankish army.'

Paul raised an eyebrow. 'Sigwulf, you're beginning to act like a true Roman in the devious ways your mind works.'

'There's more,' I said. 'Last night's attempt was intended to kill the Pope. Yet the attack on Leo in April last year was only meant to frighten him, to silence him, not kill him. That's what I reported to Archbishop Arno when I took the warrior flagon back to Paderborn before it vanished again.'

'And now you think you know the reason why things have changed, and someone, presumably the Beneventans and their friends, want to kill the Pope, not just frighten him?'

'Yes. Because they have selected someone else to place on St Peter's chair.'

Paul's lively, intelligent eyes searched my face. 'And you know who the intended occupant might be?'

'When Beorthric and I were in the monastery to meet with the Beneventans, there was an old man, a monk, there. He came into the room while Beorthric was receiving his instructions, and listened in.' I licked my lips, fearing that what I was about to say would sound far-fetched. 'He's party to the murder plot, even though he might be blind.'

Paul had always been quick-witted. Now he excelled himself. His expression went from curiosity to one of amazed understanding. 'Are you suggesting that this elderly monk is Constantine, the former pope who was driven from office? That the Beneventans are preparing to put him back in the Vatican?'

'I am. There's that link with the Lords of Nepi, and you yourself told me that Constantine was tucked away quietly in a monastery.'

Paul puffed out his cheeks in amazement. 'You should have told me before. Had I known, I would have warned you not to go near the Forum of Nerva and Caecilia Signorelli's house. I would have insisted you go straight to Archbishop Arno with your information.'

'Archbishop Arno was out of Rome,' I reminded him.

'With luck that's changed,' Paul snapped. Suddenly he was bustling with energy. 'If Leo came back into Rome, there's a chance that Archbishop Arno accompanied him and will be at the Lateran, even as we speak. As soon as Beorthric is comfortably settled, the two of us should go there.'

He paused and gave me a critical glance. 'Before then, I think you should change your clothes. I doubt that the Family of St Peter would let you in through the door.'

I looked down at my jerkin. One side was streaked with Beorthric's blood.

# Chapter Seventeen

IT WAS MY THIRD visit to the Lateran Palace, and this time the guard sergeant broke into a broad smile the moment he recognized the former Nomenculator. It was plain why Paul was popular. He remembered the names of all three of the sergeant's children and asked after them, paused to tease a particularly handsome soldier about his reputation as a lady's man and whether he had yet found himself a suitable wife, and gave a friendly wave to the others. Then we hurried inside.

'Everything seems very relaxed. Not what I'd have expected after an attempt to kill Leo,' I commented.

'Leo won't have told anyone. He doesn't want people wondering why he was visiting the Forum of Nerva late at night.'

We retraced the now familiar route down the long corridor to Arno's office, and I was relieved to find the archbishop's secretary alert and on duty in the antechamber, not half asleep like the last time. He, too, recognized Paul and confirmed that Archbishop Arno had returned to Rome the previous day and was now at work. The former Nomenculator could go straight in.

Archbishop Arno was seated at his desk with his back to the windows, their shutters closed to keep out the noonday glare. He had reverted to wearing the plain brown vestment that I had first seen in Paderborn, and the bars of sunlight slanting through the shutters made stripes of dark and light on the garment. Coupled with the fierce look he gave me as I entered with Paul, the archbishop reminded me of the fearsome striped cat-beasts, bigger than the royal leopards of Paderborn, that were caged in the Caliph's zoo in Baghdad.

Arno ignored my companion. 'Sigwulf, I trust you have a good excuse to burst in like this,' he growled.

'I have, my lord. Last night there was another attempt on the life of His Holiness.'

Arno rubbed his eyes with the heel of his thumb. He looked tired and I wondered if he had been catching up on paperwork all night. 'Tell me about it.'

Once again I recited what had happened, starting with the summons to visit the monastery at Monte·Cassino and ending with Leo's narrow escape from death.

When I finished, there was a long silence while Arno considered my report. Finally, he said, 'I need to discuss this with Leo himself.'

He was reaching towards the small handbell on his table, about to summon his secretary, when Paul interrupted. 'If I may make a suggestion . . .'

Arno glared at him, bushy eyebrows raised.

'His Holiness will be in denial about the whole affair,' Paul said smoothly. 'He'll have told his staff to make sure that he is unavailable.'

Arno gave a snort of frustration. 'They're experts in being obstructive. But we'll have to deal with them if we're to get to see Leo face to face. I've learned to my cost that trying to track anyone down in this labyrinth of a building is a waste of time.'

Paul looked towards the window. 'The procession and litany of St Symphorosa started at ten o'clock and it's now about an hour after midday. I believe I know exactly where to find him.'

'Then lead the way,' grunted Arno, heaving himself out of his chair and coming round the desk. Together the three of us marched out of his office and Arno told the hovering secretary that his assistance was not required. Then, led by Paul, we set off along a succession of corridors, through a kitchen area smelling of boiled cabbage, and up two short flights of stairs at the back of the building. On the upper floor we took a short cut through what appeared to be a library archive and then emerged into yet another corridor.

'Where are you taking us?' Arno asked.

'To the papal private chambers,' Paul answered. 'It's a back route that one remembers from forty years of service.'

Several times we met papal staff: scribes and notaries in shabby black gowns, small groups of junior officials standing together and gossiping near open windows, domestics of various sorts. All of them either ignored our little group or we swept by them before they could ask what we were doing in the papal quarters. The only time we might have been questioned was when we encountered a plump, officious-looking priest dressed in a fine planeta who made as if to stop us. 'Official business,' Paul said to him, brushing him aside.

'Who was that?' I asked in an undertone as we headed on.

'The assistant to the Vicedomus, the head of the household. I knew him as a pimply *cubicularius*, a creepy youngster. He's done well for himself.'

Finally we came to a set of imposing double doors at the end of a short passage. Without pausing, Paul pulled them open and we stepped into a large, high-ceilinged room with luxurious carpets spread on the floor and its walls hung with embroideries. In the centre of the room stood a single throne-like wooden chair with a high back. Distributed around the room were a number of large chests and cupboards while half a dozen free-standing wooden racks were hung with an array of garments that caught the light pouring in through glazed side windows. I saw damask, fur trimming, silk, fine wool, cloth of gold, laundered white linens.

We were in the palace robing chamber.

I had forgotten that, despite his night-time adventures, Leo still had to wear his most gorgeous regalia and officiate in the procession for St Symphorosa. Now that the ceremony was over, he had retired to remove the heavy garments and put on clothes more suitable for a summer's day.

He was standing by the chair, wearing nothing but white socks and a light undershirt. When I had seen him at Carolus's banquet, I had thought him unremarkable. Now, dressed in such simple garments, he was even less impressive. At first glance, he would have been taken for a petty shopkeeper getting ready for bed. He had turned to face us and was gaping in surprise, as were his attendants. There were at least a score of them. I presumed that they were underlings of the vestararius, the official responsible for the safekeeping of papal vestments and treasures. Most were *cubicularii* like the lad who had first escorted me into the palace. One still had the Pope's tall white processional hat in his hands and two others were holding up a splendid damask cloak, edged with bands of cloth of gold, so that it could be inspected for damage or dirt by the pot-bellied, bearded man I took to be the vestararius himself. The other attendants were standing around idly and looking on. One of them, a much older man and soberly dressed, caught my eye. He was close to Leo and slightly to one side. I was fairly sure that he was the same man who had escorted Leo on his visit to Caecilia Signorelli. More important, his nose had once been broken, leaving it slightly off-true. Months earlier, I had sat beside him at a meal in an Alpine monastery, then later across the table at a banquet in Paderborn when he had recognized the Avar flagon. His house was where Paul and I had found the hidden items from the Avar Hoard. He was the papal chamberlain – Albinus.

Arno took advantage of his moment of surprise. 'Forgive the intrusion, Your Holiness,' he announced loudly enough for everyone to hear. 'I felt I should come to make sure of your well-being.'

With a visible effort, Leo recovered from his initial shock. He drew himself up straight and assumed an air of mild outrage, though I noticed that his eyes had darted nervously around the room. 'I thank you for your concern, Archbishop Arno, though you should be aware that these are my private apartments.'

'I thought that after last night . . .' said Arno, deliberately not completing his sentence and allowing his voice to trail away so that only those standing close to us could hear him.

If Leo was planning to deliver a rebuke, it died on his lips. He went pale and, after a pause of several heartbeats, he addressed the vestararius. 'Leave us. The disrobing can be completed later. I'll send for you.'

The vestararius responded with a slight nod that did little to hide his look of disapproval mingled with curiosity. He set aside the hem of the papal cloak he had been examining, then began to usher his staff from the room, fussing around while making sure that they did not carry with them any items of value. Albinus the chamberlain, I noticed, remained where he was, and without consulting Leo. Finally, when all the other staff had left the chamber and the doors had been closed behind them, Leo turned to Arno and demanded, 'Pray, tell me what is this all about?'

'I think you know, Your Holiness,' Arno told him bluntly. 'Your personal safety is of great concern to King Carolus.'

'Do you serve the King or the Church?' The slight quaver in his voice marred Leo's attempt to remind the archbishop that he was in the presence of his superior.

'I serve both. Their interests are the same,' answered Arno bluntly.

Standing off to one side, Albinus was staring at me. I knew that he had recognized me.

'Paul, what are you doing here?' Leo enquired, treating the former Nomenculator to a sour glance.

'I am here in a private capacity, merely to assist,' Paul answered. 'I have known Sigwulf for some years.'

Leo looked in my direction and was about to ask me a question when Albinus stepped in closer to him and whispered in his ear. Leo listened intently, then shot me a mistrustful glance. Albinus must have told him enough to make me out as some sort of threat. No doubt the chamberlain had made the association between all three of our meetings, first in the Alpine monastery, then at the banquet in Paderborn and most recently in the Forum of Nerva.

Archbishop Arno broke the awkward silence. 'Your Holiness, please accept my apologies for this unannounced interruption. I shall report to King Carolus that you are unharmed.'

And with that he bowed, turned on his heel, and led us out of the robing chamber and back into the corridor where a cluster of curious *cubicularii* were gathered, wondering what had been going on inside, and probably trying to listen at the door.

The encounter with Leo had taken less than three or four minutes and as we walked back the way we had come, I realized that the archbishop had failed to mentioned any details about the attempt to kill Leo outside the house of his mistress.

'What was all that about?' I asked Paul after Arno had dismissed us at the door to his office, leaving us to find our way back to Paul's villa.

'Giving Leo a warning,' Paul replied. 'I thought it went rather well.'

'But shouldn't Leo be told who his enemies are, so that he can take precautions for his own safety?'

Paul laid a finger against his bulbous nose and gave me a conspiratorial wink. 'As far as Arno is concerned, it is enough to let Leo know that he's well aware of the Pope's visit to his mistress.'

Nor would he speak any further on the subject. As we strolled quietly across the city and back towards his villa, I wondered just how much the former Nomenculator knew but was not prepared to reveal. The presence of Albinus the chamberlain in the robing chamber had left me confused. I was in no doubt that sixteen months earlier Albinus had been involved in, or at least warned about, the first attack on Leo, yet I had a distinct impression that the chamberlain had not anticipated last night's attempt to murder the Pope in the Forum of Nerva. I was now even more puzzled as to whether there could be any connection between the recent turn of events and our discovery of the warrior flagon hidden in the chamberlain's house.

I was still attempting, and failing, to make sense of these new developments when we arrived back at Paul's villa to be told that Beorthric was awake and in great pain. Paul's gardener confirmed that the dagger blade had been poisoned. He had packed the wound with wadding soaked in a concoction of herbal remedies, but he did not know what type of poison had been used and could do no more than hope that he had applied an effective antidote. The big Saxon was sweating and groaning on his mattress and mumbling incoherently.

'You realize that both Beorthric and I are now targets,' I warned Paul as we went to his study. 'Whoever is behind the plan to murder the Pope will want to silence us as witnesses to what happened. The plotters will be looking for Beorthric, in particular, and they won't take the risk that he has shared his information with me.'

'Then you must both stay here with me until Beorthric recovers,' Paul replied without a moment's hesitation. 'My staff are discreet and I will give instructions that they don't speak about your presence. I'll also send word to Archbishop Arno so that he knows where to find you when he needs you.'

'What about the chamberlain, Albinus? He saw you with us this morning. If he's involved in this latest plot against Leo, he'll guess where we are staying.'

'That's a risk I'm prepared to take,' said Paul. 'As I once told you, I have my own reasons for stirring up trouble in the Lateran and muddying the waters for the bureaucrats up there. I confess that today it was a real pleasure to watch Archbishop Arno making Leo squirm.'

\*

It was six weeks later that events took an unexpected direction. By then Beorthric's convalescence had progressed to the point that he could shuffle very slowly around the garden, using a walking stick to steady himself, and I was less worried that the men who had tried to murder the Pope would trace us to Paul's villa. Paul had been keeping us up to date with all the latest gossip from his visits to friends and contacts in the city: Leo was now being accused of land speculation and blasphemy as well as the theft of Church property and simony. Someone had even started a wild rumour that Leo was in negotiations with the Byzantine Greeks to form a united front against the Roman nobility. As a result, the beleaguered pope was losing popularity with every passing week. In this whispering campaign against Leo I detected the hand of the Beneventans and their Roman allies. It seemed that they were further undermining Leo's reputation before they made their move to replace him.

Then, one evening at the end of August, Paul brought momentous news.

'Carolus is coming to Rome,' he announced as he joined Beorthric and me on the porch overlooking the garden. Beorthric had over-exerted himself that afternoon and was lying down on a day bed to rest, wrapped in a light blanket.

'When's the king due to arrive?' I asked.

'Sometime in late November or early December. He wishes to celebrate Christ's Mass in St Peter's Basilica, with his family. He made the announcement at the great assembly of the Franks earlier this month. The news came this morning by official courier.'

Then it had to be true. Each summer Carolus summoned all his vassals to an enormous field camp at which he hosted a succession of banquets, watched army exercises and announced his plans for the coming year.

'There is more,' said Paul, giving me a sharp look. 'Carolus has made it known that he's distressed to hear that the Church is in such turmoil. He wishes to heal its wounds.'

'And that's going to involve Archbishop Arno?' I guessed.

Paul nodded. 'Arno is chairing a tribunal to examine the allegations being made against Leo and will report to Carolus when he gets here.'

'Will his investigation include the circumstances of the attack made on Leo in April last year?'

'My contacts in the Lateran tell me that our suspects, Campulus and Paschal, are on the point of admitting that they were involved.'

His face was so carefully blank that I could not resist saying, 'Were they confronted with evidence gathered by your very persuasive investigator Theodore?'

Paul ignored my question. 'I expect that both men will be sent into exile.'

'What about Albinus the chamberlain?'

'Albinus is a rather special case.' Paul was choosing his words with great care. 'There is no evidence against Albinus except—'

'. . . The warrior flagon that Beorthric and I took such trouble to obtain,' I interrupted, finishing for him.

He spread his hands wide to indicate that the matter was beyond his control. 'So I expect you may be called to appear before the archbishop and his tribunal. They meet in the triclinium, that splendid new banqueting hall that Leo has added at the side of the Lateran Palace.'

*

Sure enough, a messenger arrived within the week bringing a summons from Archbishop Arno: Beorthric and I were to present ourselves at the entrance to the east wing of the Lateran, one hour after dawn the following morning. Beorthric was still too sick to attend, so while it was still dark I set off without him, though accompanied by Theodore; Paul had arranged for him to act as my bodyguard in case I ran into trouble on the way. An usher was waiting for me in front of the triclinium's double doors and, while Theodore was left outside, he escorted me through the grandiose interior resplendent with painted ceiling, triple apse, marble and porphyry, mosaics and bright new frescoes. At the furthest end, he turned through a low archway and let me into a much smaller and unfinished side chamber, a functional room with recently whitewashed walls, windows not yet glazed and a floor of raw new terracotta tiles. A faint smell of fresh plaster hung in the air, and the dawn chill lingered. I wondered if the summer warmth ever penetrated this far.

Paul had told me that the leading members of the investigating tribunal were two archbishops, one of them being Arno, plus the Duke of Spoleto, who was regarded as a reliable vassal of

Carolus. So I was surprised to find Arno alone, without even a secretary to take notes. He was seated behind a long table on which lay writing implements and a thin pile of documents. As his paperweight he was using the only exotic item in the room – the polished and gleaming warrior flagon.

The usher withdrew, closing the door behind him. An empty chair with heavily carved arms was placed directly across from Arno but he merely pointed a thick finger towards the corner of the room behind me and immediately to my left. 'Stand over there, Sigwulf,' he ordered, 'and stay silent.' He did not enquire after Beorthric.

Nearly half an hour must have passed while Arno ignored me as he read through various documents and occasionally drafted a note. I might as well have not existed and I found my attention wandering from the archbishop's scratching stylus, to the top of his grizzled head as he bent over his work, to a patch of sunlight slowly moving across the squares of the tiled floor, to a small, brown insect crawling along the edge of one of the windows.

Always my gaze returned to the warrior flagon.

Eventually, there was a soft knock on the door and Arno called out 'Enter!' It opened inwards towards me so that I could not see who was coming into the room. When it was pulled shut, presumably by an usher from outside, the newcomer was already well into the room, his back to me. It was Albinus the chamberlain. Arno had got to his feet and indicated that his visitor was to take the empty chair facing him. Albinus was completely unaware of my presence no more than two or three yards behind him. I realized that this was exactly what Archbishop Arno had intended. I found myself taking shallow breaths and keeping very still.

I regretted that I was not standing where I would have seen the chamberlain's expression as he laid eyes on the warrior flagon on the table directly in front of him. What I did observe was a very slight hesitation in his gliding step, a momentary flicker of uncertainty before he moved forward again. It was his only reaction. His hands had been tucked into the sleeves of his gown when he entered, his arms folded across his chest. As he took his place on the chair, I watched the hand closest to me as he placed it on the arm of the chair. It was absolutely steady.

'This interview is strictly informal and should not take long,' began Arno briskly. He discarded any attempt at politeness. 'His Majesty King Carolus has asked me to look into allegations of improper behaviour made against Pope Leo. Doubtless they have also come to your notice.'

'My duties keep me too busy to be listening to such calumnies,' murmured the chamberlain. His voice was as I remembered: flat, toneless and unemotional. He might as well have been a low-ranking clerk in some office reading off a page.

Arno wasted no time in getting to the heart of the matter, 'I'm interested in learning if there is any truth in the accusations levelled against His Holiness and contained in certain letters sent to His Majesty's councillors.' At this point the archbishop lifted the gold flagon and set it to one side so that he could take the top page from the sheaf of documents in front of him. 'Those letters were written in Rome prior to the unfortunate incident when Pope Leo was attacked in the street.'

Albinus sat still, utterly composed. 'Those complaints were discussed at the time of His Holiness's visit to King Carolus soon after the attack. They were set aside.'

'Since then you have no fresh thoughts on these complaints?'

The chamberlain gave an obsequious bob of his head that somehow also managed to be subtly disrespectful. 'All I have to add is my gratitude for the generous hospitality shown to us during our stay in Paderborn.'

If Arno was frustrated by the chamberlain's glib evasion, he did not let it show. He shifted his position and leaned back as if to make himself more comfortable. 'I must advise you, in confidence, that some of those letters of complaint were written by two of your very senior colleagues, Sacellarius Paschal and Arcarius Campulus. They are now prepared to admit that they were aware that His Holiness would be assaulted on that day.'

'How truly regrettable –' Albinus admitted, then he paused – 'if it is true.'

'Certainly it is true.' Arno allowed a harsher tone to creep into his voice now. 'What I now ask you is whether, from your personal knowledge, there was any justification whatsoever for those allegations of misconduct.'

The chamberlain sounded very sure of himself. 'They have no basis in fact. Nor, as you will note, does my name appear amongst those who wrote letters of complaint.'

'So you recognize the authority vested in Pope Leo?'

'I have always served His Holiness faithfully, and believe him to be blameless.'

'And you are prepared to sign an affidavit to that effect?'

'I am.' Albinus's voice was firm and clear.

'I have a document ready,' said Arno. He selected a paper that he had drafted earlier, and slid it across the table towards the chamberlain, together with a stylus and ink.

Albinus leaned forward in his chair and was about to pick up the stylus when he caught sight of me out of the corner of his eye. His head jerked round, his eyes narrowed and, for one instant, I saw a look of pure venom as he realized that I had been standing there throughout his conversation.

'Sigwulf is here as a witness to your declaration. He is a trusted and loyal servant of His Majesty,' Arno told him.

For the first time Albinus's hand trembled, but only very

slightly, as he reached for the stylus. I wondered if it was from anger or shock or, possibly, relief that the archbishop had not questioned him about the flagon. He signed his name and placed the stylus down on the table. 'If that is all, my Lord Bishop?' he said, his voice icy. 'I'm already overdue for my next meeting. The cellerarius wishes to discuss the ongoing refurbishment of the papal residence.'

'Yes, that is all,' said Arno flatly.

The chamberlain rose to his feet and headed towards the door and I was again raked with a hostile stare. This time it was of cold, menacing calculation.

'Sigwulf, you are to stay in Rome, pending His Majesty's arrival, when I want you to be on hand in case there are last-minute complications,' the archbishop told me as the door closed behind the chamberlain. He picked up the flagon. 'I'll see that this is returned to where it rightly belongs, to Carolus's treasury.'

I was dumbfounded. The brief meeting between Arno and Albinus had turned out exactly the opposite of what I had antici-pated. I had expected Arno to confront Albinus, accuse him of stealing Church property, and then to follow up by cross-examining the chamberlain about the extent of Pope Leo's corruption. But not a word had been said about Albinus's theft of valuables from the papal coffers. Instead, Archbishop Arno had only obtained Albinus's assurance that Leo was innocent of any charges of misbehaviour. That, as Arno and I both knew, was an outright lie.

\*

'The chamberlain's sworn statement is worthless,' I grumbled to Paul as I told him what had taken place. Theodore had escorted me back to the Viminal Hill by a route different to the one we had used earlier in the day, saying it was for my safety. With the hostile look from the papal chamberlain fresh in my mind, I did not object.

'There you're wrong,' said the former Nomenculator. 'It keeps Albinus under control for the next few months.'

I must have looked baffled because Paul laid a hand on my arm and said in a serious tone, 'Think about it, Sigwulf: Campulus and Paschal hold two of the most senior posts in the Lateran, heads of their departments. When they confess in public that they knew Leo was about to be attacked while on his way to celebrate the Litany, they will be disgraced. That leaves the chamberlain as the obvious Lateran candidate to succeed Leo if he is deposed.'

'You think Albinus has ambitions to become Pope himself?'

'If he does, the document he signed for Archbishop Arno makes it impossible for him to be involved in any scheme to remove Leo. He can scarcely plot against someone he swears is so virtuous.'

'And what about the warrior flagon? Why didn't Arno tackle Albinus directly and accuse him of stealing it?'

'Because your archbishop is a master of hidden menace. He was letting Albinus know that he can be accused of theft at any time of the archbishop's choosing.'

'That's blackmail.'

Paul shrugged dismissively. 'I prefer to describe it as good politics. When you know a person's weakness, it is wise to use that knowledge sparingly and not squander its effectiveness.'

His remark confirmed what I had begun to suspect since our visit to the robing chamber. 'And that's also why Arno never mentioned Caecilia Signorelli's name when we called on Leo? It's all about putting pressure on other people, the quiet threat.'

Paul patted me on the shoulder. 'Bravo, Sigwulf. Without your help Arno would never have been able to manoeuvre Leo, and now Albinus, into the position where he now has them.'

His compliment failed to lift my spirits. I thought of Beorthric, still struggling to throw off the effects of poison, and of the miserable winter I had spent as a prisoner of the Avars. The two of us had paid a high price so that Arno could pull the strings that controlled what went on behind the scenes in St Peter's and the Lateran. Also, I was left with a vague feeling of unease. I recalled the clandestine night-time meeting in the monastery at Cassino with the Beneventans and their aristocratic Roman ally and, hovering in the background, the elderly monk that Beorthric had seen. I had my doubts that Arno's reach extended that far or was enough to thwart whatever plot was being hatched there. Finally, there was no word about the man with the fur hat who had knifed Beorthric. He was still on the loose and unidentified.

# Chapter Eighteen

SUMMER TURNED INTO autumn and, worryingly, Beorthric began to suffer random bouts of dizziness and there was a continuing numbness on his left side where he had been stabbed. The shorter days and colder weather obliged him to spend more time indoors and he became morose and tetchy. To escape his bad humour, I took the risk of making brief excursions into the city, choosing times when it was raining so that I could wander the streets wearing a workman's horsehair cape with the hood pulled up to conceal my features.

In taverns and shops and on street corners I eavesdropped on the changing mood of the ordinary citizens of Rome. Two topics dominated their conversations: Pope Leo's future and the impending visit of King Carolus. Leo's reputation was in the balance. People talked openly about his lax behaviour. They grumbled that he was bringing the Church into disrepute. Harsh words were spoken, threats that if the Church did not set its own house in order, then lay people would take matters into their own hands. The more cautious responded that Leo should be given a chance to mend his ways because Rome could not afford another dispute over his replacement that might lead to open fighting in the streets, as had happened with false Pope Constantine.

Invariably, the conversation then turned to the role that King Carolus might play in resolving the situation. There were those who said that Carolus had a legal right and a duty to intervene because he was *Patricius Romanorum*, a Patrician of the Romans, a title bestowed on him by Pope Stephen II. Others objected scornfully that the title meant nothing. Carolus had been barely into his teens at the time, and both his father and Carloman, his three-year-old younger brother, had been similarly honoured. A Frankish king had no business meddling in the affairs of Rome. The arguments went back and forth, and grew so heated that, with each passing week, the tension grew until, as reports came in of Carolus's progress towards us by way of Ravenna and Ancona, it felt as if a thunder cloud was approaching and about to burst.

The Feast of St Chrysogonus, 24 November, was set as the day that Carolus and his entourage would make their grand entry into the city, and by then all of Rome was on edge. It dawned with a clear sky and no wind, yet it was cold enough for me to see my breath on the air as I mingled with the immense throng that had clustered at the Flaminian Gate since first light. The atmosphere was a combination of awe, excitement and anticipation mixed with some unease at not knowing how the king and his small army of followers would behave. Pope Leo had left the city the previous evening to greet the king at the small town of Nomentum some twelve miles outside the walls, and the guilds, churches and ordinary people had been preparing their reception for months. Drawn up on foot to greet the king were robed senators, noblemen and senior *palatini*. With them in the front rank stood the representatives of the four major foreign colonies – the Franks, Frisians, English and Lombards – holding up the insignia of their guilds. Behind them were massed the officers and men of the city militia. Jostling in the background were tradesmen and apprentices.

Carolus's entourage could be seen approaching with outriders and heralds. The royal carriages in the centre of the column shone with gold leaf and bright paint. Even the baggage carts rolled on gilded wheels. A stage had been built on one of them where an attendant stood holding up a white satin cushion on which rested the keys to the shrine of St Peter. Next to him a city official brandished a flagstaff with the banner of the city. Leo had presented both the keys and the flag to the king as an act of homage. The royal escort of armoured cavalry were mounted on big-boned Frankish horses, their coats brushed and gleaming and with saddles and bridles of dyed, embossed leather. The cold, crisp weather gave the horsemen an opportunity to flaunt their magnificent furs and gorgeous winter riding costumes, and it took more than an hour for the cavalcade to filter in through the city gate. It was a triumphal procession worthy of a barbarian potentate rather than a Christian king because Carolus had brought along his current concubine, Regina – his fourth wife, Luitgard, had died the previous June – as well as a brood of illegitimate offspring born to his string of mistresses. The noise from the onlookers was stupefying – a hubbub of shouts, trumpet calls, hymn singing and cheering. Rome hadn't seen anything like it in generations.

The newcomers spilled into the city, spreading out through various homes and lodgings that had been prepared for them. Carolus and his family stayed near St Peter's Basilica. Frankish barons took up temporary residence in the houses of leading Roman nobility while the bookkeepers and notaries that always accompanied the king on his travels moved into a row of offices in the Lateran which Archbishop Arno had already requisitioned for them. I retreated back to Paul's villa on the Viminal Hill to bide my time until I heard from Archbishop Arno that he no longer needed me. Then I planned to report to the royal household, ask if a role could be found for the sickly Beorthric and resume my duties as a *miles*, a courtier-soldier.

While I waited, Paul kept me informed of what was going on.

A week after his arrival, Carolus held a grand meeting of the clergy, nobles and leading citizens in the great basilica of St Peter. The king presided, dressed in the toga and gown of a *Patricius Romanorum*, and not his usual Frankish costume with its leggings, breeches, tunic and a short cloak. It was a signal of his intentions. He announced to the assembly that he had come to Rome to restore good order and discipline in the Church and to punish the outrage committed on its Head. Seated next to him, Leo managed to look fair-minded and self-righteous at the same time. According to Paul, who attended that day and was watching him closely, the Pope's expression quickly changed when Carolus went on to say that he also proposed to hold an inquiry at which he and a panel of experts would hear the complaints of those who accused the Pope of impious behaviour.

'That must have shaken Leo,' I commented.

'He went pale and stared straight ahead,' Paul said. 'He has no idea what is planned.'

'And you do?'

He grinned. 'I can guess. It's what Archbishop Arno has been preparing all these weeks. The inquiry should be well worth attending and I've arranged for both of us to be watching from the side-lines.'

Two days later, the friendly guard sergeant at the Lateran smuggled us up onto a balcony overlooking the great chamber of the triclinium where the tribunal of inquiry was going to sit. We had to be in our places very early, long before the clergy assembled, and, to pass the time, I puzzled over a large mosaic on the curved roof of the main apse. It was a work-in-progress and the artist had only got as far as sketching in the outline of the scene with charcoal on the smooth plaster. It was a familiar arrangement with a seated man in the centre, shown oversize, draped in a gown and with the circle of a nimbus around his head. Two smaller figures knelt on either side, facing him as each received a gift. It reminded me of the damaged fresco that I had seen in the abandoned chapel at Monte Cassino, but this triclinium scene carried a different message. Two crossed keys above the central figure signified that he was St Peter. His two companions were identified by the gifts they were receiving. One gift was the pallium, the long white woollen band decorated with crosses that the Pope wore as his badge of office. The other man was receiving a crown.

I had succeeded in solving what the finished picture would represent when Paul leaned across to whisper. 'Leo must be disappointed that the mosaic's not ready for Carolus to see.'

'If that's St Peter appointing Leo as Pope and granting Carolus the crown, Leo's being over-confident as well as rash. He doesn't know the outcome of this inquiry. Maybe his accusers will present a good case against him.'

Paul merely chuckled.

Below us the audience had begun to arrive, and Paul kept up a running commentary identifying those whom he recognized. Apart from a handful of Frankish courtiers, everyone permitted to attend was a churchman of one sort or another. Many were staff from the palatium, the papal household, others were titular priests and canons and monks working within the papal administration. There were also deacons and sub-deacons from the seven ecclesiastical regions of the city, dispensatores and patres from the xenodochia, the charities run by the Church for the sick and needy, and an abbot or two. The most senior found seats on two rows of benches positioned in front of the platform on which the king and his tribunal would preside. Everyone else had to stand.

I peeked cautiously over the rail in front of our balcony and ran my eye over the congregation of black-clad figures. Amongst those who had seats, I recognized Albinus on the front bench and, for a moment, I believed that I saw the grey beard of Pelagius, the praepositus from Monte Cassino. But when he turned round to speak to someone on the bench behind him, I realized that I was mistaken.

'Where are all the others?' I asked Paul quietly. 'I thought there would be more. This can't be all the churchmen in Rome.'

'A lot of them are staying away,' he explained. 'Down there are the priests who belong to Leo's faction. The opposition are frightened to show their faces.'

After a while the Lateran attendants closed the great outer double doors, signifying that the hearing was about to begin. A side door opened, and the congregation hushed as the members of the tribunal filed in and took their places on the table looking down into the room. All of a sudden I was reminded of the very similar scene at the banquet in Paderborn when Carolus had hosted Leo and his delegation at his high table on the evening when the warrior flagon had been lost and I had been waylaid and beaten up. Once again, the king sat in the centre. On this occasion he had chosen to dress warmly as a Frankish monarch, bareheaded but wearing a long cloak of lustrous marten skins with a wide ermine collar. On his right was Leo in the place of honour; to his left was the Duke of Spoleto. Three bishops – Franks, to judge by their complexions – completed the panel together with Archbishop Arno, who sat slightly apart from the others and looked on, stone-faced. He was, I presumed, to act as convenor.

A royal herald stepped forward and called for silence, though this was unnecessary as the hall was already silent with a sense of uneasy anticipation. Without moving from his seat, the king spoke up. As always, his voice was unexpectedly high-pitched and thin and it did not carry well. Several of the more elderly priests in the crowd had to raise their hands and cup their ears to hear what he was saying. He announced that the sacellarius Paschal and the arcarius Campulus had both pleaded guilty to the charge that they had helped to organize the disgraceful attack on the supreme pontiff, and it was his duty to pronounce punishment. Carolus paused, and there was a general intake of breath as his listeners waited to hear what he would say next.

'I therefore sentence both men to death.'

Carolus let the words linger. There was a low murmur from his audience, a rustling of clerical gowns as men shifted nervously. The sentence of execution, of two senior *palatini*, had come as a shock.

The silence lengthened, broken only a sudden loud sneeze from someone in the hall, probably troubled by the plaster dust. I scanned the crowd, trying to pick out individual reactions, wondering if anyone else had been involved in the attack on Leo, and who might now be in fear of discovery and punishment.

At that moment Leo rose to his feet. He coughed to clear his throat as well as to draw attention to himself, turned and bowed towards Carolus, then addressed the crowd.

'I ask His Majesty to show clemency,' he called out. 'I forgive these two men for their crime, and I request that they be sent into exile, never to return and trouble this city again.'

He turned back to face Carolus, who nodded gravely in response.

'Pure theatre,' whispered Paul into my ear as Leo resumed his seat.

Now it was Arno's turn. All eyes turned in his direction as he got to his feet and stood glaring down at the congregation from under his bushy eyebrows. More than ever, he looked like a labourer, truculent and burly, who had just arrived from a building site.

'It is the wish of His Majesty that anyone who bears witness against His Holiness should now state their case,' he said in a rough, almost threatening voice.

Again there was a long silence in the room. A few priests and monks cast worried glances at one another, anxiety showing on their faces as they waited for anyone to speak up. Most looked straight ahead, fearing to attract the archbishop's searching gaze that swept over them. Arno waited for a full minute, and then he repeated the appeal: anyone who had reason for complaint against Leo was to speak up, and would be heard by the tribunal.

This time a quavering, elderly voice came from somewhere deep in the centre of the assembly. It cut through the silence, and a sudden nervous shiver ran through the crowd. But it was only an ancient abbot so hard of hearing that he was asking his neighbour what had been said, unaware that his own voice was raised.

Arno was looking down, straight at Albinus seated on the bench below him.

'Chamberlain, are you aware whether anyone within the palatium wishes to bear witness against His Holiness?'

Albinus stood. There was a general shuffling as those immediately behind him moved back, allowing open space so that others in the crowd could see him better. A stranger would have thought that the chamberlain was somehow unwelcome in the gathering, a possible plaintiff.

'My Lord Archbishop,' Albinus declared in his emotionless, flat voice, 'I speak for my colleagues and for myself when I say that we have no complaints against His Holiness. Nor, I believe, does anyone who is here assembled.'

Arno scowled out over the massed congregation. 'Does this express the view of all those who have gathered here?' he demanded.

'It does,' came back the mumbled response, hesitant at first from a few voices, then repeated more firmly and loudly as the agreement spread throughout the chamber. Many in the crowd crossed themselves as if to confirm their pledge.

Arno sat down. When it seemed that no other member of the tribunal was due to speak, all tension in the chamber began to drain away. A number of priests and monks in the audience turned to one another and began to exchange their comments on what they had just witnessed.

Then Carolus startled them. He raised a hand and the chatter stilled.

'It is not my place to pronounce judgement on Christ's vicar on earth. His power comes from the Lord,' he said. 'I look forward to celebrating Christ's Mass in the great basilica of St Peter, to give thanks and to see you all on that joyous occasion.'

With those words, Carolus got to his feet, and left by the same side entrance, walking from the dais side by side with Pope Leo. Paul and I watched the other members of the tribunal leave the hall, Arno bringing up the rear, and the former Nomenculator muttered softly, 'Very astute. If fresh evidence emerges later that proves Leo is unworthy of his office, then no one can say that Carolus had pronounced him innocent.'

Below us there was a general movement as the audience began to file out of the triclinium. I moved with Paul further back into the balcony, in case someone looked up and caught sight of us.

'What about the Beneventans?' I asked, looking across at the unfinished mosaic on the ceiling opposite.

He waved a hand dismissively. 'Even if that blind monk really is Constantine, they won't dare move against Leo now that they see he has Carolus's support. Neither the Duke of Benevento nor the Roman nobles would risk a direct confrontation with the King of the Franks. That would be madness.'

But Paul had not been at Monte Cassino, I thought to myself, and seen how purposeful had been the plotters who met under cover of darkness. They were neither mad nor risk-takers; they were ruthless and determined. They would not easily be deflected from what they wanted to achieve. Once again, I regretted that I had not yet told Archbishop Arno what Beorthric and I had witnessed that night in the derelict chapel and I feared the consequences.

\*

'Christians lie as they breathe,' had been Beorthric's response when I reported that the assembly of churchmen had found no fault with Leo as Pope. For the Saxon mercenary the only way to ensure Leo's survival was to recruit a company of professional papal guards and replace the useless amateurs of the Family of St Peter. A well-trained papal guard would shield the Pope from men with daggers and be ready to intervene if the Beneventans attempted an uprising in the streets.

He brought up the subject yet again a few weeks later, as we shared a light breakfast of hot milk and bread with Paul in his library. The servants had lit a fire to keep out the winter dampness and chill, and it was the morning of what was much anticipated as the climax of Carolus's visit: Christmas Day, when he and his family would attend a magnificent service led by Leo in the great basilica of St Peter's.

'Nobody is going to try to kill or depose Leo while Carolus is in Rome,' I assured him. Beorthric snorted with disbelief. 'The greatest risk is when people think they're safe. That's when they lower their guard.'

'So what do you think is the risk now?' asked Paul. He had risen from the table and gone to stand where he could see his reflection in a mirror held up by a servant. Paul was dressed in his finest planeta as he was due to leave for the church of San Pietro in Vincoli. He would have much preferred to attend the extravagant Mass in St Peter's; the basilica could hold as many as four thousand worshippers. But all the leading figures of Roman society, as well as the most important churchmen, would be in attendance, and the demand for places had been so great that Paul, even with his influence, had been unable to obtain an invitation.

Beorthric put down his clay drinking bowl and reached across with his right arm to knead the muscles on his left side where he had been injured. 'The Beneventans will not give up easily. I've seen men like them before, ruthless in the pursuit of power. They plan carefully and if they employ professionals, they strike at precisely the right moment.'

I knew that he was thinking of the massacre at the Avar spring ceremony when Khagan Kaiam's throat was slashed open in front of the assembled Avar chieftains.

Paul turned to me. 'Sigwulf, I'm sorry neither of us will be at St Peter's today. This event is going to be unique, something that makes history. The palatium has been making great efforts. A contact in the Treasury tells me that they're bringing a great treasure out of storage. It's something that is displayed only once in a lifetime.'

'I'm surprised there's anything of value left in the treasury that Albinus and his friends haven't stolen,' Beorthric observed caustically.

Paul chose to tease him. 'Maybe they're hiding another masterpiece from the Avar Hoard, even more spectacular than your gold warrior flagon.'

Something echoed in my memory: another ceremony, another ritual, a gold-plated skull, and what had happened to the man who had drunk from it. I felt my insides contract in a sudden spasm of fright. The same thought must have occurred to Beorthric. He sat up straight, a wariness in his eyes, all his attention fixed on the former Nomenculator.

'Do you know what this special item is?' I croaked.

Paul heard the change in my voice and looked at me curiously. 'I've no idea. No one would tell me. It's being kept secret.'

'Who's going to be at Mass today?' Beorthric asked sharply.

'Senior priests, Roman nobility, foreign dignitaries. Carolus's family will also be there, looking on. Everyone will want to see the king on such a grand occasion.'

Beorthric gave a little hiss of alarm. 'And what exactly happens at this Christ's Mass?'

'As Bishop of Rome, Leo enters the basilica with all pomp, surrounded by his staff. He is escorted up the central aisle to his position by the altar. From there he turns to face the congregation and pronounces the first words of the service. His assistants do the rest, leading the prayers, directing the choir, and so forth. At the end of the Mass, Leo again stands by the altar and pronounces the final blessing on the congregation.'

'Alone?'

'On this occasion he will undoubtedly deliver a special blessing for the king himself, probably with a laying on of hands to emphasize the bond between them in front of this great audience.'

Paul's voice trailed away. Finally, he had grasped what both Beorthric and I had been thinking. 'You believe that Leo will be attacked in church, right in front of his altar?' He sounded shocked.

'Not Leo,' I said quietly, 'Carolus.'

Paul's jaw dropped. 'That's unthinkable.'

With an effort I kept my voice steady. 'Remember what Beorthric heard the plotters in Monte Cassino say: they wanted Leo disposed of before autumn. If not, then they would have to take more extreme measures.'

Paul was staring at me, his eyes narrowed.

'This has gone beyond getting rid of Leo,' I told him. 'You yourself said all along that this is a matter of high politics. It's about getting rid of Carolus instead. In coming to Rome, the king has become vulnerable. He's not in the safety of his own palaces, protected by his loyal vassals. The Beneventans and their allies will take this chance to be rid of him.'

Paul let out a slow breath. 'Maybe they've a good reason. I've heard that several squadrons of Frankish cavalry are on the way here. People are saying that they are to join up with the Duke of Spoleto's troops. Together they will cross the border into Benevento, and force the duke there to recognize Carolus as his overlord, and that all this talk of Carolus wanting to celebrate Christ's Mass in St Peter's is just a ruse. He's planning to extend his control of his borders.'

'The duke will have spies in Carolus's court. He must know about this too. He will strike first,' I said.

Paul was frowning, concentrating on what I had just said. Suddenly he slapped a palm against his forehead. 'What a dolt I've been! That elderly priest whom Beorthric saw shuffling into the room at Monte Cassino wasn't the candidate to replace Leo. He's the person whom the Beneventans will put forward as the rightful ruler of all the Franks.'

The awful sick dread that had been gathering in the pit of my stomach became a hard lump. 'But who is he?'

Paul took a deep breath to calm himself. 'This goes back to the way Carolus's father Pippin succeeded to the Frankish throne. Many said that it was underhand and that he had no right to rule because he had an older brother by the name of Carloman. There was a power struggle between them, and Carloman travelled to Rome to get the Pope to support him. But Pippin engineered it so that Carloman was held back for several years as a monk at Monte Cassino. Only when Pippin was safely installed as King of the Franks was Carloman allowed back to Frankia. He died there and later his remains were transferred back to the monastery.'

'A dead man isn't a threat,' said Beorthric.

Paul made a dismissive gesture, silencing the Saxon. Plainly the former Nomenculator was thinking hard. 'Carloman had a son, Drogo, who would now be about five or ten years older than Carolus. Drogo, too, was banished to a monastery, tonsured and became a monk. Nothing more is known about him.'

'You think he is now at Monte Cassino?'

'The monastery would have taken him in, as it did his father –' he paused – 'and it gets worse. There are those in Rome who claim that Carolus is illegitimate. He was Pippin's first-born son, but Pippin was not married to his mother in any church ceremony. It strengthens the argument that the true King of the Franks should be from the senior line, Carloman's son.'

'Surely no one is going to expect an elderly monk to turn overnight into a monarch who is competent to rule a kingdom as vast as the one that Carolus has,' I objected.

Paul grimaced. 'It doesn't really matter. Carolus has gone through so many wives and mistresses that there's an entire brood of his sons, bastards or legitimate, any one of whom might lay claim to the throne. The Duke of Benevento could enter the fray, claiming that he was fighting on behalf of Drogo, the rightful heir, strike Carolus down in public, claim that it was an act blessed by God as Carolus is an affront to the Church, and then there would be bloody chaos.'

'You're wasting time, Sigwulf,' Beorthric snapped. He was on his feet and limping towards the corridor leading to his room. 'Get down to that ceremony as fast as you can and warn Carolus's bodyguards. They'll know what to do.'

Paul was calling for a cloak and boots to be brought for me, and I was putting them on as Beorthric reappeared. 'Here, take this with you,' he rasped, holding out his scramseax in its leather sheath, 'just in case you come across our friend in the fur hat.'

# Chapter Nineteen

IT TOOK PAUL and me the best part of two hours, half running, half walking, to reach the great square in front of the basilica, and by then a cordon of soldiers, mostly Frankish men-at-arms supported by a handful of the Family of St Peter, had sealed the entrance to the basilica. The invited congregation had gone inside already, and Lateran clerks at portable desks were double-checking their lists against those who had been admitted. Paul hurried up to them.

'You must let us through. A matter of state importance,' he wheezed, purple in the face.

The senior of the clerks looked at him coldly. 'Not possible,' he said with more than a touch of malice. 'The service has begun. The doors are closed.' He made a show of looking down the list. 'Besides, your name's not here.'

Paul pulled me aside, out of earshot. 'I know that swine. He's one of Campulus's underlings. Bears me a grudge.'

I looked about me; my heart was pounding. 'What about your friend the sergeant from the Lateran? If we can find him, he might get us through.'

We hurried along the cordon. The line of soldiers was relaxing, the guards were stamping their feet and blowing on their hands to keep warm, for a raw wind had sprung up, carrying a few icy specks of rain. The troops gave us curious looks but made it clear that we would not be allowed to pass. Eventually, we found the sergeant, at the far end of the line, and Paul blurted out to him that we had to be allowed into the basilica.

'It's a matter of life and death,' Paul pleaded.

The sergeant looked taken aback. 'I'm not in charge. You'll have to speak with that officer, over there.' He nodded towards a humourless-looking Frankish captain who was already watching us suspiciously.

Paul and I hurried over to the man, and Paul repeated his request. The captain gave us a hard stare. 'No one is allowed inside, except those on the list. Those are my orders,' he said flatly. He glanced towards the senior Lateran clerk who gave a smug nod of agreement.

'I'm on the royal staff,' I said in Frankish, trying to sound official.

'Haven't seen you around before,' the captain drawled. 'Not with the court when we came here.'

'I'm on special duties, working for Archbishop Arno.'

'He's already gone inside. You can wait for him to come out and vouch for you,' said the captain unhelpfully. His eye fell on the scramseax. 'If you're on royal staff, what are you doing carrying that barbarian weapon?' He held out his hand. 'Give that to me.'

I surrendered the weapon, feeling more frustrated than ever. Paul came to our rescue. He reached inside his planeta and pulled out an elegant gold cross on a chain around his neck. 'Here you are, captain,' he said, holding it up. 'I am a genuine priest. And I'm prepared to leave it in your safe-keeping as a pledge if only you'll allow us inside. We just want to witness the ceremony.'

The captain hesitated, and I could almost see the thoughts going through his mind. He was being offered a bribe, and I wondered, if Paul tried to reclaim his gold cross, whether it would be given back.

'All right,' the captain said at last. 'You can pass.' He took the cross and chain, slipped them into a pocket and then added slyly, 'But you won't get inside. The doors are shut and bolted. The service is almost over.'

Paul and I scurried up the long flight of shallow steps leading to the great doors. 'That was quick thinking,' I said to him.

'If I can bribe a guard, so can anyone carrying a hidden blade,' he answered grimly.

He guided me around the side of the great basilica to where another guard was stationed outside a side door. This time we were lucky. The guard was from the Family of St Peter and recognized the former Nomenculator. Paul used the same excuse that we were anxious to witness the spectacular ceremony for ourselves, and, with a conspiratorial nod, the guard eased the door open and Paul and I slipped inside.

*

I had been in St Peter's before – on my trip to Baghdad escorting the king's beasts – but the splendour of the interior still took my breath away. It was larger than the largest royal palace, and even the dull December light pouring in through the high windows of the clerestory lit up the bright array of silks, flags and draperies strung between the famed marble columns – one hundred of them, mottled green and grey and red. Everywhere you looked the walls of the nave were painted with scenes from the Old and New Testaments, or covered with glittering mosaics. The basilica was full to capacity. A great throng dressed in their finest clothes stood listening to the full-throated singing of a choir somewhere towards the far end of the building, the sound of their canticles rising and falling.

But what struck me most was the underlying atmosphere of tension. It was not true of everyone. Many in the congregation

were acting normally, craning their necks to get a better view of
the grandees closer to the altar, jostling to find a little more space,
occasionally muttering comments to one another. But there were
others who were clearly on edge. They were mostly priests and
some, I guessed from their rich clothes, were Roman nobility.
They shifted and fidgeted, making small nervous movements, or
else held themselves with a strained, artificial stillness, as if they
were waiting for something to happen that no one else expected.
The hairs on my neck prickled as I scanned the dense mass of
people. It was achingly cold inside the church and people were
dressed in the same outdoor clothes that they would have worn
on their way to the basilica. Everywhere I looked I saw warm,
heavy garments of felt and thick wool, padded cloth and expensive leather. Fur was in profusion: marten, fox, squirrel, wolf and
badger. One burly man was wearing a bearskin cloak that must
have been unpopular with those standing beside him for it bulked
him out even more. And, of course, there were fur hats. Within a
dozen paces of me there must have been three or four men tall
enough to be the hired killer who had stabbed Beorthric in the
Forum of Nerva. All of them wore fur hats. I felt confused and
impotent.

Paul had me by the elbow and was steering me into an aisle
that ran parallel to the nave, pushing our way forward. Despite
his clerical dress we met angry glances and an occasional profanity
as we elbowed a path through the congregation, the worshippers
giving way reluctantly. Eventually, after several minutes of ruthless shoving, we reached the front of the congregation, within
view of the great altar under its massive silver arch. Here were the
nobility of Rome and the great office holders of the Church. Off
to one side, the women of the royal family had been placed in a
row of seats in the transept, looking on. Now I felt the tension
even more acutely; there was a sense of excitement in the air. It

made me sick with apprehension, knowing that Paul and I were the only two people who were aware of the looming catastrophe, and an awful knowledge that there was probably nothing we could do to intervene.

Not ten yards away from me was Archbishop Arno. He was wearing a white dalmatic hemmed with purple bands. In place of his usually severe expression, he looked serene and unruffled. I wanted to grab him by the elbow and tell him to stop the service, but it would have been futile. It was too late. He was standing amongst six or seven senior churchmen closest to the altar. With a sudden stab of shock I saw that Albinus, the papal chamberlain, was part of the same group. My mind was in turmoil. I had the distinct impression that the two men, though ignoring one another, were well aware of each other's presence.

I was trying to puzzle out what was going on when the choral song gradually rose to a crescendo, then died away, and in the silence that followed I heard a high, light voice – I presumed it was Pope Leo's – call the congregation to prayer. Leaning forward I was able to look to my left and see that Carolus had taken up a position by himself, several paces in front of the congregation and directly in front of the altar. The time for the final blessing had come. Pope Leo was before him, standing on the raised step of the altar platform, facing down the length of the building.

Once again, Carolus had chosen to wear the costume of a *Patricis Romanorum* for the occasion – a long white tunic and, over it, a chlamys, a flowing ankle-length cloak pinned at the shoulder. That morning Carolus's chlamys was of heavy purple silk edged with white and gold embroidery. His shoulder brooch had a central gem, the size of a large walnut and blood red.

Unarmed and alone, Carolus was the perfect target for a killer.

As we knelt for the final prayer, I delayed going down on my knees so that I could see over the heads of those around me and look towards the king. He was in the same spot, by himself right in front of the altar, and already kneeling, his shoulders squared, his broad back towards the congregation, and presenting an inviting target for a blade or an arrow. He had his hands clasped in front of him as he faced Pope Leo to receive the final blessing. Carolus was bare headed, his grey hair cut in the Frankish style, shaved clean in front and long locks hanging behind, almost to his shoulders. My glance fell on the king's shoes. His feet were protruding from the edge of his cloak. Incongruously, he was wearing vivid purple boots.

Beside me Paul hissed, 'Kneel Down!' I ignored him. Now was the moment for a killer to strike. The palms of my hands were sweaty with fear. I gathered myself, ready to throw myself forward and protect the king. If someone attacked Carolus, I would have to intervene bare-handed.

Leo finished the final sentence of the blessing and lowered his arms. Behind me I heard the abbots, bishops and archdeacons getting to their feet, rising with a rustle of silken vestments, and one or two grunts of effort from the more elderly.

Leo turned and, removing the cloth that hid it, picked up something from the altar, then held it high for all to see. I had expected a religious item, perhaps a chalice or a cross. But it was a wreath of gold, the leaves crusted with gems that glittered. In one smooth movement Leo placed it on Carolus's head.

For a couple of heartbeats, all was still; there was absolute silence through the huge basilica. Then from the immense audience came a great shout: 'To Carolus, the most pious Augustus, crowned by God, to our great and pacific emperor, life and victory!'

Three times the crowd repeated the acclamation, and when the cheering died away, I knew why Carolus had come to the basilica wearing purple boots. They were the symbol and privilege of an emperor. The King of the Franks had been crowned as Holy Roman Emperor.

*

'It was all a sham,' I commented to Paul later that afternoon after we had got back to his house.

My friend chuckled. 'What do you mean, a sham – the coronation of an emperor or the attack on Pope Leo?'

We were back in the library, the same room where I had first asked him to help investigate the assault on Pope Leo. Beorthric was nowhere to be seen, and I supposed he had gone to his own quarters to lie down and rest.

'Both,' I said.

'A matter of politics, my friend, but you did give me a bad scare this morning. I really did believe there was a last-minute threat from the Beneventans.' The former Nomenculator was in a noticeably good mood, relaxed and smiling.

I pressed on. 'The allegations against Leo were true: he was diverting money from the Church treasury, selling Church appointments, lining his own pocket in every way he could, and Albinus was helping him.'

'Of course,' said Paul over his shoulder. He had gone to the wall where he stored his scrolls and was reaching up to the topmost shelf. 'Nearly everyone who gets to sit on St Peter's Chair seeks to enrich himself. You saw that when you visited the Church of Saints Stephen and Sylvester. That palazzo was a bonus a pope awarded to his own family.'

'And Campulus and Paschal had also been dipping into Church coffers, even under Pope Adrian beforehand. Am I right?'

Paul pulled down a couple of scrolls and laid them on the table. He turned to face me. 'Yes. Campulus and Paschal expected everything to continue as before when Leo became Pope. They still held their senior positions in the Vatican, and for a while the money flowed. Then Albinus took over, and their share gradually dwindled.'

'So they set up that attack on him to frighten Leo into continuing with the arrangement.'

'Again, Sigwulf, you are correct. It was a falling-out amongst thieves.'

'And a chance for Carolus to bring the Pope to heel just like one of his hunting hounds.'

Paul grinned. 'Alcuin always said that you were a sharp one. When did you realize?'

'After we found that Avar gold in Albinus's house, I asked myself why Carolus had sent such a large amount of the Avar Hoard to Rome if the Church was so obviously corrupt. Perhaps someone wanted to see if it was stolen, by whom, and where it went.'

'Quite a leap of the imagination,' said Paul.

'Not really. A gold vessel decorated with a pagan warrior is an odd choice for a gift to the Christian Church. But it is unique and far easier to trace than gold coins.'

'Indeed, Albinus obliged us by stealing it,' Paul agreed.

I drew a deep breath. 'Which means, my friend, that you were involved in this charade all along, right from the beginning. That was the real sham.'

A slight smile played around Paul's lips. 'Now that we have Carolus crowned as the first Holy Roman Emperor for many centuries, I am happy to admit my role.'

'And would I be wrong in thinking that Alcuin was part of the plot too? He recommended me to Archbishop Arno.'

Paul chuckled. 'Before you work out the details for yourself and perhaps get them askew, perhaps I should explain.'

'Please go on.'

'It was largely Alcuin's idea: he had come to the conclusion that the complaints made against Leo were justified. Leo was corrupt and immoral. But to expose him risked doing huge damage to the Church. It would be better to use Leo's immorality for a higher purpose.'

'Like establishing Carolus as a new Holy Roman Emperor – ruler of the Western world under God.'

'Exactly. Carolus had already sent a good portion of the Avar Hoard to Leo's predecessor, Pope Adrian, as a gift for the Church. Now Alcuin suggested sending some of the finest pieces like the warrior flagon that Carolus had been keeping for himself. It was bait, knowing that Leo and his cronies were likely to steal it for themselves. If it could then be proved that they were thieves, they could be offered a choice: either be exposed or agree to crown Carolus as emperor.'

I shook my head in wonder. 'So when Leo was attacked and fled to Carolus, looking for help, he was putting his head into the lion's mouth.'

Paul had gone back to the shelves, carrying a low stool which he set down. 'It was too good an opportunity to miss,' he said to me over his shoulder. 'Alcuin suggested sending you to Rome while Leo was out of the city. He thinks highly of your ability.'

He hitched up his gown, hopped up onto the stool, and reached to the back of the shelf. 'When you had identified exactly who was involved, Archbishop Arno would take over.'

'And now that Arno has sent Campulus and Paschal into exile, it means they'll no longer be able to put their sticky fingers into the papal treasure.'

'Then we have something to celebrate,' Paul announced. He had found what he wanted to take from the back of the shelf. He turned to face me. In his hand was the elegant gold chalice with the exquisite fluting that we had removed from Albinus's house. I had forgotten all about it.

'Shouldn't it be returned to the papal treasury?' I asked.

'All in good time,' he answered. 'This isn't Avar workmanship. It's a superb Roman copy of a Greek original. I can make a good case that I bought it from a local dealer here in Rome. One day I'll donate it to the Church and be thanked for it. Until then I will enjoy it.'

As he twirled the chalice, admiring it, I was reminded of an unsolved mystery that had led to my captivity amongst the Avars. 'Do you remember those runic letters on the base of the golden flagon, the maker's mark? Apparently, they spelled out the word Zoltan. I never found out whether he was still alive.'

Paul stopped spinning the chalice. 'Is that what the writing meant? Who told you that?'

'The Khagan of the Avars, Kaiam himself. He read the letters that I had copied down. I had carried them with me into Avaria.' Into my head came a vivid memory of the khagan seated on his wooden throne and surrounded by his obsequious attendants, as he puzzled over the scrap of paper, and pronounced Zoltan's name.

'I wonder if he knew what he was talking about,' said Paul slowly.

'No one questioned him. His courtiers were all too terrified of him. He was a hot-tempered, dangerous tyrant. He ripped up the paper in a rage.'

Paul sucked in his cheeks. He was deep in thought. 'Do you remember that Avar gold buckle that the thief Gavino had in his possession, the one he stole from Albinus's house?'

'Of course.'

'While you were away on your travels to Avaria, I took it to a dealer in exotic jewellery to see if he could tell me anything more about it. He confirmed that indeed it was Avar workmanship and he told me that the Avar craftsman who made the buckle would have described it as "zolto". It means yellow, but is also the word used for precious gold.'

He tapped a finger on the rim of the chalice to emphasize the point he was making. '"Zoltan" was not a maker's mark at all. It was badly written and meant to read "zolto", an assay mark, if you will, to indicate that it was made of solid gold. No wonder you failed to find the mysterious goldsmith.'

Dumbfounded, I stared at him, thinking that if this simple fact had been known earlier, perhaps I would have avoided much of my suffering at the hands of Kaiam and his people and several Avars unlucky enough to have the Zoltan name would have survived the khagan's hunt for traitors.

Paul was too pleased with himself to note my reaction. The side of his face twitched in an enormous wink which could have been deliberate or might have been involuntary.

'With Paschal no longer in charge of the papal secretariat,' he said, 'I doubt anyone will bother to trouble me about the return of this villa to papal ownership.'

I would have voiced my resentment at being constantly manipulated had not Paul forestalled me. 'I'm thinking about Beorthric,' he added. 'Now that we have Leo under control, I'm sure he will agree if Arno suggests that he establishes a proper papal guard. I wouldn't be surprised if Beorthric isn't appointed as its first commander. And what will you do, Sigwulf?'

'I'll report back for duty as a *miles* with Carolus's household troops,' I told him, trying to sound positive. 'It won't be long before the king – I mean our new emperor – will be travelling north, back to his own capital. I'll be glad to be away from all the complications of politics in Rome.'

Paul's blotchy face broke into a knowing grin. 'As you pass through Milan, you should pay a visit to Saint Ambrose's shrine.

He was the one who said, "*Si fueris Romae, Romano vivitio more, si feuris alibi, vivito sicut ibi.*"

It took me a moment to do the translation in my head: 'When in Rome, do as Romans do, and if you are somewhere else, live as the people do there.' It left me with a feeling of vague unease. The calculating manner in which Carolus had made himself Emperor of the Western world showed that he and his advisors were capable of cunning, ruthlessness and deception. I had a premonition that this was not the last time they would employ me as an agent of their ambition.

## Historical Note

The two main events in Sigwulf's story did take place: on 23 April, AD 799, Pope Leo was viciously attacked and beaten up in a Roman street outside the church of Saints Stephen and Sylvester. The motive and identity of the plotters behind the attack remain obscure, though two high officials of the Church administration, Campulus and Paschal, were later identified as being involved. Following the attack, Pope Leo fled to the court of Charlemagne – or Carolus – the King of the Franks at Paderborn, seeking his help. Charlemagne gave Leo his support and sent him back to Rome with a military escort. He also despatched Arno, the Bishop of Salzburg, with other Frankish churchmen, to conduct an inquiry into the ongoing unrest within the Church in Rome. Eighteen months later, Charlemagne himself arrived in Rome, claiming he was there to put an end to the discord. Soon afterwards, on Christmas Day 800, Pope Leo crowned him as Holy Roman Emperor in St Peter's Basilica. Historians have long differed as to whether the coronation was a ploy by Pope Leo to show that the emperor owed his position to the Church or it was Charlemagne's deliberate acquisition of supreme authority.

Charlemagne did donate part of the Avar Hoard to the Roman Church, though the finer objects in the great 'Avar Hoard' captured by Charlemagne's troops seem to have been melted down for their value as precious metal. A solid gold Avar 'warrior flagon' of the period is on display in the Kunsthistorisches Museum in Vienna.

The figure depicted on its surface has been dubbed 'The Triumphant Prince' or 'The Horseman from the East' and shows a horseman
in heavy chain mail and helmet which resemble armour from
Persia. His face has been described as having a mix of European and
Mongol-like features, while the captive he is dragging along by the
hair, half running, half walking beside his horse, looks much more
European, as does the face of the severed human head attached to
the rear of the saddle of the victorious rider.

The Old Turkic script, which Sigwulf has difficulty in reading
on the base of the Avar flagon, was used by the Avars in the eighth
century. It is strikingly similar in shape and style to futhark or rune
writing of Northern Europe, and is sometimes described as runi-
form, though most scholars believe that it evolved in central Asia
and there is no link between the two alphabets.

The Avars, a semi-nomadic people, pose one of the great myster-
ies of central European history. For 250 years, their khaganate, or
confederation of tribes, dominated much of the Danube basin. They
created no permanent structures and left no written records. Even
the precise location of their famous stronghold, the 'Ring', with its
massive wooden palisade, has not been traced beyond doubt. What
little is known about them mostly comes from the archaeological
examination of their graves containing their skeletons, horse goods,
weapons and simple domestic implements – and from the Byzantine
chroniclers who describe their alarming raids across the border and
threats to Constantinople. Their khaganate collapsed with astonishing swiftness, probably through internal squabbling though this
too has never been fully explained. In a single generation the Avar
khaganate vanished so utterly that there is a Russian proverb for
complete and sudden oblivion that goes: 'They perished like the
Avars, and left neither progeny nor heir.'

\*

A note on the title of this book: The word 'assassin' was unknown in Europe in the age of Charlemagne. Very likely it entered the language at the time of the Crusades. But it seemed so appropriate for the title of this book of Sigwulf's adventures that I decided to ignore the anachronism.

*The first book in Tim Severin's*
*thrilling historical adventure series set in Saxon times*

# SAXON

VOLUME ONE

## The Book of Dreams

A *haunting premonition.* A *deadly betrayal.*

Frankia 780AD: Sigwulf, a minor Saxon prince, is saved from execution after his family is slaughtered by the ruthless King Offa of Mercia. Sigwulf is exiled to the Frankish court of King Carolus, the future Charlemagne.

He gains the friendship of some – Count Hroudland, Carolus's powerful and ambitious nephew, but – mysteriously – several attempts are made on Sigwulf's life. When he obtains a Book of Dreams, a rare text giving understanding to their meaning, he attracts the attention of Carolus himself. But the Book proves to be a slippery guide in a world of treachery and double dealing. Sent into Spain to spy on the Saracens, Sigwulf becomes caught between loyalties; either he honours his debt to new friends among the Saracens, or he serves his patron Count Hroudland in his quest for glory, gold and even the Grail itself . . .

The second book in Tim Severin's
thrilling historical adventure series set in Saxon times

# SAXON

## VOLUME TWO

### The Emperor's Elephant

*A perilous journey. A treacherous promise.*

Sigwulf, a Saxon prince exiled to the court of Carolus, King of the Franks, is summoned by the royal advisor Alcuin of York. Carolus has received magnificent gifts from the Caliph of Baghdad and is determined to send back presents that will be equally sensational. White is the royal colour of Baghdad so the most important gifts will be rare white animals from the Northlands.

Having proved himself as a royal agent to Moorish Spain, Sigwulf has been chosen to obtain the creatures. He must find white gyrfalcons and two white polar bears, and – as Carolus has seen its picture in a book of beasts – a unicorn.

He and his companions travel far into the north. Though they obtain some of the animals, they quickly realize that not all are even real. Setting out for Baghdad with their menagerie, they encounter danger after danger until it seems that someone is trying to wreck their mission – with each stage of the long journey bringing a new and unexpected peril . . .

extracts reading groups
competitions books new
discounts extracts
competitions
books
new
events
extracts discounts
reading groups
books
extracts
new titles reading groups
interviews
events extracts
discounts
new books events
events new events
discounts extracts discounts
**www.panmacmillan.com**
extracts events reading groups
competitions books extracts new